Tanya Ata... ... n general medicine ... ...ering in ...lawi. She now specialises in psychiatry. Outside of her medical ...vriting is her passion. She studied Creative Writing at Bath ... niversity and has previously been longlisted for the Mslexia ... Competition and Bath Novel Award. Tanya lives in Bristol ...her partner and two children. *Things My Mother Told Me* is ...rst novel.

Things my Mother Told Me

TANYA ATAPATTU

sphere

SPHERE

First published in Great Britain in 2018 by Sphere
This paperback edition published in 2019 by Sphere

1 3 5 7 9 10 8 6 4 2

A CIP catalogue record for this book
is available from the British Library.

ISBN 978-0-7515-6949-0

Typeset in Electra by M Rules
Printed and bound in Great Britain by
Clays Ltd, Elcograf S.p.A.

Papers used by Sphere are from well-managed forests
and other responsible sources.

MIX
Paper from
responsible sources
FSC® C104740

Sphere
An imprint of
Little, Brown Book Group
Carmelite House
50 Victoria Embankment
London EC4Y 0DZ

An Hachette UK Company
www.hachette.co.uk

www.littlebrown.co.uk

To my own mother,
for the typewriter when I was twelve.

Prologue

There are some things I'll never tell Mum. About that tender feeling I get beside a drift of lavender, beside the heavy heads of sunflowers drooping in the light. About how it wasn't me, but Jack, who once arranged those flowers in the chipped vase on her dining room table. About how I felt afterwards when she warned me against him, when she said he would break my heart.

About how my heart is broken.

'It was just sex, Anj, it never meant anything.'

It's funny. He's standing right here in the lounge and he must be talking, because his mouth is moving, but it's like I'm somewhere outside it all and the words are kind of disconnected, floating above our heads.

'I don't know what I was doing.'

We've been together for ten years, but now he's like a stranger, darker pinpricks of stubble beneath his jaw, a first strand of silver, fine and sparkling, in the bowed crown of his head. Someone else's lips at his ear.

'Say something, Anjali, for God's sake.'

But if I'm a Buddhist, then there can't be a God.

The crumpets have dried out, the espressos are cold, rings of black beneath the cups on the coffee table. When we first moved in, I scrubbed that table with vinegar, scrubbing out my old life. Now his phone rests beside the food and the coffee, with that message inside. *Baby, I love our weekends.*

'You need to go,' I whisper.

'What?'

'You have to go now.'

On the mantelpiece are the photographs of my family: my mother, my sister. My sister's eyes shine. It's odd too that I have an urge to call Shanthi, to tell her what's happened. Ten, fifteen years ago I might have done that. Before I moved in with Jack, before the coffee table was clean. From somewhere buried comes an image of my sister and me, skinny teenagers, lying in a sea of grass, picking clover. We grew up without a garden, were two years apart at school; I can't remember where we were. Our words now long lost, drifting upwards like dandelion seeds. It's hard to believe we were once that close.

'Can I come back?'

Jack's skin is pale as milk, the hole in the knee of his jeans a little bigger – the only things Mum could really hold against him. His eyes are still as mesmerising as the clearest sky.

The roses he gave me a couple of weeks ago are on our dresser. Twenty-nine rugosa roses, one for every year of my life. I gaze at the wilted white flowers, fallen petals blurred, their edges swimming. If he doesn't come back, what will I do?

'You have to go,' I whisper again.

One

A week later, our shop is bursting with dahlias. The buckets brim with fluted plumes of scarlet, magenta, flushed pink, burnt orange. The air is spicy. Dahlia, the goddess of fate in Baltic mythology. Standing for dignity and elegance.

And betrayal.

I kick a bucket and a dahlia goes flying.

'Yikes,' I say, to Clara and the flower.

Clara rescues the dahlia; tucking it into her dreadlocks, she disappears inside the kitchenette. Instead of tea, she brings out a silver hip flask. Seeing my face, she waves me away. 'It's for emergencies. Like right now.' Pouring two fingers of golden liquid into a thick tumbler, she sits us both down on stools behind the counter.

'Drink,' she instructs me.

The dahlia is an orange flame in the thick wads of her hair. Clara's my boss; I have to listen to her.

'One year. I can't believe it was going on so long,' she says. 'What if you hadn't seen that message?'

I down the whisky and my head explodes.

Clara refills my glass. 'Do you know her?'

I nod. There's a sharp pain piercing my skull. *Baby, I love our weekends.* My throat is clogged, her name breaking into syllables as my tongue tugs it out. 'Ju-li-a.'

Julia. I met her once. Stood gazing at the roaring mouth of the dragon that covers her right shoulder. Its wings apparently spread over the full expanse of her back, although when she turned, you could only catch the deep blue strokes visible above her low-slung black dress. Julia, a friend of Jack's best friend; Julia, who happens to be, among other things, a burlesque dancer. Maybe Clara won't remember.

'Oh, Anjali,' she says.

She remembers. She hardly ever uses my full name. I down more whisky. I hate whisky. But Mum said it was my dad's favourite drink, so it's worth another try. And if I tilt my head to one side with my index finger pressed to my right temple, very, very hard, the tears won't come.

'All those times he said he was working ... What an absolute ... What did he expect you to do?'

'He asked me to forgive him.' My voice sounds distant now, like it's coming from someone else. But there's no one else here; Clara's locked the shop. The early-evening sunlight burns through the window, the flowers are intensely bright. I'd booked holiday; Jack and I were supposed to be away this week, camping in the Cumbrian mountains, celebrating the last year of my twenties with anoraks and mugs of champagne. When I'd left the shop behind, it was full of blushing, submissive stocks, all pink and blue and baby-comforting. Now the dahlias are clamouring around me like dazzling, slightly diminutive Daleks.

Are there some infidelities that are easier to take than others? What if she didn't look so intimidatingly cool? If she didn't have a size 8 body, supple as elastic? What if she had dimples in her thighs and a little too much curve in her belly – what if she was just a little bit more like me? When I saw that message, all I wanted to do was overlook it somehow. To not have to face the mornings alone with a pack of reduced-price Warburtons crumpets.

'But you just couldn't forgive him, right?' Clara says.

Sometimes, your body won't do what your mind thinks it can. I've known this ever since the Bristol Half Marathon, Autumn 2012.

'Right, I've heard enough.' Clara removes my glass and drags me to my feet. Six foot and big-boned, she towers over me. She tugs the dahlia from her dreadlocks. Plucking off the fiery head, she tucks it behind my ear. 'I'm taking you out.'

'I can't go anywhere now, Clar. I need to go home and kill myself.'

'I'm taking you out,' she repeats.

'But look at me!'

She looks at me. This wouldn't be the best time for introductions. My black hair is wild and my eyes are still swollen. My brown skin can't go blotchy but it's doing its best. And that may well be snot on the sleeve of my grey top.

Clara glances again at my tiny green retro-print skirt. I saw her clock it as soon as I walked into the shop, just as she was closing up, surprise on her face not just because I wasn't supposed to be here. In all honesty, this isn't my typical kind of skirt. It's the kind of skirt that would frighten my mother's beta blockers.

'You sort of look like you're on the pull,' she says.

I'm not on the pull. I'm not sure why there's gold dust on my bloated eyelids and a plum-coloured lipstick in my bag. My partner has been having an affair and there's no way that meeting another man could ever make me feel better. It would be like that one time the hairdresser sheared off my curls: it was glorious until Mum told me my face wasn't symmetrical.

It's July. I used to think summer in Bristol was magical. The harbour glistens with evening sunshine, people cluster outside the waterside cafés with wine and burgers, watching the sway of the moored boats, listening to the buskers and the music pumping from the bars.

There's a couple walking across the bridge, hand in hand, stooping to examine the padlocks that others have fastened to the steel railings. A couple of years ago, Jack and I wandered over this same bridge, talking about buying a houseboat and living life in a different way. The kind of thing you talk about when there's vegetable chilli in the slow cooker and you think you'll be with someone for ever.

I gaze as the couple cross the bridge and fade into the evening. I don't want to lose the summer. I don't want to stare at the water and watch the shadows dissolve; I don't want to watch my world fall apart.

'Come on, Anj.' Clara tugs gently at my sleeve.

'I just don't get it – why risk everything, if it didn't mean anything?'

Clara's pouring our second bottle of wine. It's two hours later and we're in a bar on Park Street, up the hill from the harbour, crammed onto a bench at a table surrounded by exuberant people.

'I guess she must have meant something.'

I pick up my glass and focus on the meniscus of the wine. It's a good word, 'meniscus'. I remember telling Jack how it comes from the Greek word for moon. It occurs to me that I might vomit.

It wasn't as bad as it sounds, Anj. It was just a few weekends.

How many weekends?

What?

How many times, Jack?

Does it matter?

'Of course it bloody matters.' Clara's voice is a little high-pitched, her dreadlocks swishing as she shakes her head. I gaze at her blunt nose, the dark border around her clear green irises, the glinting silver hoops that pierce her eyebrow and lower lip, the stud in her cheek. It's been ten years since I got together with Jack; ten years since I walked into Clara's florist's shop looking for a job.

'But maybe he's right.' I swallow. 'It could have been five times, a million times. The fact is, it wasn't just a drunken thing. So there must have been something wrong with us. With me.'

'There's nothing wrong with you, mate.' Clara's eyes are shiny. My heart is thumping; if she starts crying then I won't be able to stop. 'Fuck him.' She rubs her eyes. 'Scratch that, fuck someone else.'

We look around the bar. There's a gang of skinny lads in a corner singing football anthems and taking it in turns to down tequila shots, lemon juice dribbling from their mouths.

'This is the whole problem with relationships.' Clara pushes the wine bottle back so that it teeters for a moment on the edge of the table before settling onto its base. 'They take everything from you, and what are you left with? Bugger all.'

It's the rant she gets into after this much Shiraz. Clara's only ever been in one relationship, yet it was significant, lasting from the age of fourteen to twenty-one (she's thirty-two now, three

7

years older than me). After it had run its natural course, she fell apart. Not because breaking up had been so hard. But because it was only then that she realised how *bored* she'd been. She'll go on dates now, but the fear of more wasted years means she'll bolt at the first hint of commitment.

'Do all relationships have to be like that?' The alcohol won't get rid of the images inside my head: of my silent flat, the barren side of the bed, the food going off in the fridge, flaky mould on the cheese. Can it all go back to normal if I just try to work things out with Jack? I down my wine. The low-cut dress of the burlesque dancer flickers again, her cleavage shining beneath the tongue of the dragon. It doesn't feel possible for anything to be normal again. My head's dizzy; it feels like everything's falling away from me. 'Clara, is the bench moving?'

She reaches out for my hand. The table gets a fraction steadier. 'Christ, I'm sorry, Anj. The last thing you need is me going on.' Her fingers are longer and broader than my own. Her nails are still rimmed with soil. 'Listen, what are you going to do now? About the flat and everything?'

'He took some things. It's rented under my name.' I pick a tiny price tag off the edge of her sleeve, absent-mindedly. 'Not that I can afford it on my own. I need a plan.' Except the wine's giving everything a hazy sheen that the answer isn't easily emerging from.

'Sod it then. Play the field.'

I look up to see if she's being serious.

'That's not a plan.'

'Why not?' There's a smile growing on my friend's face.

We look around the bar once more. The skinny lads have ordered another tray of tequila, and it looks like one of them has just thrown up on his mate's shoe.

'Why not?' Clara repeats, seizing my hand again. 'Maybe this could be the best thing that's happened to you. It's just been you and Jack, in that flat, all this time. Maybe this could be a chance to cut loose for a bit.'

I know what she's doing. It's the same thing I do when other friends are at the point of despair. It's too hard to see them going through it; you think of anything, everything, to put some joy back into their lives. Then you walk away, worry edged with a very, very slight feeling of relief, because it isn't happening to you. You're still with the person who will be there for ever, plus there's a new box set on Netflix and a plate of fresh cheese.

But now it *is* happening to me. I swallow hard, trying desperately to remember the schoolmates and uni friends who somehow made it through their break-ups, who met new people and came out on the other side, to sparkling yards of wedding lace, and vanloads of John Lewis crockery, and vaginas loosened by hordes of screaming babies.

'Anj, can you hear me?' Clara's voice sounds faint, coming from somewhere above the pit I've fallen into. 'Anjali!'

The dahlia is burning my ear. The skinny lad who has thrown up is now having his back rubbed by a skinny mate, a poor staff member making his way over with a mop. 'But I don't even know what cutting loose means,' I say, finally.

'Exactly.' Clara nods.

I think of my days up until now: the long hours in the shop, coming back to cook dinner with Jack, listening to the pitch for his next journalism piece, worries running steadily in the background, about the rent, about what I should be doing with my own life. Marriage and babies seeming too far away to reach, even then. But no time to think any of it through because suddenly it's morning and time to do it all again.

'You don't need to think about that now,' Clara says.

'About what?'

'About what you should be doing with your life.' Clara's been reading my mind for years; it's not clear how she does it. 'Just have some fun for a change. Forget sodding relationships.'

Goose bumps are dotting my bare legs; I'm cold in this packed bar. I'm cold whatever. Me, my sister, my mum, it's the downside of getting your genes not too far from the equator. I wonder what Mum will say when I tell her about Jack. Will she throw open her arms and welcome me back into the brown fold? Or will she shriek hysterically and ask what's going to become of my spoiled body now? I shiver. My cardigan is discarded on the shop counter, my tights are jumbled on the floor of my bedroom. A memory comes of spending a whole day in thick socks before peeling them off and realising they belonged to Jack; that moment felt somehow more meaningful than each celebrated anniversary.

'Clara?' I say. 'What about love?'

Clara picks up her glass. For a while, she is silenced. I wonder if she's remembering that first and only relationship of hers, the renovated van that became their home, the nights they stayed up to hear the first notes of the finches.

She downs her wine. 'Remember what Tina Turner said.'

I think confusedly of the last eighties night I went to. 'We don't need another hero?'

'No, you dimwit. What's love got to do with it?'

Going to the bar, she gets swallowed up by the throng of bodies. The skinny lads have been ushered on now, the poor staff member still cleaning up the vomit. This tiny place is crammed with students; it was where I used to come too, before I dropped out of uni. There's a picture of Che Guevara on the wall, and an old Budweiser poster; a vase of daisies on the windowsill standing straight and tall. When I touch the stems, they're plastic.

Nothing feels real. I look over at the bar again. Clara's disappeared. There's a thin Asian woman in the corner who might be my sister, and for a moment the relief is overwhelming. I'm about to fight my way over to her: *Shanthi, it's me!* But the woman turns her head and her eyes are ringed in kohl and her earrings are balls of glitter – she isn't Shanthi; she's nothing like her. My sister would never come here. I don't know any of these people. The guitar music's swelling, the voices around me becoming more raucous, the chasm growing deeper. My chest starts to thud and my breath is coming quicker. I've never had a panic attack before, but it's going to happen, right now.

'Are you OK?'

There's someone beside me. There's a gentle voice, a kind hand on my shoulder. I feel the strength and warmth radiating from his palm. I want this person to be Jack.

I turn my head, and there is the Architect.

Turns out the Architect is just a fledgling, only twenty-one years of boyish construction. He's in the third year of a seven-year course. Jack, on the other hand, is a few years older than me. I wonder how important age is. The Architect has a heart-shaped face and gentle green eyes; he is talking to me softly, like I'm a child who's grazed her knee.

He's telling me a tale of architecture. It's a fascinating story with words such as voussoir, vermiculation and flying buttress. His neck is long and pale and his hands are slender and expressive; he uses them to emphasise the processes of planning and presenting and problem-solving. And something called perlustration, which should be an exciting combination of frustration and intense sexual desire, but on further clarification turns out to be a survey.

'What do you do?' he asks me.

A clump of dreadlocks surfaces above the crowd of heads at the bar. Clara hasn't disappeared. The pounding in my chest is starting to settle.

'I'm a flower girl,' I tell him.

He tilts his long neck to one side and surveys me. 'Straight up?'

I nod. 'Like Eliza Doolittle.'

'Who?' he asks.

Jack would have known that. He'd remember that as kids, my sister and I watched *My Fair Lady* every Saturday afternoon while waiting for Mum to finish her supermarket shift, terrified of being discovered alone in the flat and taken into a children's home run by white people. *Never open the door!* Mum reminded us sternly every Saturday morning, while filling the fridge with enough curry to last us for the rest of our lives, just in case.

'Here, for you.' The Architect pours the last of his pitcher of beer into his glass and passes it to me. I stare at the drink, feeling oddly touched by this gesture. Looking back up, I take in the smooth curves of his face, the dip of his chin, a little nick from a shaving blade at the edge of his jaw. So maybe he isn't familiar with Eliza Doolittle, but there's a sense of kindness that accompanies this man; like he might one day put a hot-water bottle beneath my side of the duvet, or maybe heat up a bowl of chicken soup for the end of a long shift. Never mind that I'm a veggie. Suddenly it feels like this is the only thing I need – just to feel a little bit warmer.

'See this?' He points towards an alcove beneath the stairs

where two wooden arcs meet in the middle. 'We call that an ogee arch.'

And Jack might not have known that.

'Tell me more.' I shift towards him and then realise that our thighs are touching. But it feels surprisingly OK, good even, to be in contact with another body. Something to hold onto. Even if his leg isn't like Jack's, even though it's bulkier, his jeans heavier, not softened yet by years of wear. Looking at the Architect's face again, I note a distinct lack of lines, clear skin beneath his eyes.

Clara emerges from the throng, but she's deep in conversation with another youthful man. I've never thought that much about our ages before, but looking around the bar, it's becoming evident that Clara and I are approaching death.

'So, if the lower curve is convex and the higher one is concave, that's known as a Roman ogee.'

'Oh, right.' Do I look as old as I feel? Are people glancing at me and the Architect, wondering if I'm a cougar?

'Wait a minute, did I get that the wrong way round?' The Architect frowns, scratching his forehead.

'It doesn't matter?' I suggest, hopefully.

'No, you're right.' He stops scratching, relieved. 'So what about you? Are you ready to tell me what's wrong?'

The inky body of a burlesque dancer begins writhing away in the back of my mind.

I falter.

Maybe I can tell this stranger what's happened to me. Maybe he'll say, *Let's get out of here*, and take me somewhere to drink tea. Maybe he'll remove his architectural disguise and reveal himself to be a shining oracle, before going on to soothe my aching head with wise, buttress-shaped sentences.

'Are you OK?' he asks again.

I gaze once more at the glass of beer, seeing my thoughts swirling round and round in the golden pool. No, I can't talk about Jack. I can't think about any of this yet. I just need a way out, someone to help me get over to the other side.

Finishing the beer, I put the glass down.

'It's nothing, I'm just drunk.' I lift up my voice to sound more confident. 'Anyway, what brings you out tonight?'

The Architect studies me, as if debating whether to probe further. I wonder what he sees: the deep pouches beneath my dark brown eyes, maybe the tremble in my bitten (but plum-coloured) lip. He waves his hand towards another group of guys at the bar.

'Exams are long over. The lads wouldn't let me stay in.' I glance at his friends. They're egging each other on to down pitchers. In that moment, I see Jack and his mates on one of their weekends away, drinking pints and pints of beer while in the middle of the throng Julia might have been swaying in a tight-fitting bodice, fishnet stockings clinging to long, slender legs. But these images are more than I can bear; I have to stop doing this to myself.

'Listen, are you really all right?' the Architect asks.

The thing is, I know that pain and misery and the depths of despair are fast approaching, but maybe they can be delayed, like a government bill for high-speed rail. Maybe you can avoid the story of your life if you stick to the bus, or another slowly moving metaphor. Or maybe you can avoid transport analogies altogether and just find a whole different story, featuring a youthful architect in scratchy jeans, for example.

'Did you *want* to stay in, then?' Turning back to the Architect, I take his hand. There are calluses at the tips of his slender fingers, as if he plays the guitar. When I look up into the green of his eyes, I see that they are warm, like Clara's.

14

'Not any more.'

Is it possible I'm going to have sex with this man? Now that I've let him sit at my bench in this crowded bar, now that I've drunk his beer? Now that we've engaged in a conversation about Roman construction? Now that my hand has slipped into his? His fingers are bonier than Jack's, but his palm feels secure, pressed against mine.

It wasn't like this for Jack and me. We'd known each other a while before we slept together. I was nineteen; before him there'd only been one other boy, a short romance at sixth-form college that could never go anywhere because of the watchful eye of my mum. We'd had sex only twice, on his bunk bed. Even so, it had taken weeks to get to that point, and afterwards, walking back to Mum's place, I'd cried. I was convinced she would know the truth as soon as she looked at me, and that once again there would be disappointment in her eyes.

I think of Mum's watchful eyes now as the Architect gazes back at me, this geeky, kind, studious person, keen to help rebuild foundations and who seems to find me, despite my swollen features and rampant hair, attractive.

Cut loose, Clara said.

'Take a walk?' the Architect asks. We stand up abruptly, our hands still pressed together. I smile at Clara's salute as we slip out of the door, trying to ignore the stabbing voice inside my head: *Anjali, are you seriously going to do this?*

It's early in the morning. It's a freezing July and I am regretting my tiny skirt. Bristol seems full of the drunk, scattered about the pavement like a scene from a post-apocalyptic HBO series. Everything looks faintly blurred, and there's a stale odour of beer and vomit. At the top of Park Street is the magnificent Wills Memorial Building, its soaring front of Bath stone gleaming in

15

the lamplight. The Architect lifts my face towards the tip of the tower and tells me about its octagonal lantern, which holds the sixth largest bell in England.

'Are you single?' he adds.

There are three missed calls and four unanswered texts from Jack in my phone. I'm not entirely sure if I'm single or not. The stabbing voice is getting kind of persistent: *Why are you doing this, Anjali?*

As the Architect presses his lips on mine, I imagine the bell chiming. But it stays still and silent, wherever it is in that hazy sky.

It's the first time I've kissed someone else in ten years. Jack's face lodges in my mind, blue eyes penetrating, refusing to budge even with the hint of the Architect's tongue.

After a few seconds, I break away.

'It's so beautiful up here,' my companion is saying. He waves his arm at the lights of the city sprinkled below us. 'Down there, there's way too much brutalism.'

The kiss has shaken me. It was deep and warm, but I don't know these lips, their contours are too unfamiliar. I wonder how it might have felt for Jack, when he first kissed the burlesque dancer. Where were they? Perhaps a bar, at his mate's house, maybe a party I hadn't gone to. In every image it's the same: her taut arms around Jack's neck, red-painted nails meeting at the nape, her full lips against his, Jack kissing her back with no thought of me at all.

Don't go there, Anjali. The stabbing voice pauses and changes tack, becoming softer, a little kinder. Beckoning me away from that dark place. Because if I set foot in there, chances are I'm not coming out.

The Architect is watching me curiously. He holds out his hand.

I can do this.

And anyway, Mum always told me to be polite to outsiders.

I take his hand and hail a taxi.

'My flat's down there. Want to come?'

There's a beauty in brutalism as well. Maybe.

'Can't wait to see your place,' the Architect says as we stumble through the front door of my flat.

My place is all over the place. I haven't cleared up in a week, and there are still things on the floor that shouldn't be on the floor, including framed photographs, cheap crockery and three ebony elephants. After Jack left, the last few days have been a bit hazy. But there might have been some throwing.

In the living room, the Architect picks up one of the elephants and runs his long fingers along its haunch. 'Where's this from?'

'Sri Lanka.'

'Is that where your family are from?'

I nod, feeling a bit naked. Now that we're here, it occurs to me that I really don't know this guy. I'm not sure if I want him to touch my things. My body, maybe, but not my elephant.

'Were you born there?' he asks.

'My mum and sister were. I was born in Bristol.'

'Is this your mum?' The Architect has now picked up one of the photographs. My mother's cinnamon eyes charge out of the cracked frame and I swear that for a moment I can hear her. *Who is this white man, Anjali?* I gently remove the picture from the Architect. Families are surely best reserved for proper relationships, when the honeymoon is over and you need to explain your neuroses.

'And is this your sister?' I didn't throw my sister on the floor, but the Architect has worked his way over to the mantelpiece. 'She's pretty. Is she older than you?'

Two years older, but I'm not about to open up this discussion with the Architect. My sister won't take her eyes off me. *Anjali, what are you doing?* Oh Jesus, not her too. It's not often that my sister and I talk, but this doesn't seem a good place to start.

There's nothing to do but have sex. It's the only way to change the subject. I steer the Architect away from my sister's searching gaze and into the bedroom, where the olive duvet is half on the floor and the sheets are still ruffled on one side from the weight of Jack's body.

Before lowering the Architect into Jack's place, I note the dent in the pillow where Jack's head should have been.

I push the Architect slightly away from it.

OK, what next?

Now that we're here, I'm not sure how to go about this. I know I have to peel off my skirt and remove my knickers, and I'm probably supposed to do something with his penis. But inserting it into my vagina seems a bit odd. In fact, the whole concept of sex feels a little overwhelming, alarming even, like the Ebola crisis, or a Tory prime minister.

The Architect pulls off his T-shirt. Perlustration of his mid-section reveals an incredible set of abdominal muscles. I stare at them for a moment.

Somehow, I get his penis in.

Then, once on top of the Architect, I start to bounce.

'Man,' the Architect says. 'You're good.'

'Really?' I pause for a moment, flattered.

'Yeah, man, but keep going. This is better than St Peter's Basilica.'

No, no, I'm kidding. He doesn't really say that.

But he does think I'm good.

He takes *ages*.

18

Jack and I tended to be pretty quick once we got going. That didn't bother me. Somewhere along the line I must have started taking our sex life for granted. I always needed to be somewhere: the shop, the traders' market, my mother's. After ten years, sex had stopped being a priority. The burlesque dancer returns to my mind. Dancer legs, dancer arms, dancer chest. Ribs outlined, pert breasts, with silver tassels on the nipples. How does a tassel even attach to a nipple? Is it like a plaster, or is there some kind of suction thing, or a clamp?

Stop thinking about it, Anjali, stop thinking about it.

Trouble is, there isn't much else to do except think, and bounce, as the Architect seems capable of going on and on, and on. I wonder if he'll notice if I just quickly text Clara, to confirm if this is what she means by cutting loose. And whether she has any thoughts on the tassel thing.

I also find myself wondering again what Mum will say when she hears about me and Jack. This probably isn't the best time to be thinking about her either, but the Architect really is busy down there, and there's never exactly an ideal time to consider my mother.

Mum never approved of Jack. Although we can rarely afford to visit Sri Lanka, and have no extended family in the UK, she continues to hold traditional Sri Lankan values close to her heart. She was never able to reconcile herself to my relationship with an English guy, and was deeply suspicious of Jack's career in journalism. 'Why could you not meet a nice doctor? Or accountant? Or lawyer?' she used to wail. These are among the top five South Asian careers: ask any second-generation South Asian immigrant.

Where do architects feature in the list? I wonder. Just then, the one underneath me performs an impressive acrobatic manoeuvre to reverse our positions. I am shifted, penis *in situ*, down onto Jack's side of the bed, my head in Jack's pillow. Something sinks in my chest. What would Jack say if he could see me now? I try to push him out of my mind, but my mother just slips in to take his place. The image of Mum, hovering beside the Architect, shaking her head and tutting, *You must make something of yourself, Anjali!*, is suddenly overpowering.

Maybe the Architect picks up on this because he pauses. 'Everything all right?' he pants.

'Fine, fine.' I nod vigorously. 'As you were.'

No, no, I don't think I said that. But the Architect resumes his thrusting.

The thing is, Mum wanted me and my sister Shanthi to also become doctors, accountants or lawyers and to marry our Asian colleagues to produce scientific or judicatory brown grandchildren. But she was forced to give up on this fantasy early on, when I would only read novels and Shanthi would only paint pictures. Still, I managed to make it to university, even if it was only to study English.

'All is not lost, Anjali. You can still achieve!' She told me this with glee on the eve of freshers' week.

So I totally let her down by dropping out, getting a job in a flower shop and moving in with a non-scientific Caucasian.

'Is this good enough for you?' the Architect puffs.

Is it? A severed education and a broken heart?

'Yes! Yes!' I assure him.

At this point he starts to wheeze, approaching either the end of his performance or, I suddenly fear, his short life.

Also at that moment, my mobile starts to ring on the bedside table. Clara. She must be checking up on me. I try not to look as if I'm glancing over.

Jack.

Oh God.

'Ignore the phone,' I instruct the Architect, trying to cast aside both Jack and my mother and get back to where I am, underneath a mass of muscles, attempting to shift into a position that eases my genitalia.

Ring, ring.

Fuck off, Jack, I'm being fucked right now.

No, no, I can't say that, not even in my mind.

The phone eventually stops and the Architect eventually comes. Our bodies make a funny smacking sound as we pull apart, because of the sweat that has bound us together. I watch him slide the condom off his penis. It's odd to see his semen, a thin, paltry collection for such a feat of activity.

'Do you have a bin?' he asks.

The exercise has sobered me up and my stomach is heavy. My phone is silent: no message, no voicemail. The Architect and I lie side by side, no longer touching. Even though I'm not alone, it feels suddenly colder in here than it has done over the past few nights, lying in this bed by myself. I close my eyes. It was only last Saturday that I woke here with Jack. Kissed the bend of his neck, traced the curve of his broad back. Rested for a moment on the mole beneath his right shoulder blade, like I always did, to make sure it hadn't changed. How warm a person's skin feels, when you know them.

'I thought I knew you,' the Architect says.

'What?' My eyes blink open. Did he just read my mind?

'When I saw you at the bar.' He is concentrating on the ceiling. 'For a minute, I thought I recognised you.'

'Oh, right.' I'm watching the ceiling too, following the swirls on the yellowed paper.

'You didn't look like you belonged in that place.' His voice is soft, his words coming slowly, while my eyes follow one circle, then another, then another. 'Then I knew I didn't recognise you. I just recognised how you felt.'

He tells me a few things then: about his parents' divorce, about growing up on a council estate with his mum, about his dad not caring less, about how hard he's worked every day of his course, because one day he's going to be somebody. His mum has a dream to visit San Francisco; for what reason, he isn't sure. But he'll make enough money to take her there every year for the rest of her life, if that's what she wants. He swallows, his Adam's apple bobbing up and down. His course is hard. It's not just maths and science; it's art and history and geography and everything else too. None of this comes easy to him. He works through the night while his mates hit the bars, downing their pints. He runs a hand through his fine brown hair. A little tuft grows awkwardly above his ear, the tiniest of scars beneath.

I don't speak for a while. Then, when the silence grows too heavy, I tell him a couple of things too. About my mum on the tills at Tesco, doing the night shift, ringing up people's groceries, stacking the shelves for as long as I can remember. About how I sometimes shop there too, standing at the end of a line while the customers in front gather their items without noticing the woman scanning them through. My words are almost a whisper, not quite wanting to come out. I tell him there's not much money to be made as an assistant florist either; my mum ain't never going to San Fran. I almost tell him about my dropped degree, but the ache is filling my head again. I think about my sister's photograph out in the lounge. I don't tell him about her; I wouldn't know where to start.

'I've never really talked to anyone like this,' the Architect says.

I get a strange sensation then. Looking down at our bodies a centimetre apart, it's like our loneliness is tangible in the channel between us. If we'd only touch, maybe this really could be the start of a story, and not just one where I'm a victim of Jack's choices. There's a part of me that wants to edge closer to the Architect, to feel the firmness of his thigh against the soft one that is mine. But Jack's clear blue eyes are still there in my mind, and when my mouth opens, nothing more comes. The words are balled up in my throat, tight.

Anyway, I can't possibly have sex with this man again. Not without a personal trainer.

We stay where we are.

'Do you want me to call you a taxi?' I ask him, after a while.

'It's fine, I can walk,' he says. 'My place isn't far from here.'

There's disappointment in his voice. I should have listened to my mum, I should have been more polite.

'Do you want a cup of coffee?' I ask.

But maybe he knows it's a half-hearted offer, and he shakes his head. He pulls his clothes over his dried-out body and I get a last glimpse of his shiny muscles. Another time, I'd like to tell him they really aren't bad at all.

'So long then,' he says.

'So long.' I've never used this phrase before, and the words repeat inside my head. There's something peaceful about them.

'I'm going to an evening on Gothic architecture next week,' he tells me. 'A few of us are going to walk around Bristol.'

'Oh, right.'

'You could bring an umbrella in case it rains.'

'You want me to come?'

'Why not?'

The Architect stands at the door. His face really is kind. It's sensitive and symmetrical, and another time, I would have been glad to have a coffee with him.

'I'm sorry,' I say. 'It's just I'm . . . I'm getting over someone.'

And once the words are spoken out loud, it's true. My relationship is over.

'So this was just a one-night stand?' the Architect asks.

'I guess so.' I think about how Clara loves the ease of never seeing someone again, of never allowing anyone to bother her. I wonder if she's ever felt like I do now, like there's a piece of myself that's going to slip out of the door with this stranger, that won't ever return.

'Just sex and nothing else?'

Nothing else. The end of this decade creeping away into a void. The future looming ahead, cavernous.

'I guess.'

'And you just want me to go?'

If you tell someone to go, do they ever come back?

'I'm sorry.'

For a moment, he doesn't speak. Then, as if he's made a decision, he changes his expression and looks suddenly cheered. 'Don't be sorry. It was awesome. The lads will be thrilled for me.'

'Really?'

'Yeah.' He picks up a book from the pile on my windowsill. 'I don't have many notches.'

'I'm glad I could help.'

He opens the book. It's my copy of *The Professional Florists' Manual*.

'You're not like Eliza Doolittle.'

'Eh?'

'She never went back to the flowers, did she? They weren't her real passion.'

'I thought . . .'

'My mum's favourite play. I must have blocked it out. It came back to me.'

Hang on, does everyone think about their mother during sex?

He lays down the book and puts on his jacket. 'Well . . . so long.'

'So long.'

It's nice to say it again.

When the front door closes, I wrap myself in the duvet and hobble over to pull the chain across. Hobbling back to the bedroom, I stand at the window, watching the Architect make his way to the end of the road, a broad shadow in the lamplight. Will his mates already be home, waiting to slap him on the back when he returns? Or maybe he doesn't live with them. Maybe he lives alone in a student room, getting in to fix himself some toast and instant coffee before heading to his single bed. On his bedside table, a pile of art history books. The guitar that bruises his fingertips resting against the wall. A photograph of his mother on the shelf, the same heart-shaped face, tired green eyes. *Have you been to the gym, son?*

I take a shower in my small bathroom, standing under the falling stream for a long time. The temperature's right up but the water can't quite burn away the pinpricks of guilt that are starting, that I know will keep coming back. Drying off, I go back to the bedroom and pull on my pyjamas. An elephant has found its way in here; picking it up, I gently set the smooth ebony body on the windowsill. Its proud black eyes watch me curiously.

I gaze around the room, at the piles of books; some mine, some Jack's. The chest of drawers containing my jumpers, but also Jack's jeans, his T-shirts. He packed only a small bag when he left. The shirt he was wearing last Friday night is still bundled in the laundry basket. Lowering myself to the carpet, I pull out the checked cotton and breathe in the smell that can only belong to Jack. The trace of his sweat, the leather of his cologne, his cigarettes. There's a knot in my throat. If I hadn't read that message on his phone, none of this would have happened. Not yet, anyway. We'd be sitting cross-legged on the grass outside his two-man tent, bathed in firelight and the small glow of head torches, maybe the only two people left up on the campsite, in the mountain shadows of a Cumbrian sky.

The orange dahlia lies at my feet, exterminated.

A knock at the door.

Springing up, I go out into the hall, looking round for something the Architect might have forgotten: his wallet or his keys.

But reaching the door, I stop.

'Anjali.' Jack's voice is low and urgent. 'Are you there?'

Two

When Jack and I first rented our flat, the only thing growing out-side was a skinny lavender bush. The garden was mostly a small patch of weeds and concrete. I set myself working out there for weeks. Now, amongst the weathered garden furniture, there are forget-me-nots, lupins, stocks. But it's the lavender I love most. Flooded with sunlight, the plant has spread into mounds of grey leaves, bursting into fragrant spires of purple with the first hint of summer.

I told Jack how lavender was revered across the ages, not just for its scent, but for its healing and its magic; legend has it that the plant can protect and seduce. It's how Cleopatra got Caesar and Antony, so they say.

It's how Jack will get me back, he says.

I'm sitting against the front door, listening to his voice on the other side. I put my hand up to the keyhole. Maybe the scent of his bunch of lavender is trickling through here, meeting my fingers. Flowing across my skin, diffusing into my chest. Circling my heart.

'I know you're there, Anj. I saw you, through the glass.'

He's got his keys. The flat is still half his. The chain's pulled across the door, but if he uses his keys, I will take it off.

'Open the door, Anj, please. We can sort this out.'

But can we, now? My heart is beating hard, my eyes are hot. If he'd arrived only fifteen minutes earlier, he would have crossed paths with the Architect.

'It was a big mistake. I just need to explain.'

What will he say if I tell him what I've done? My checked pyjamas can't hide what my body's been up to underneath. I feel grubby, like it's me who's been unfaithful. What chance do the two of us have now? The stinging behind my eyelids won't go away.

I hear a heavy brushing down the door; he's sitting down too, on the other side. There's a click and a hiss. He's lighting a cigarette. If not for the thick plank of wood separating us, we'd be leaning against each other. I'd borrow his fag for a couple of tokes, even though I don't smoke.

'D'you want one?' he asks, through the wood.

I think of his slender fingers gripping the cigarette, I think of his full lips against the tip, the cleft that will appear in his forehead as he inhales. I think of his broad back against the door, my fingers aching to check the mole beneath his shoulder blade. I think of a week ago, two weeks, three, when his arms were around me, no hint of this horrible feeling, wobbly like vertigo, that won't be steadied by alcohol, or an architect.

But I must stop. If I keep on doing this, I'll have to get up and go to him.

'Remember the time you chucked my cigarettes in the sea?'

It was an early morning three years ago in Porthcawl, Wales. *If they sink, you quit!* Except my glee was instantly replaced by panic about what would happen to the mammals and seabirds that might mistake the cigarettes for food. I plunged fully dressed into the water to rescue the sodden pack, Jack rolling up his jeans and following me in. Afterwards, sitting on the shore, our patch of sand darkened by our dripping clothes, surrounded by the glistening washed-up bodies of moon jellyfish, Jack tried to light a floppy fag. *Well they didn't sink.*

'That was one of the best days, Anj. There were so many days like that.'

Against my will, my mind is showing me pictures: a daisy chain tied around my ankle, buttercups scattered across a plate of scones, forget-me-nots on my pillow. There are so many things Jack has done for me.

'Forget the lavender. What about a tattoo? I'll tattoo your name anywhere you want me to. Just give me a sign.'

And then there's the thing that he has done to me.

My mind shows me another picture. Julia again.

I remember that house party where I met her, two years ago. The dance music, the strangers, the smoke. The heads that turned when Julia walked past, low-cut silky black dress swishing above her knees. The worst thing? I liked her. She was funny and self-deprecating and kind. It was hard not to stare at the dragon on her shoulder, to stop my gaze dropping to the snake etched along her slim, pale calf.

I don't even know if I like tattoos, but I had nothing but admiration for someone who could alter their body so elegantly and irreversibly.

'So shall I get one? Your whole name, if you like. That's a lot of letters. It'll hurt.'

I have no works of body art. I will never be a burlesque dancer. I have a fairly motionless kind of dance style myself. I don't even own a low-cut dress. Most of my outfits cover up

29

the curve of my belly and buttocks; I don't have a back that is worthy of ink.

'Anj, talk to me.'

I guess when your partner is unfaithful, you know you won't be alone again in your relationship. You know this other person will follow you around, sit on your shoulder. They'll never take sex for granted, they'll be athletic in bed, their slender thighs will be hard as diamonds. Especially if they're burlesque dancers.

He sighs. 'You can't keep ignoring me.'

I turn my body slightly and press my hand to the frame. I imagine the warmth of his fingers holding mine. But I'm in another person's hands now. A person with an orange breath of fire billowing over a strong arm, the grey-blue body of a snake disappearing up a thigh, beneath the folds of a dress. A person who doesn't know me, or care about me.

Another brush against the wood; Jack is standing up.

I turn back, keeping my limbs folded inside the outline of the door, so that he can't catch my shadow through the glass. In front of me, I can see into the bedroom. A tiny skirt on the floor; bed sheets covered in another man's sweat; a condom in the bin.

Guilt washes over me again. I don't know how either of us can go back now.

The front path is covered in gravel. I listen to Jack's footsteps fade away.

Sunday evening, carrying the bunch of lavender I found on my doorstep, I make my way to Mum's.

I've spent most Sundays with my mother, and my sister, for most of my life. My dad died when I was three, so it's been just us for a long time. I don't really remember my dad, but sometimes I have conversations with him in my head. *You can be whatever you want to be. You are strong. You are stronger than the burlesque dancer.* That kind of thing. If you're going to talk to a dead person, they may as well be supportive.

Mum and my sister live in the two-bedroom flat where I grew up, near the top of Ashley Hill in the north of Bristol. It's packed with Victorian terraces and is a desirable area now for the hip middle class, but it was more run-down in Mum's day. The building's still fairly dilapidated. Pieces of duct tape hold the gate together as I push it open and go through.

Shanthi's sitting on the step, smoking. She's another person I couldn't persuade to quit. Even shorter than me, and thin-boned, she's enveloped by her baggy jeans and oversize jumper. The jeans are spattered with drops of paint. Her curly black hair is as wild as mine, raked back into the same scruffy bun she's worn since we were kids. Her face is smaller than mine, dark eyes shaped like almonds, eyebrows two heavy curves, skin stretched taut across her cheekbones. There are drops of paint on her narrow wrists, too.

When we were young, and not hiding from the white people who'd take us into a children's home, I was often out here, playing with the other kids who lived in the flats. Shanthi was always inside, drawing. In my earliest memory of her, she's holding a pencil, our bedroom littered with sketches. Didn't I mind, my friends asked, that her pictures crowded the wall and there was no room for my posters? But I didn't. My favourite bit of the day was lying in bed, waiting for Mum to turn the light out, listening to Shanthi tell me the stories her hands illustrated.

'Mum banished you?' I sit down beside my sister on the step, dislodging a cracked piece of concrete. The sky is a sheet of grey, the paving stones darkened with drizzle. The forecast is for an unsettled July.

Shanthi looks up at the first floor. 'She might not know I've gone. She's deep in the curry.'

The weekly curry has become a bit of an institution, ever since I moved out. Mum never works a Sunday shift; her managers are convinced it's the Buddhist Sabbath. It's a good thing they've never looked deeper into it or they'd realise the Buddha was a fairly chilled kind of guy who might not have interfered too much in Sunday trading hours.

'You OK?' Shanthi's looking at me closely. I know there's a map of red lines in my eyes and dark circles beneath them. After Jack left last night, I changed the bedding, but the dents in the pillow wouldn't shift and I couldn't stop thinking about what I'd done with the Architect. I could have given tonight a miss, lied and told Mum it was too much after camping. But for one reason or another I've missed the last couple of Sundays too, and a further absence would only send her over the edge.

'Late night,' I say. 'What's new with you?'

Shanthi pauses, still sizing me up.

'Nothing much,' she says, finally. 'Although I've got to head out in a bit.'

'Oh.' My chest falls. 'You're not staying for dinner?'

'I'm meeting a friend.'

'You are? What friend?'

She doesn't answer. Now it's my turn to study my sister. Her jeans are paint-spattered but the oversize jumper must be new, second-hand new anyway, a deep emerald green I haven't seen her wear before. Instead of faded trainers, she has on the lace-up boots that rarely leave the shoe cupboard; when she stands up, she'll be the same height as me. For a moment I see us as teenagers, going through Mum's gold sandals, heads bent together, curls indistinguishable. After Jack, those times together seemed to drift away.

'So who are you meeting?' I ask again.

'No one you know.' She stubs out her cigarette.

Shanthi's two years older than me, but after getting her degree in fine art at Goldsmith's, years ago now, she has stayed at home. All I know about her time at uni is in the first-class certificate framed in the hallway. There's no graduation portrait, no other university paraphernalia, no friends she keeps in touch with. When she returned home to live, for a while everything stopped for her. Then a couple of years ago she got a waitressing job in a community café; through that a space to paint in a local studio. But otherwise she's in the flat, tucked up with pencil and paper, to the soundtrack of Mum's droning. If she ever dreams about leaving, the way I yearned to, she's never given a sign. But sometimes I look at that certificate on the wall, the gleaming gold frame that Mum polishes every week, and think about how it might feel to catch your reflection in it, to wonder whether things could have been different.

'Is it someone from the studio?' I ask.

Shanthi nods.

'What's their name?'

'You're asking a lot of questions.' She raises her heavy eyebrows.

Her eyes are bright. There's a faint shade of grey powder on the lids. But my sister doesn't wear make-up. When I was a teenager and wanting to experiment with clothes and eyeshadow and hair gel, I hunted through her drawers and found only paper and pencils and card and bottles of paint from Miss Harrison's art cupboard. Shanthi never went to school discos, never needed to line up awkwardly against a wall with the other girls; she never needed to fit in. It was only me who felt awkward, watching her standing apart from the crowd, eating lunch by herself in the canteen.

'It's a guy, isn't it?' I'm getting more intrigued. 'Come on, who are you meeting?'

'So, Anjali, you have bothered to turn up?'

We both swing around to see Mum at the door.

Facebook, Spotify, my mother. Three things to avoid when you break up with someone.

Mum ushers me upstairs and into the flat, Shanthi following behind. Immediately I am bathed in the smells of home. Curry, first and foremost. Cumin and coriander and turmeric have infused their way into the seventies carpet, the fading wallpaper, the floral curtains, the saggy brown settee, and probably our DNA. There's no escaping it. Not even with the incense, burning sandalwood fumes beside each Pledge-polished statue of the Buddha. And there are a lot of Buddhas. There's even one next to the cat's basket.

I pick up the cat and stroke her soft grey hair. Ordie's not a Buddhist, not the way she watches the pigeons. There are bald patches in her thinning fur; she's twenty-three years old. Her full name is Ordinary. Don't ask me why, I must have been a precocious six-year-old.

'So you have decided to grace us with a visit?'

OK, enough about the cat, onto my mother.

'Here you go.' I pass Mum the bunch of Jack's lavender. It's in a sorry state, dampened by the drizzle, but I couldn't throw it away. Plus most Sundays I bring my mother flowers from the shop, but today was still holiday.

I missed the shop this morning. As Mum takes the lavender without one sniff of its fragrance, I'm recalling my first day of work ten years ago. The roomful of sunflowers smelling of freedom, conversations with Clara that seemed far away from the

34

curried confines of home, from the expectations of university seminar rooms. From all expectations really. Clara never seemed to ask anything of me, except to love flowers. (And maybe to go to the traders' market, sort and deliver the stock, update the website, keep the inventory and work fifteen-hour days, come to think of it.) I wish I were at the shop now, trying to refuse Clara's whisky, picking up fallen petals.

'I don't know why you must always forget your family.' Mum's ongoing accusations boom through my wandering mind.

'Oh Mum, please stop going on.' I put Ordie down on her favourite spot beside the fireplace and look to Shanthi for support. But she's disappeared into her room.

'There she goes, with her English words.' Mum presses the long edge of her index finger against the tip of her forehead, her favourite gesture for when her younger daughter is showing off her Western ways.

I hate it when she talks about me in the third person. 'Well, what other words would I use?'

We aren't getting off to the best start, but to be honest, that isn't unusual. Mum marches off into the cramped kitchen, where she chucks the lavender on the counter, switches on the kettle and begins lifting and thudding saucepans onto the worktop as if she'd rather be banging them over my head.

So this is my mum: she's wearing a huge dress that clings to her vast bottom and substantial thighs, patterned in red and blue so that from afar you might mistake her for a Persian rug. It's her favourite look of the past decade, after deciding saris were too impractical for Bristol's rain-soaked pavements. Her hair is very short and very dark, thanks to Tesco own-brand jet-black hair dye. Maybe all three of us have the same almond-shaped eyes, but Mum's irises are little fires, burning into you with each word she utters.

'What did I do wrong, to have you talk back to me like all of these English girls?' Mum stares at me fiercely now over the tea, triple chin and thick arms wobbling as she pours milk into the mugs.

My sister comes into the kitchen, a brown corduroy jacket that also looks new slung over her shoulder.

'Are you going out for food?' I ask, for diversion.

'And now she is gone too!' Mum passes out our mugs and then raises both hands in the air, fingers shiny with the Sri Lankan gold handed down by my deceased grandmother. 'Where on earth are my daughters these days?'

Mum's language tends towards the melodramatic. Since coming to the UK, she has learnt English from all available sources: Radio Bristol, waiting-room posters and the *EastEnders* omnibus.

Shanthi and I catch each other's eyes in silent understanding.

'I'm not quite gone yet,' Shanthi points out.

'And why you must go tonight, I don't know,' Mum continues, unhindered, picking up her mug and taking several heavy slugs before composing herself. 'When Anjali has finally graced us with her presence.'

'Give it a rest, Mum,' I sigh. 'It's not like Shanthi's out all the time.'

'And I don't like these people from that art place.'

From where I'm standing, I can see the new painting hanging in the hallway. It's of the St Mary Redcliffe church in Bristol, dark and bold, heavy grey lines of spires and spikes. The Architect would be impressed, the church being an excellent example of Gothic construction. I was glad when Shanthi found the shared studio. It's a part-time space, discounted because of her work in the café. Too many years she's been stuck in this flat, her talent hidden away. At school, while I was giving her those awkward glances in the canteen, she was just hurrying to finish Mum's carrot and beetroot sandwiches so she could get back to Miss Harrison's art room. Miss Harrison had a sheet of mahogany hair and a collection of velvet scarves, and she's maybe the only person who's ever got my sister. Shanthi was always in her studio, even when she was supposed to be in double maths.

'You haven't met these people,' Shanthi reminds Mum.

'I know what they do.' Mum shakes her head, tea sloshing inside her mug. 'They draw on the *outside* of the buildings.'

'It's called street art.' There's a little smile on Shanthi's lips. Somehow Mum's criticisms don't get to her quite the way they get to me.

'Do they not have any paper?'

Mum was furious about Shanthi's missed lessons at school. On parents' evenings, other mums (and dads) would pause to look at my sister's paintings displayed across the art room. Miss Harrison would raise her shiny head hopefully when the three of us trotted in. *Mrs Chandana* . . . But Mum never stayed long. She just shot a quick glance at the teacher she was sure was messing up her elder child's scientific future, then bailed.

'Well it's great you've made friends at the studio,' I say, noting again my sister's new jacket, new jumper, the firm, unfamiliar sound of her boots on the kitchen lino and the fact that I still don't know who she's meeting.

'It is not great.' Mum downs the rest of her tea. 'Both of you now always off gallivanting, and who is going to look after me in my old age?'

'It's just one dinner,' Shanthi says mildly.

'That is not the point.' Mum waves a chopping board in front of my face, rather than my sister's. 'It is what it will become that is the point.'

'What will it become?' I ask, since I'm on the receiving end of the wood.

'Your mother alone on her deathbed.' She thuds the board down.

I should mention at this point that Mum is fifty, working full-time, and probably some years away from expiration.

I've read lots of stories about Asian mothers, seen various send-ups of them on TV programmes and watched all the standard Asian coming-of-age films. I've seen lots of send-ups about mothers in general, Asian or not. I don't want to make my mum out to be just another caricature. But sometimes she can make it bloody difficult.

'Right, I need to find my wallet.' Shanthi throws me a look of apology. I brace myself for the evening ahead.

'What can I do to help?' I turn round to Mum brightly, and am handed an aubergine. For a few moments there is a blissful quiet, just the tapping of our knives on the chopping boards, the sound of Shanthi gathering her things. In a bit we'll be eating aubergine curry, lentils, deep-fried chilli potatoes, bright red coconut sambol. I might be able to keep something down for the first time in a week. Maybe tonight won't be so bad after all. I need a decent meal.

The spray of purple lavender rests on the kitchen counter. I wonder if Jack is looking at his watch, thinking about this food. Despite the lack of meat, he was never able to get enough of Mum's cooking.

'Where is Jack?' Mum asks suddenly, as if picking up the thought as it travels through my mind.

'He's busy,' I mumble, starting on another aubergine.

'That boy is always busy,' Mum mutters.

I wait for the usual questions that are about to pour from my mother's mouth. I say 'questions', but they come with a subtext that in my mother's case is always obvious.

'Does Jack visit his own family?' (Or is he as neglectful and uncaring as I think he is?)

'Yes. Sometimes. His dad. You know his parents are divorced.'

'And his mother is a . . . cleaner, isn't she?' (I know I only work in a supermarket myself, plus the pile of other odd jobs I used to do on top, but that's because I had to bring up two children all alone. Otherwise I would have risen to an immense greatness. What is Jack's mother's excuse?)

'She runs a cleaning *company*. She's very successful. And so what if she was just a cleaner, anyway? Wasn't Dad a cleaner?'

'Have you told Jack's family that?' (You'd better not have told the truth to outsiders, who can never be trusted with such information. Your father would have risen to immense greatness as well, were it not for the fact that he died.)

'They wouldn't care about stuff like that. They're not judgemental.'

'You don't think these people are judgemental?' (I am ashamed of your misplaced trust in these outsiders, who, admittedly nice as they are, are nevertheless waiting for an opportunity to destroy me.)

'Mum, "these" people could never be as judgemental as you.'

'You think you sound clever, using all of your English sarcasm?' (I supported your education, and now you are just using it to destroy me.)

'Stop it, Mum. You've been here for almost thirty years. Stop it with your 'these' people and your English sarcasm and just . . . get over it, can't you?'

'You think I wanted to come and live here?' (Are you so stupid as not to understand that these people divided our people so that we all fought each other and ruined our economy and had no choice but to move here to look after our children, and now all you want to do is try and destroy me?)

'Anyway, I don't want to talk about all of this again, Mum, I know what you did for us, so can we just move on?'

'Yes, look what we did for you, and instead you throw your education down the dustbin and live in sin with a white man.' At this point Mum usually dispenses with the questions altogether.

'Would you stop saying it's a sin? We live in the twenty-first century, Mum.'

'It is a sin. It is the biggest sin.'

'Well, you don't need to worry about it, because it's all over.'

'What do you mean?'

'I'm not living with Jack any more.'

'Where are you living?'

'I'm still in the flat; he's moved out.'

'He has left you?'

'I've left him.'

Now there is the heavy tread of Shanthi's boots at the door. I keep my eyes on the chopping board.

'He has moved out?'

'I told him to go.'

'You told him to go?' Mum puts down her knife.

'Yes.'

'You told him to leave?'

'Yes.'

There's a moment of silence. I force myself to look at Mum. If it's possible, and I'm not sure that it is, her face has turned

40

from brown to grey. She presses her forefinger to the tip of her forehead.

'*Anay*. Oh no. Oh *anay, anay*.' *Anay* is her expression of pain/bewilderment/incredulity.

'What? What's the problem? I thought you'd be happy I'm not living in sin any more.'

'But at least you had a man.'

'What do you mean?' Except I know exactly what she means. She's picturing me in an alternative Oz, yellow-brick road replaced by concrete and a barren city at the end, its spinsters being picked off by flying monkeys. For a moment I see the Architect's face again. It's a bit hazy on account of lost brain cells, but something kind and gentle is shining through. There's a knot in my throat. I could have taken his number.

'*Anay*, my Anjali.' Mum presses the edge of her finger further into her skin, possibly imagining me now high up in the sky, legs dangling from a screeching winged primate. 'Soon you will be thirty.'

'Hold on a minute, Mum,' Shanthi's voice cuts in quietly. Looking across, I see her small face, its frown of concern.

But Mum can't stop. 'What will she do now? After living with that boy for so long? Who will she ever meet now?'

Beside me, the lavender gives off its clean, pine-like scent. My head is aching. The oil from this plant is sometimes used for migraines. But against my mother, it doesn't stand a chance.

I don't want to make my mum sound like a caricature. But as I said, sometimes it's bloody difficult.

The thing is, I know she is being ridiculous. I know that being almost thirty is not a bar to my future happiness. I know this because as soon as I set foot outside the flat I'm typing: *Is being almost thirty a bar to my future happiness?* into the search engine on my phone, and the answer I get is: *Your mum is being ridiculous and you are still, in modern-day terms, a foetus.* Or thereabouts. Well actually, there are several pages about social networks and midlife crises, and one entitled: *Why happiness is not everything!*

I know Mum is a small woman who looks like a Persian rug and who's mistrustful of a group of people because, in times past and present, they have done some pretty bad things to her group of people. I know she comes not only from a different country, but from a different generation altogether, who probably did all die by the age of thirty-two. It's therefore likely that the outlook of their lives cannot be compared to mine and it's possible that I might live until, I don't know, at least thirty-four, and I *know* when putting together all of this information that I can disregard everything she says and get on quite happily with my own future.

But I can't.

She's my mum. And she believes everything she says. And somehow, though I fight against it and say all kinds of things about Persian rugs to prevent myself from taking her seriously, I somehow believe everything she says as well.

Who will want me now?

'Anjali?'

My sister's standing at the door, watching me with that same look of concern.

'I'm OK,' I say. 'Can you tell Mum I'm sorry I had to go?'

'Come back in? I can delay my plans.'

But we don't talk any more, I want to say. You won't even tell me what your plans are.

'It's fine, I'm OK. Please don't worry.' I push out of the gate, duct tape falling off onto my hand.

*

42

'You know what your mum's like.'

Clara watches me take another sip of wine. Her eyes are heavy with our late night and a full day's work. After Mum's, I should have gone straight home to bed. I should have eaten something. I shouldn't have stopped Clara poring over the accounts and made her come out with me. I shouldn't have bought the second glass of wine. Or the glass after that.

'Maybe she's right,' I say.

'But you know she isn't.'

'Who am I going to meet now, Clar?'

'You didn't exactly have any trouble last night.'

There's a pang again as I see the Architect at the door, his hazy but gentle face looking back at me. How would it have been if I really had taken his number – would I have been staring down at it, wondering whether to call?

'But last night didn't make me feel better,' I say, in the end. A different pang comes now, this one heavy with shame. As the hours pass, sleeping with the Architect is making less and less sense. Whatever I wanted, it didn't work. There's still a tight band around my head; my chest still hurts.

Clara traces the thin stem of her glass. 'It's early days, Anj. And you just can't let your mum get to you so much.'

'The thing is, I *am* almost thirty.' The wine is pooling in my empty stomach and the room is starting to sway a little.

'I'm thirty-two.'

'But you're different.'

'How's that?'

'You said no to all the conventional stuff years ago.'

'Do you want the conventional stuff?' Clara folds her arms.

'We talked about it once.'

'You mean you and Jack? Marriage?'

43

I nod. Four years ago, another July day, lying on the grassy slope of St Andrew's Park. The words slipped into the conversation as naturally as what we would have for dinner. Why not? Jack said. It had been six years. The next step.

'But you didn't want to?'

Not then. Not when I was still trying to figure out what to do with my life. I think of Jack moving on each year, his master's degree, his internships, his first journalism assignments. What was it like being with me, working in the shop for so many years, never finding my path? I wonder where he is now, where he might be staying. Julia feels heavy on my shoulder tonight. Her legs wrapped around my arm, the snake slithering open-mouthed across her calf.

Later, I'm standing outside an old building off Gloucester Road, aware of the plastic peeling off the guttering, the walls lined with grime and spray-painted with punk figures Mum would not approve of. There's a series of buzzers on the front door; the studio is on the first floor. I look up at the dim glow coming through the window, barely enough for anybody to work by. A security light maybe. My sister probably went home after her dinner. It's gone ten. The place looks empty.

Someone comes up behind me. I turn, half expecting Shanthi, excuses about why I'm standing here running quickly through my mind. My sister's never brought me to the studio, she's never shared this space with me or Mum. I don't really know what I'm doing here.

But it's not Shanthi. It's another woman, tall, skinny, with short, spiky, burning red hair, the sort of hairstyle that stares at you and says: No, *your head will never support this arrangement, you are simply not this cool.*

44

'Yes?' she asks. She's got a set of keys out, ready to open the door. I realise I'm staring at her.

'Sorry,' I mumble. 'I was looking for … I thought that … maybe my sister was here.'

The woman screws up her eyes. 'You mean Shanthi?'

Now she's looking at me closely. I have an urge to defend myself. *OK, OK, you're right, I've pretty much worn my hair like this since the age of twelve, but that's because every year before that Mum sat me naked in the bathtub and cut off all my curls till I looked like a small Asian member of the Beatles. So you wonder why I don't choose a more adventurous style? Safe and long, my friend, safe and long.*

'She's not here now.' The woman looks up at the window.

'Oh, right.'

'She'll probably be back tomorrow.'

I wonder again what I'm doing here, what I hoped to find.

'I'm Donna,' the woman says.

'Oh, right.'

Another pause, and then I remember my manners. 'Oh, sorry, I'm Anjali.'

'Anjali.' Donna nods. 'Shanthi's mentioned you.'

'She has?' It surprises me. I can't imagine what my sister would say about me.

Donna opens the door. She hesitates, maybe because I'm still standing here and she's wondering what on earth to do with me. I'm wondering why I don't move. I shouldn't have had those four glasses of wine. Or at least I should have got chips and gone home, like Clara.

'Did you want to come up?'

I follow her up the stairs, our boots echoing on the wooden boards. Four of them share this space, I'm told, and when I go inside, I'm surprised to see how small it is. I can't imagine my sister in such close quarters with three other people. The place smells earthy, sharp, of paint, oil, methylated spirit, clay, wood, glue; desks are crammed into each corner, a couple covered with bottles and brushes and palettes, easels and canvases wedged alongside, another with a sewing machine and folded textiles, a fourth pushed out of the way to make room for a sculpture of the swollen head of a woman with a giant mouth.

'That's Shanthi's desk.' Donna gestures to one of the painting corners near the window.

The final streaks of light have crept out of the sky. I touch my sister's desk, running fingers over the stiff bristles of brushes, the heavy paper laid out for sketches. The paintings beside the easel are different to the ones she brings home, the colours bolder, thicker, blended into blocks and lines that make me feel something I don't really understand. Something that makes me shiver with panic, like I'm standing on the edge of a cliff, stones giving way beneath my feet. My heart's thumping inside my chest and I don't know why.

I shouldn't be in this studio, invading my sister's space. She's never invited me in, she hasn't wanted me here.

I start to back out of the room, forgetting to look for clues to the person who might have gone out with Shanthi for dinner, almost stumbling into the sculpture, turning round into the big gaping hole between its lips.

'Are you OK?' Donna asks, her face seeming fine and sculpted too, pale eyebrows arched, eyes amber, scorching, like her hair. She's taken off her jacket and I can see a tattoo above her collarbone, a peacock feather, iridescent, wispy black tendrils around an eye of green, yellow, a centre pit of deep blue.

'Thanks for letting me come up.' I'm trying to smile while fumbling for the door.

'I'll tell Shanthi you stopped by.'

'No.' I think we're both surprised by the vehemence of my reply. I swallow. 'No,' I say again, more softly. 'Could you maybe ... could you keep this to yourself?'

'Why?' There are three eyes on my skin, Donna's and her peacock's. My cheeks burn and I get an odd feeling, like I'm face to face with the burlesque dancer.

'This is her space. I'm sorry.' I find the handle and leave the studio, hurrying down the steps, out into the night.

Three

The days pass. Dahlias turn into delicate blue delphiniums, then asters with starry purple heads. The messages from Jack become less frequent. Sometimes I find myself logging on to Facebook, Twitter, Instagram, wanting some kind of connection with him, even just a picture or a status he has liked. But he stays quiet. And social media is dangerous, threatening every second to unleash something worse, maybe a photograph of him with Julia.

I deactivate my accounts.

I work as much as I can, begging Clara for shifts on my days off, missing a couple more of Mum's Sunday dinners, burying myself in scent and water and brown paper.

In early August, I tear open my palm with a thorn.

I gaze at the spot of my blood on a pure white damask rose. Breathing in the petals, the faint undertone of honey, I'm back in my tiny garden a few weeks ago, a row of Jack's shirts dancing on the fraying line. I'm pruning the pot of damask roses, telling him how in Greek mythology, it was Aphrodite who gave the rose its name, who created it from the tears and blood of her lover, Adonis. I'm seeing Jack store this fact in his mind, then seeing us again, when he is presenting me with a bouquet of his tears and blood for my birthday. The twenty-nine rugosa roses, one for each year of my life. I'm placing the flowers in our vintage vase, thinking that I'm happy.

I wonder about that happiness. Wonder if it could really have existed, when Jack was shagging the burlesque dancer the week before, the week after. Even if I didn't know it.

'That's it. I can't spend another day like this with you.'

'What?' Clara's voice startles me out of my memories. I suck the blood from my palm, metal on my tongue. Clara's looking at me from the shop counter, green eyes narrowed, the silver hoops glinting in her eyebrow and lip. 'You're sacking me?' I ask.

'No, you bloody idiot. I'm taking you on holiday.'

'You're the idiot. We can't both leave the shop.'

'We can. My mum said she'd help, and I've lined up Anna.' Anna is the student who works with us some weekends and at peak times of the year. 'She's got a reading week or something coming up; she can manage this place while we're away.'

'What about her reading?' I'm not sure when I switched from being Anjali Chandana to being Professor Chandana, Anna's educational supervisor.

'For God's sake. Are you coming or not?'

'Where to?'

'Rome. I've found a last-minute deal.'

'I can't.'

'You can.'

'I'm rubbish company at the moment, Clar. You can see that.'

'Yes, I can. And as I've got to be with you anyway, I'd rather be somewhere a little more exciting.'

'When?'

'Monday.'

'Monday?' (I should point out that it's Friday today.)

'You've got three minutes to think about it.'

And at that very moment, my phone flashes on the work surface.

I know you don't want to hear from me. But I have to collect my stuff. I'll come over next week. If you're home, can we talk? J

My chest starts to thud. Sometimes the universe conspires to help you make up your mind.

'Monday it is.'

I've never been on holiday with a girlfriend. Apart from Jack, the only people I've been away with are Mum and my sister. And even Shanthi's gentle presence can't take away the fact that holidays with Mum are more like a community sentence than a vacation.

I'm apprehensive about this break with Clara. The fact is, since splitting up with Jack, I am not good company. Every event, every conversation, every flower is now linked to my broken relationship in some way. Maybe this is just what happens to everyone after a break-up, maybe everyone's world constricts into one narrow, miserable existence, but I can only imagine that from the outside, it's very dull.

And Clara, as I said, has a terror of the dull.

Still, she seems able to overlook this in my case.

'Anjali Chandana, your mission, should you choose to take it, is to not think about Jack, or Julia, for half an hour each day. Just half an hour. You achieve that, and I'll keep quiet.'

I raise my eyebrows.

'OK, maybe not quiet as in the original definition of the word.'

I assent to my mission.

'And you never know.' Clara winks. 'I've heard there are a fair few men in Rome.'

The Architect makes an appearance inside my head, standing in a corner, weighing it down. I try to shake him out. 'I'm not interested in any of them.'

'We'll see.'

'No way, Clar, not one single Italian.'

I'll remember those words.

We stay in a place called Trastevere, over the Tiber river and outside the main city. Clara wants somewhere artistic and bohemian that's suited to our artistic and bohemian natures. I'm dubious about my nature but decide not to object.

Our apartment turns out to be a tiny converted stable. We step into a hideaway lined with worn flagstones and dusty wooden beams. The furniture is dark and heavy, the room scented with the papery musk of ancient things. The only downside of our new home is the lack of a second bed.

'You're kidding me.' Clara holds up the printed email, which clearly states the apartment is for two people.

I take it from her and study it. 'I think by two people, it maybe means a couple.'

We appraise the narrow bed.

'This is going to bring us closer together,' Clara tells me.

So in those first squashed, chaste days, Clara and I wander around the ancient city with our arms linked, like a long-time married couple. We do the things a long-time married couple might do: lifting our heads in awe inside the Pantheon, eating gelato beside the Trevi Fountain, climbing the Spanish Steps, taking too many photographs of St Peter's Basilica (which incidentally turns out to be far more impressive than my sexual technique). We visit the Colosseum so that I can gaze on the arena where bodies have been torn apart and put my own problems in perspective. Where

I don't imagine stabbing a burlesque dancer in the heart with a gladiatorial spear, not once.

We hang out in cafés and drink little cups of powerful coffee, while I impress Clara with my knowledge.

'That, over there, is composed of two ogees,' I inform her, pointing towards the arch above a doorway. I see the Architect again, his toned body leaning against the frame, nodding. For once, there's less guilt pooling in my stomach. A little less, anyway. He's looking at me like a friend would, maybe even a bit proud.

Clara is proud of me too, for different reasons.

'You're going to be just fine,' she says.

'D'you think?' I lift my cup to the light and catch the shadow of my generous nose.

'Of course you are.'

But Jack's never far from my mind, as much as I try to keep him away. I wonder how it's possible to be fine without him.

'I keep thinking, Clar, how long would it have gone on for if I hadn't found out? Did he ever plan to stop it?'

'Did you ask him?'

'I started to.'

'What happened?'

'I was worried he would tell me the truth.'

'Anj. Mate. You've got to stop killing yourself.'

I gaze at the little dimple of Clara's silver cheek stud, wishing that I knew how.

'And listen, maybe this is going to be the making of you.'

'How so?'

'Well, you always said you needed space to figure out what to do with the rest of your life.'

'Or just to drink till this decade's over.'

'Anj.' Clara lays her hand across mine. She always seems to see the good in me, even when I can't.

I lift her hand and kiss it. 'Right now, I just want to work in your shop for the rest of my life.'

By rights, we should at this point be sitting at a table on a sun-drenched cobbled pavement, sipping espresso from delicate cups. Perhaps while watching water gush from the genitalia of stone cherubs.

But Clara has a dread of the busy cafés and restaurants on the popular squares, of drinking overpriced coffee in front of accordion players, portrait masters, and gold-painted mime artists. Every drink and meal is a planned effort to avoid the crowds and seek a more authentic experience. So at the present time we're sitting on cracked plastic chairs in a back alley with a definite whiff of . . .

'Fish?' Clara wonders, nose in the air.

'Urine,' I correct her.

'Anyway, the thing is,' Clara holds out her chipped cup and signals to the bored waiter for more coffee, 'I might not exactly have the shop for the rest of your life.'

Flowers and Clara came together unexpectedly. Her aunt Samantha had owned the shop on Gloucester Road for many years. Clara had, by dint of her aunt being the prime babysitter, spent many afternoons and weekends in the company of petals. She knew the names of all the flowers before she ever set foot in school. But then the years passed, she got busy with uni, went travelling for a while, and forgot all about the blossoms until a phone call brought her back from Bali, where she was almost about to break her no-relationship rule with a one-handed percussionist. The phone call was from her mum, to say that Aunt Sammy had died.

Clara never expected to inherit the flower shop. At first she considered selling it. But she wanted to do something for her aunt. And for herself, before she wound up married to the percussionist. The shop seemed the perfect solution in the end, providing both work and a home, in the flat above the foliage.

That was ten years ago.

'I think the time might have come to do something different,' Clara says.

It's been a tough few years. Flowers are like people: they suffer in austerity. Clara has spent many hours looking over the accounts, her head in her hands. But we've worked hard. She supported me to get my NVQ, and the pair of us, along with the local blooms, a decent website and an accidental counselling service (a fair few troubled souls seem to wander into florists), have somehow kept the business flourishing.

Clara talked about shutting up shop before during my years with Jack, and even though I knew I should be moving on, those conversations provoked mild terror. Now, in these days post-infidelity, the smell of the shop seems to be about all that's keeping me going.

I finger the rough edge of my chipped saucer. 'I guess you were never supposed to be there forever.'

'Neither of us was,' Clara says. 'If it wasn't for you, I might have closed up a long time ago.'

We sip our espressos. I think of the first day I wandered into the shop. I was looking for a summer job, something to tide me over between university terms. I didn't know then that I wouldn't be returning. It was easy, with Jack, to keep going along with the flow.

'Maybe that's why he chose her,' I say.

'Jack? The dancer? What?'

'I wasn't going anywhere, was I? Just doing the same stuff, every day.'

'I keep telling you. It wasn't your fault.'

'I mean, you can only get so excited by a new box set.'

'Anj . . .'

'What if *they* watched box sets?' The new thought makes me shiver in the August warmth. 'I mean, what if they did couple stuff? What if she, like, made him spaghetti bolognese? Proper bolognese, with actual meat in it?'

'You have to—'

'How can I compete, Clar? With a real-life burlesque dancer? Who watches Netflix too and has no policy on cows?'

Clara grabs my cup and sets it down with a firm thud. 'Don't even think about competing. You have to stop doing this to yourself.'

The waiter comes along again with two more espressos. He must sense that we need them. His apron is a coffee-stained Italian flag, secured with a green and red striped ribbon. I wonder how long he's been working in this back alley.

'I just thought I'd have it all figured out by now,' I say, watching him saunter back inside the café. 'This whole life thing.'

'You and me both.'

We down our coffees.

'I wonder where we'll end up,' Clara muses, looking out on the vista of scaffolding in front of us. She turns to me. 'What did you always think you'd be when you grew up?'

It's a funny thing. When you're raised in the shadow of someone else's expectations, there isn't much space of your own to think about what you might want to be. I assumed one day I'd turn out to be a doctor, accountant or lawyer, just as Mum told me. Now, finding myself none of the above, it's hard not to feel lost.

'But was there anything you ever thought *you* wanted to do?' Clara asks. 'When you were at school? I mean, really want to do?'

I pick up the flyer that's been left on our table. It's advertising a jazz night in an artistic and bohemian bar, not far from our new artistic and bohemian home. There was once a very vague, very unformed idea that came to me sometime in my teens, midway through a music lesson.

'Saxophonist,' I tell her.

The only lesson at school I ever took seriously was English, so this dream was always going to end up lying with the corpses of my mother's fantasies. And it's doubtful I'll be a saxophonist now, given my ongoing lack of musical ability, and saxophone.

But as Clara and I study the flyer, working out just how far the bar is from our new home, it is possible we'll meet one.

Well two, actually.

So this is us, Friday night, our last night in Rome, in a crowd, in the cellar of a cramped and musty bar. The brick walls are dripping with sweat. Our clothes are drenched. Clara has gathered her dreadlocks into a gigantic bundle on top of her head so that the people behind have to jump up to see the bands. They don't seem to mind. Nobody seems to mind anything in this place. Everyone just seems happy that it's still warm outside and that the jazz is still playing.

The bands started at ten, and it's now the early hours of the morning. There are no famous names, just a run of talented musicians, with members of the audience intermittently pulling out brass instruments from behind their sweaty backs and leaping up onto the stage to join in. I'm watching Clara smiling and dancing; I'm watching the rest of the crowd whooping and cheering.

Jack would like this place. It's his kind of thing, the hidden underground bar in the city that doesn't feel made up for the tourists. I remember the two of us in another place like this, somewhere else, maybe in Paris or Berlin or Prague, one of the cities we visited together. He's standing beside me with a beer in his hand, his body swaying next to mine, an arm around my waist. I can feel the warmth of his grip, the jostle of his thigh.

He's looking at the band, but then he's drifting to the people in the crowd, to the women. After a while, he breaks away from me to go to the bar. While getting a drink, he talks to a pretty woman with a ponytail. I look over to them from time to time. Jack laughing, the woman responding, her red mouth opened wide. He wasn't flirting, he'll insist, when I ask him about it later; he was just having fun.

I close my eyes. The heavy notes are twisting a pain deep in my gut. I wanted so much to be happy. I was so pleased the day we moved into our own place, had our own tiny garden. I was so grateful for my stocks and lavender and pot of damask roses. I told myself I was just jealous, and days later, I'd forgotten about the woman with the ponytail, just like I'd forgotten about the other women who sometimes tried to creep into my life. If I told myself I was happy, it would be true.

I feel my eyes becoming hot. I keep them closed, breathing in the sweaty brick, focusing on the drums, the trumpet, the piano.

I'm concentrating so hard, I almost don't notice the hands on my shoulders. I feel myself being turned, and let my body move.

Another mouth touches mine.

I open my eyes.

There's a man in front of me. Skinny, goateed, with a glinting dark expression.

He's a saxophonist. I realise this as soon as he grabs the case that's been balanced against the wall, and runs up the steps onto the stage. He pulls out his instrument and adds to the music with a tremor of notes.

'Did he just kiss you?' Clara appears at my side.

'I'm not sure.' I'm confused.

He seems to be playing just for me. (This isn't me being self-absorbed; it's just that the room has started to empty, everyone seems headed to another club.) I stare at this man who may or may not have kissed me, as he leans back, eyes tightly closed, muscles flexing in the thin arms gripping the golden body of his saxophone, the deep hum reaching a crescendo – and for a moment anything seems possible. Maybe this could be a ticket out of the painful memories. Maybe this guy can give me the answer the Architect couldn't.

The Saxophonist has a brother. It turns out that they are, sadly, British, albeit of Chinese origin, both buskers from Basingstoke who, fed up with the paucity of donations from the supermarket crowds, decided to pack up their woodwind instruments and busk their way around the world. They boarded a plane to Rome, this being the first EasyJet flight they came across, and haven't really moved on since then.

'The tourists here are generous,' the brother explains to Clara, while gazing at her gigantic hair arrangement. 'And our hostel is cool. And there's a steady supply of ganja.'

They figure they'll stay until the cannabis or the tourists run out, neither of which seems to be showing much inclination to do so.

All of this we find out from the brother while the Saxophonist is still mid-melody. The brother offers us a spliff, and Clara slips away with him. This pretty much leaves me the last person on the floor as the Saxophonist's final cadenza draws to a close. I feel bad; he's pretty talented.

I clap as enthusiastically as I can.

He puts away his saxophone and drops down to the floor beside me.

'I think you kissed me,' I say.

'I did,' he replies.

It seems as good a beginning as any.

We toss euros, and Clara and the brother get our apartment for the night. My saxophonist picks up his instrument and beckons me out of the club, over the bridge, running across the river Tiber.

I wonder if we're heading for his hostel. The water is dashing by on either side of us, and the cool early-morning air is drying out our damp skin. As we run, thoughts of Jack seem to be whipping away, falling off into the ripples. I can almost feel the pain slipping from my body, leaving me lighter, faster. I want to run for ever.

He slows me down and takes my hand.

From time to time, I glance over at the stranger beside me. His is a skinny elegance, skinnier than Jack, and I like the feel of his long, artistic fingers. They make me want to say odd things. *Play me like your instrument. Let me touch your reed. Can I blow into your . . .*

'I'm glad to see you smiling,' the Saxophonist says. 'You looked so sad in the club.'

'Is that why you kissed me?'

'Did it work?'

'A bit.'

'Why are you so sad?'

'Because of a boy.'

'He's not worth it,' the Saxophonist says at once.

'I know that.'

'I was sad because of a girl,' the Saxophonist says. 'That's why I left Basingstoke. Well that, and its large quantity of roundabouts.'

'Did it help? Are you over her now?'

'If I went home, the answer would probably be no.'

'So ...?'

'So, I'm staying in Rome.'

'Are you in touch with her?'

'That would be suicide. Are you in touch with yours?'

'No.'

'Should you be?'

I'm not expecting that question. It's a difficult one to answer, and I avoid a reply by kissing him again. If I just keep on kissing this man, then I don't need to let Jack in. And the Saxophonist has this tender way about him, a way of holding the sides of my face with those long musical fingers, keeping me steady. Though I guess Jack sort of did that, too.

It occurs to me that even though my arms are around this stranger, at some point I'll have to start working things out. After all, the Colosseum reminded me how many thousands were destroyed by beasts and gutted with spears. At the Forum we saw the spot where Caesar was cremated, after the Senate had turned on him. The history of our world is formed by the terrible things that happen to people, burning brightly for a moment in our minds, then forgotten. In the whole scheme of things, what's happened to me can't be so bad. An affair with a burlesque dancer. It hadn't felt real to him, Jack said – it had felt somehow separate to everything else; it hadn't mattered. Not until he'd realised what it had done to us.

I think about how I brushed off the Architect after one night together. How I've hardly been back to Mum's, even though she wants to see me. I wonder if we are all just as capable of hurting someone. I wonder why I can't give Jack a proper chance to explain, why I can't even answer the phone to him.

The Saxophonist pauses to tuck a stray curl behind my ear. His lips meet mine once more. But even though I'm pressing back firmly, my ex-boyfriend won't go away.

I think of the things I once told Jack about me. The good things, but also the bad. My lack of direction, for a start. Letting Mum down and never amounting to anything. Never really being there for my mother or my sister, especially with Dad not being around. Sometimes it feels as if there is a hole inside me, round about my chest, where all these things have been.

It's too hard to dwell on this.

The Saxophonist lowers his hands and draws away from me. 'You're running, too,' he says.

Damn it, he's going to make me talk.

So I give in, and we talk. We are in Piazza Navona now, and even Clara wouldn't have minded. The crowds have gone. The waiters are packing up the tables. A long-stemmed red rose has been left on one of the chairs. You can't escape the roses here either. Hawkers tend to follow you around Rome, desperate to sell you romance (and umbrellas). I watch a waiter pick up the rose and tuck it into his waistband, a little flash of red every time he turns. I wonder where it's going to end up tonight – with his lover, or his mother? Beside him, a few stragglers are smoking and laughing. We approach one of the fountains and find a space for ourselves in front of a sea creature that is being viciously speared.

I tell the Saxophonist about Jack. I tell him about the other attractive girls who sometimes came into our relationship, how confused I got over my jealousy. I tell the Saxophonist I don't know how to forgive the person who has left me with a burlesque dancer to compare myself to.

'Is that why you can't see him?' my companion asks.

I look down at my lap, the fading leaves printed on my dress. 'Maybe. Probably. I guess I'm angry. That after so long, this was how it ended.'

'You have a right,' the Saxophonist tells me.

I look up. 'But I've made it sound like it was all bad. And it wasn't.'

I find myself telling him about the other times. Those times with Jack in the early hours of the morning, lying with our bodies turned into each other, my head on his chest. How Jack also made me feel beautiful. How easy he was to talk to; how well he listened.

When I've finished, the Saxophonist cups my right hand in both of his, warms my palm inside the cradle of his slender fingers. For a moment he doesn't speak, and then he asks me, 'Why are you lonely, Anjali?'

It's unexpected. It's like the painful parts inside me are suddenly there, exposed. Images flood my mind, of my mother at the dining table, waiting for Shanthi and me to come home. Of my sister, those first nights alone in our room after I moved out. Maybe staring at my empty bed, my empty wardrobe, bare shelves. I let his question drift into silence, while he holds my hand tightly.

'It must be nice, to be here with your brother,' I say, after a while.

'It's useful,' the Saxophonist says. 'He brings in the money. He was always the good-looking one.'

'Which one were you?'

'The one who took all the money.'

I smile. 'What's the age difference?'

'Two years. He's older.'

'Like me and my sister,' I say. 'But we'd never take off round the world together.'

'You're not close?'

I pause. 'Maybe once. Before Jack.'

'Was Jack the problem?'

I hesitate again. I'm seeing myself ten years ago, lifting up my suitcase and walking out of Mum's flat. Walking down the stairs, out of the front door, along the concrete path, out of the gate. Not looking back. Walking to Jack's, but it was before we'd got together. He was just a new person then, still a stranger.

'No. I don't think so.'

I face the Saxophonist. 'But what about you? It's your turn to talk.'

He holds up his hands. He tells me about his girl. This girl cares deeply for him, that much is clear, but she doesn't care for his lifestyle. She doesn't want to watch him be ignored by the supermarket crowds, but she doesn't want to watch him be admired by the Italian ones, either. She wants to have the thing. The marriage, the babies, the security. She wants him to put his saxophone on the shelf, and bring it down sometimes, at parties. Play a little tune to the kids before they go to bed. Play to her when she can't sleep.

'But even if nothing ever comes of this,' he says, 'if I'm here till I die and never make a penny, I can't regret it. I can't regret trying. She accepted that.'

I wonder how it feels, to know so clearly what you need.

In the end, it was an amicable split: the Saxophonist and his girlfriend wanted different things: it just couldn't work.

Now he plays to the tourists with a hole in his chest.

The waiters finish for the night, turning the lights off behind them. The stragglers have left the square. The red rose is gone. It's odd to listen to Rome without its crowds, its accordion players, its fast, relentless traffic. Just the quiet, and the pouring of the fountain. The water never stops.

'I don't want to go home,' I say. I think about walking back to the apartment, Clara and me packing up our suitcases, waiting for the taxi. Heading towards the airport, queuing up to board our flight. No Jack at the other end, flask of tea at the ready in case his old Fiesta breaks down on the A38.

'Then don't go. Come travelling with me.'

'I don't have enough knickers.'

The Saxophonist is smiling. I look into his face, his glittery eyes, the rounded nub of his nose, the dark hairs so fine on his goatee. Skin an olive brown, a couple of shades lighter than mine. I wonder whether it would be brown enough for my mum. I wonder how it would feel to follow a dream, without knowing how it might turn out.

But this dream is his.

In the deserted square, listening to the water, we sit by the fountain and kiss. Our hearts are still broken, but for now this is a gentle reprieve.

In a few hours, I will be on a plane, looking out of the window. I'll be remembering how it felt to have this man's slender arms around me, his careful hands steadying my face. This moment will burn as brightly as all of the others, and then it will fade.

Back in Bristol, the summer sun shines along my street, the pavement glistening, light reflecting off the windows of the packed cars and crowded terraces. I put down my bag and listen to the gentle breeze rustling the branches of the gaunt silver birch outside my flat. My chest feels a little less heavy than when I left, the dull ache a little easier.

I put my key in the lock.

The flat is different. I know it before I see it.

Crossing into the lounge, there's an empty space where the TV used to be, where the espresso machine used to be. In the bedroom, there are empty drawers in the chest, Jack's wardrobe cleared out, only bare boards beneath my fingertips. His books and papers gone, an outline on the wall where the old football poster was tacked.

I walk slowly back into the lounge, my heart thumping. The three ebony elephants have vanished, too. I touch the round, dust-free patches on the mantelpiece where they once stood, where I often ran my hand along their firm, heavy haunches. We bought those elephants together in Sri Lanka, the one time Jack visited with me, the one time I was there without my mother, seeing the country through his eyes and not my mum's blinkered ones. My legs lose their power. I sink onto the sofa, remembering the day I first held those intricately carved bodies. To keep you safe, he said.

Four

'You are here?'

I slip past my mother into her living room and plonk myself on the saggy settee. I push my head into its brown cushions, breathing in decades of curry. 'Yes, I'm here.' It seems an obvious point to make, but there doesn't seem another way to put it. Ordie mews at my feet. I pick her up and cuddle her to my chest.

'You are not in Italy?'

'I'm not in Italy.'

'You didn't go to Italy?'

'I did go to Italy.'

'You have come back from Italy?'

To be fair, I was up all night kissing a saxophonist. I'm willing to admit it might be as much my fault as my mother's that this conversation is not going well.

'Mum. I went to Italy on Monday. I came back home today, Saturday. I came here.'

'You came straight from the airport?'

It's never really clear why my mother needs to know these kinds of details. Maybe soon I'll discover that she enrolled on a top-secret project to count the exact number of steps her second daughter took from birth to thirty, and that my withholding this key information has been the source of great stress to her throughout these three decades.

'I went home first.' I nuzzle into Ordie and close my eyes. I'm trying not to picture my flat and how empty it felt. How it didn't feel like home any more.

'It is not like you to come over.' I can see the suspicion on Mum's face even without looking up. 'Did something happen on holiday?'

I wonder what she would say if she knew I'd been sitting in a public place all night snogging a busker from Basingstoke. It kind of feels like a dream now. I breathe in and try to relive that brief shelter of being wrapped inside his arms, protected from everything there was to face on getting home.

'Nothing happened.'

'Clara is home too?'

'Clara is home too.'

'So you are all right?'

'I'm all right, Mum.' I look up, finally. My mother's brow is deepened permanently by a thick line crossing right through the middle; there are deep, dark pouches beneath her eyes full of her worry about her daughters and their future. It's not clear now why I thought being here was going to be better than staying at home. 'My shower's broken.' Relief washes over me with this lie. 'I really need to have a shower.' With sudden energy, I set Ordie back down onto the sofa cushion and jump to my feet. My skirt and T-shirt are dusty, my hair is a knotted mat, my skin still coated in dry sweat. I'll stand under burning water until it's legitimately time to go to bed. I'll avoid all the cross-examination.

'You look tired,' Mum says, as I start to make my way out of the room.

'I'm OK.'

'You don't look well.'

'I'm fine, Mum.'

'Your face looks old . . .'

The days I still checked Facebook, there were so many articles on there about parenting and how to get it right. About what foods to feed your child, what books to read them, exactly how much praise and encouragement to give, how to enable them. It's like even before the internet my mum had some kind of access to a dark web, with an opposing feed. *Read this if you want to mess up your child. Remember, persistence is key!*

'Well then I must be old, Mum.'

'You must fix your shower.'

I keep on walking.

Shanthi's going out again. Drying off after my shower, I go into her room, and find her in the emerald jumper once more, that unfamiliar dust of grey powder on her eyelids.

'You seeing your friend again?' I rub my hair with the towel.

She nods. My sister has always been quiet, but there's something in her few words that seems even more closed off and secretive. I know better than to probe this time, and hope that Donna didn't tell her about my visit to the studio. I wonder about her 'friend', wonder about the three other desks in that room, the other painter, the fabric designer, the sculptor, trying to picture what kind of man could be holding the brush, threading a needle, shaping the clay.

'How was your holiday?' Shanthi passes me her comb. I go past the ornate screen that Mum once brought back from Sri

Lanka to divide the room, and sit near the window on the spare bed, the one that used to be mine. Shanthi never got rid of it after I left. I start raking at my hair, black wiry clumps coming out on the teeth of the comb.

'It was OK,' I say. 'It was good to get away.'

She picks up her wallet. 'What happened, Anjali?' For a moment, I think she's talking about the Saxophonist. Wondering what I'm up to, hooking up with these strangers in bars; what I'm trying to find. The same thoughts that kept nudging me on the plane, keeping sleep away. Clara passed straight out, tongue stud twinkling inside her open mouth, clearly not racked with any confusion about her night with the Saxophonist's brother.

But of course Shanthi's talking about Jack.

'You mean why we broke up?'

My sister nods.

'He was sleeping with someone else.'

I hear her intake of breath, see the clench of her small fingers.

'What a shit.'

It almost makes me smile. Shanthi rarely swears; it's just been me with the foul mouth.

'I don't believe it,' she says.

'Took me a while too.'

'Is he still with her?'

'I don't know.'

'Have you seen him since?'

I shake my head.

'I'm sorry,' Shanthi says.

'It's OK.' I stare at the loose white threads along the cuff of her jeans, remembering how scared I felt looking at the canvases in her studio. My eyes are hot again.

'Is there anything I can do?'

69

I look up at my sister, the tiny pucker between her eyebrows, the sharp cheekbones, the bottom lip bitten, like mine. 'Would you mind if I slept here tonight?'

'Of course not.' Then, after a pause, 'Do you want me to stay in too?'

She's still clutching her wallet. I see us as kids again, lying in our beds, only partially separated by the screen. If you look closely, the pattern of the screen is composed of the twisting, writhing bodies of tiny glittery serpents. Back then, this didn't bother us; we tapped the serpents every night, working out our special code, until Mum came in to chide us for not being asleep. After she left, we'd do a couple more taps on the screen then settle down, a warm feeling in my chest knowing Shanthi was on the other side.

I look back at my sister, the hollow beneath her collarbones, her cheeks, the secrets behind her eyes, wondering when I stopped being able to decipher our language.

'No, you've got to go out. I need to get to sleep, anyway.'

'OK, if you're sure. Night, Anjali.'

After she's gone, I lie beneath the pale covers, looking around me. It's tidier now than when I used to live here. Shanthi doesn't have much, her clothes neatly in her cupboard, her few art books stacked on the shelf. There's a plate containing two butt ends on her chest of drawers, the faint smell of cigarettes in the room. She started smoking at university and kept going, despite Mum laying into her about it. It seems fair enough to me. Living with Mum for thirty-one years would probably drive most people to nicotine.

The walls were once covered in old floral paper and tacked with her sketches; now they are painted green and there are only a couple of canvases: a bridge across a barren sky, a tiny boat on a gentle sea.

Mum comes in.

'You are in bed?'

I resist the urge for a sarcastic reply.

'I'm tired, Mum.'

She comes over and puts her heavy hand on my forehead.

'Before you ask, I'm fine, Mum.'

'All right, all right,' Mum says. Then she sighs, 'At least I know where one of my daughters is.'

'Is Shanthi out a lot at the moment?'

'Yes. And I am never knowing whether she will be wanting food.'

The distress this causes Mum is evident. But you can't phone Shanthi. She must be the only person left in the Western hemisphere who doesn't have a mobile, who doesn't check her emails, or use social media. She told me once that she can't live in constant contact with the world.

'Do you know who she's with?'

'I don't know, one of the art people.' It's clear Mum hasn't thought the relationship might be romantic, and I decide to avoid giving her a heart attack by not putting the suggestion in her head. 'I don't know, Anjali. I am not sure about these people.'

'But they might be good for her, Mum.'

Mum's triple chin wobbles; she's preparing for a tirade.

'And they could well be vegetarian.'

I see her jaw relax a little.

'They might even be Buddhist.'

There's a definite slackening in her shoulders.

'Well, you must go to sleep,' she decides. 'You are working tomorrow?'

'Yes. Early.'

'Well, goodnight. And you must fix that shower tomorrow.'

'OK, Mum.'

'Don't leave these things.'

'I won't.'

'Once upstairs's shower leaked and the ceiling fell onto our heads.'

'Whose heads?' I have no memory of this injury.

'If we had been home, it would have been our heads.'

'Night, Mum.'

'Goodnight, Anjali.'

As she goes, she pauses in front of one of the pictures on the wall, the one of the boat on the sea. 'Now I will wait up for your sister,' she says softly. 'Like I did for your father.'

I lie still. It's so rare to hear anything about my dad that when the information comes, I am aching for it, wanting to take in every detail. But my mother doesn't say any more, slipping out and closing the door.

I turn off the lamp. The curtains are open, the tails of the serpents glimmering in the pale light of the moon. My eyes close, but the snakes are somehow always there, at the edge of my consciousness. I wait for slumber, my body begging for it, but it doesn't come. Opening my eyes, I look past the serpents, staring at the blue ocean in the picture on the wall. My head is filled with images of a person I can't see but can somehow feel, a man who might once have held my tiny child hands in his great palms; who might have gently rocked me to sleep.

My dad loved boats. He couldn't sail or anything. He just liked to look at them. He used to take my mother, my sister and me down to the harbour to watch them. We couldn't afford to go inside the SS *Great Britain*, one of Bristol's tourist attractions. She's an old passenger steamship, now a kind of boat museum. She was the first iron steamer to cross the Atlantic. But Dad didn't care so much about that. He liked to look at the smaller boats.

This is all I've been able to pick up from Mum over the years. I don't know if there's a hole in her chest like mine, like the Saxophonist's, because she can hide things well. But every so often there is a certain look in her eyes, a certain set of her mouth, as if there's a gap inside her, too. Sometimes I think I see the same look in my sister, and I watch closely. But then the moment passes and it's hard to be sure; she guards herself too well.

Dad wanted to learn how to sail; he wanted to buy a yacht, he wanted to take us all out onto the water with him.

'How was he ever going to get the money, hmm?' I remember the way Mum paused in her whirlwind of housework once. 'With that cleaning job of his.'

I remember the day she might have said this. It was a year after Dad died, when I was four years old, one of my earliest memories. She'd been cleaning out some cupboards, and an old picture tumbled out. A photograph of me, Shanthi and Dad down by the harbour. Mum fell to her knees and stared at it for a long time. I don't remember her words exactly, but I do remember touching her sleeve, scared that she wouldn't stand up again.

That photo's in one of the albums now. I found it again when I was a teenager. This is my dad: he was very dark, with thick, curly hair, like mine. He had some pretty bad sideburns. He had blue eyes. You can't really tell from the photo, but Mum said that by some accident of genetics, some Burgher ancestry, his eyes were the blue of the early-morning Sri Lankan skies.

He was a handsome man, my dad.

In the picture, he has his arms about us, one around me, one

73

around my sister. I'm trying to get away; I could never stay still for long, Mum tells me. I'm not looking at the camera, I'm looking into the distance, maybe at a stranger eating an ice cream. But Dad's arm is tight around Shanthi. She has her head buried in his shoulder so you can't really see her face. She looks protected there, nestled against him.

I'm thinking about all of this a couple of weeks later, Sunday morning, sitting outside a pub overlooking the harbour. It's the end of August. After swapping some shifts around, I have a few Sundays off. At the next table is a couple, at the table beyond, a family of three kids. I watch the small food-stained faces turn towards their father as he flips up beer mats and catches them with the same hand. Their peals of laughter drift towards me.

In a little glass at my table are stems of iris, violet blue, pitted with yellow. A fine drizzle is starting, tiny drops layering the petals. Clara will be arranging the irises in our shop, dreadlocks swinging as she shifts the buckets. I think about the bulbs I planted in my garden last year, imagining the warm feeling that would come on seeing the first flicker of violet at the tip of the stalks. But none of mine made it.

My mobile starts to ring. Mum's picture flashes up, her face so round and insistent it's like she's right here on my table. I can hear her without even answering the call. *Are you coming tonight, Anjali? Why did you miss dinner last week? Have you forgotten your family again?*

I turn the phone onto silent, not quite able to cut her off.

The smallest child tries to flip up a beer mat, knocking over a glass of juice.

The temperature is starting to drop. I wonder whether it's still hot in Italy, whether the Saxophonist is out playing in a square, coins shining on the velvet lining of his instrument case. Then crossing the city with his brother, their saxophones slung over their shoulders, looking for the next place to perform. He asked me what I would do back in Bristol. 'Rome changes you, you know,' he said. 'Nobody goes home the same person.'

'Really?' I wondered.

'Probably not. I just made that up. But say it's true, what will you do when you go back?'

I didn't know that I would be standing in my small, sparse flat, seeing only the gaps where Jack had once been. The spaces between my books, his missing mugs in the cupboard, the absence of his family on the mantelpiece.

'You've got to have a dream,' the Saxophonist smiled. Gazing into his playful, glittery eyes there was a little yearning inside me to share more with him than just this random encounter, to put off the bad feelings just a tiny bit longer.

I told him I'd look for my dream when I got home.

The family finish cleaning up and leave their table, the kids trailing after their parents, the smallest running forward to take her father's hand. Behind the space where they were sitting, a square board is shining in the pale sunlight.

The Bristol Sailing School and Rowing Club. Discounts on classes available. Ask inside!

I glance again at the family. The father is lifting up his daughter, swinging her high into the air.

I wonder if I can take over where my dad left off. (Just so we're clear here, I don't mean by purchasing some bleach and pine floor detergent; I mean by becoming a sailor.)

So the sailing club is a shed with wetsuits hanging on the wall and a middle-aged red-bearded man behind a desk. I approach the desk to enquire about lessons. Red Beard hunts through his piles of paper and hands me a brochure. It makes me balk. This is my first lesson in sailing: it is, even when discounted, bloody expensive. My bank account is suffering after Rome. Maybe Red Beard understands that the woman in front of him is just experiencing the loss of a buried dream, because when I return the brochure, shaking my head, he fetches me a free paper cup of hot tea from the machine. It helps a little.

'Come back if your circumstances change.' His face is weathered, but kind.

I'm sidling out of the club, wondering what my next potential hobby can be, and if you can get cheap saxophones online, when I'm stopped by another older man who must have been watching the exchange.

'Sorry the whole thing's so expensive,' he says.

This one doesn't have a red beard, but the top half of his wetsuit is pulled down, and although there are some pale grey hairs covering his chest, there is also a pair of stunning pectoral muscles. Watching him scratch his left nipple is distracting.

'No worries.' I try not to gaze at his pecs. Except this man is pretty tall, which makes that difficult. 'I'll hunt out a cheaper hobby.' (Not the saxophone, as eBay will inform me later.)

'I could offer you a taster session, perhaps.' His words, coming from somewhere above his pink nipples, are formed carefully, vowels as well pronounced as Eliza Doolittle's.

'Sorry, you see I can't afford one of those either.' I'm now feeling a bit sheepish. At twenty-nine years old, it's embarrassing to admit that I can't shell out eighty-five pounds (EIGHTY-FIVE POUNDS) for half a day on a boat.

'No, I mean, no charge.'

'What?'

'I'm going out now. Why don't you come along?'

'Now?'

'Why not? You're dressed for it, aren't you?'

I look down at my jeans and trainers.

'But are you sure you want me tagging along?'

'Yes, of course, why ever not?'

'What if I can't sail?'

A low boom, a little like distant thunder, radiates from above the tremendous left pectoral. When I look up, I see a straight nose and fine, amused lips. 'I have no health and safety responsibilities. So I could throw you overboard, I suppose.'

I'll remember those words.

'So, are you coming?' he asks.

His eyes turn out to be as appealing as his chest. Clear grey, with dark, heavy lashes. Glancing around the foyer, I notice two women watching us from the corner. Younger than me, slender, long-legged, with tight-fitting black sweatshirts; the kind of women who look good in wetsuits.

I shift on my cheap trainers. 'Yes please.'

So here we are, just me, the Sailor, a boat and some water.

Although first of all, it's not a boat, it's a dinghy. And second of all, he isn't so much a sailor as an accountant, but that doesn't have quite the same ring to it. He's forty-four years old and runs his own accounting firm, and, watching his successful fingers handle the mainsail, I wonder if my mother would be extremely excited if I called her back right now.

'All set?' the Sailor asks.

My buoyancy aid is strapped on, my hands are gripping the orange sides and there's wind in my ears.

'Absolutely!' I tell him.

'Remember, ropes are called sheets, the rudder steers the

77

boat, the tiller steers the rudder, and always keep your back to the wind!'

The dinghy lurches off and I slide along the boat. A memory arises, of Jack trying to teach me to surf, on a weekend away in Newquay. I see the crescent-shaped bay, backed by steep cliffs. It was August then too. I glimpse a crust of sand on the curve of a brilliant blue board, feel my wetsuit saggy and cold, hear both of us laughing at my lack of balance.

'Starboard!' the Sailor says, gesticulating to his right.

'Starboard,' I repeat.

'Port!' The Sailor points to his left side.

'Port,' I repeat, since this seems to make the Sailor happy.

A breeze streams across my face. I think of finding Jack's keys on the hallway table. Picking up the bunch, no longer warm in his pale hands.

'Tacking,' the Sailor says, as the boat turns.

'Tacking,' I acknowledge, grabbing onto the side to steady myself.

The breeze is blowing harder now, shadows shifting and dissolving in the water, the smell of the harbour more intense than ever before. I sit forward and try to push away the memories of Jack. I didn't know I'd be sailing this morning. The future is stretching ahead, full of so many things I'm not yet aware of.

'Take the tiller,' the Sailor calls.

'Take the ... Oh, right,' I close my fingers around cool metal and plastic as the dinghy moves ahead, carving a little erratically through the dark water.

Are you proud of me, Dad?

Very much so.

What? The wind, Dad, I can't hear you!

Very much so, duwa!

Duwa means daughter in Sinhala. I like these made-up conversations with my father.

The Sailor takes the tiller back, frowning in concentration, wetsuit zipped up, the tiniest hint of the first sag in the firm contours of his body. Then the boom suddenly swaps sides, narrowly missing my head. The Sailor grabs my hand and pulls me to the other end of the dinghy.

'We were on a dead run,' he says.

I have no idea what a dead run is, and why we would be on it. But for a moment, he keeps hold of my hand. His own hands are large and warm; my palm fits inside his like a child's.

Back at the jetty, the Sailor moors the boat. *Starboard, daggerboard, freeboard.* It's a new language, only one that feels kind of familiar, the words safe and secure, like the shipping forecast. I consider how it might have been if I too was an accountant, or a doctor, or a lawyer, or a Radio 4 presenter, and could afford to learn how to sail for real.

The Sailor jumps down onto the jetty. The two long-legged women have come out of the club, nudging each other. They both have oval faces and poker-straight long black hair. Sisters, maybe. The Sailor stretches out his fatherly hands for mine.

'Do you want to come again?' he asks.

So I meet him a second, and then a third time. Each time is the same, a kind of cross between a sailing lesson and a language class, with me showing no particular prowess in either. Turns out I'm not a natural seafarer and really don't have a sense of balance, but if the Sailor minds, he doesn't show it, carefully explaining the rules, pointing my finger to the wind to uncover its direction. At forty-four, he's only six years off my dad, if my dad had not been dead. And he's also gentle in voice and gesticulation, as I have always imagined my dad to be. Plus, there's the very fact that he is a sailor, which my dad would definitely have been were it not for terminal cancer and a slight lack of money. Looking at it this way, the resemblance is uncanny. It's true that there is something a little awkward about sharing this small space with the Sailor, but then I never really got a chance to know my dad either, so maybe that's not so surprising. Anyway, I'm in no hurry to leave this surrogate father to return to my empty flat and my actual, real-life mother, who won't stop phoning.

On our fourth meeting, I'm helping the Sailor get the dinghy ready when the two women appear again from around the side of the club. In black leggings and trainers, luminous hair whipping around their pale faces, giant print on their black hoodies, they resemble an advert for designer sportswear, or maybe a harbour-side Hallowe'en. They confer at the water's edge, sometimes staring directly at us.

'Let's go, shall we?' the Sailor says. He's never acknowledged the females and something in his restless movements tells me he's trying to avoid them. I glance down at my worn plimsolls and wonder if he's embarrassed to be seen with me.

'Who are those women?' I whisper, once we're on the water. Their lean bodies are distant shadows on the bank, yet I can't help thinking they can still hear me.

'Rowers,' the Sailor answers. I wait, but nothing more comes.

'They seem interested in you.' I wonder if they share a crush on the Sailor. Or whether one of them, maybe even both, might be an ex-girlfriend. Although they are young enough to be his daughters. I look closely at the Sailor, the grey in his feathery chestnut hair, creeping into his eyebrows, the skin beginning to slacken in his tanned face, deep lines around his mouth and eyes.

The Sailor only shrugs.

We say even less than normal on this journey across the harbour. I fumble when given a job, looking back every so often at the distant figures, still there, watching. The Sailor stares straight on with his long-lashed eyes. I wonder what he's thinking about. Around the bend, just out of our sight, is the Clifton Suspension Bridge, high up, spanning the slate skies between the cliffs of the Avon Gorge. It's one of the defining images of Bristol, on placemats, postcards, teacups. I know that his flat is in one of the grand hillside buildings overlooking the bridge. I glance at the expensive sports watch on the Sailor's wrist. Then down at my supermarket leggings. Surrogacy aside, my being here is starting to make less sense.

Some people say they are comfortable with silence. I'm not one of those. Anxiety is clogging my throat, like a desperate, fluttering bird.

The Sailor pushes back his hair, looking at something far off in the landscape.

My hands grip the side of the boat. Oddly, an image of my sister comes into my mind. She is a little girl, five years old, sitting alone in our bedroom in a massive blue jumper, legs crossed on the floor. Whenever I see my sister, there's usually a pencil, a piece of paper, but in this image, there's nothing, just the threadbare carpet, Shanthi tracing her fingers along a circular pattern, over and over again.

'Do you mind if we call it a day?' the Sailor asks abruptly.

'What?' I come to, blinking away the image. 'Oh – yes, of course. No worries. You've been so kind, giving up your Sundays.' My chest lifts with a kind of relief. It's starting to get too awkward, sharing a boat with this guy, even if he might be my father.

'No, come back next week.'

'You mean . . .'

'I just need to stop today.'

There's a deep crease in the Sailor's forehead as he steers us back to the jetty, and I get the sense that there's something he wants to say. But the rowing sisters are watching us, and in the end, we part ways without words. I wander off, feeling myself watched over by the female eyes. My back is taut with their glances, discomfort edging my spine. Maybe they really are his daughters. Cut off from their father at an early age, they've been following him ever since, longing for him, as Shanthi and I have done for ours. Perhaps they're even planning on killing me. At the end of the harbour, I turn back to make out the Sailor, still standing by the jetty, looking over the water.

'Anjali, where are you?'

'I'm at home, Mum.'

My mother doesn't really need to use the phone. She could just lean out of the window and shout.

'Why have you not come for dinner? It is here on the table.'

'But I told you I wasn't coming tonight, Mum.' Guilt washes over my limbs. I lie heavier on the faux-leather sofa thinking of all the wasted food. Yet she knew I wasn't coming. Irritability flows along with the guilt, constant companions. I breathe in the tiny bunch of irises I'm holding.

'Why aren't you coming?'

The space in my living room is deafening, all the furniture seeming to point at the gap where the plasma screen used to be. It was too big, I told Jack. And it still is. 'I already said, Mum. I'm really tired.'

'Why are you so tired?'

Conversations with Mum are more and more starting to

resemble my chats with Clara's three-year-old godson. Except Mum is even better at the 'why' questions.

'I just . . .' I look around the room, at the corner where we kept the espresso machine, because it didn't fit in the tiny kitchen, at the mantelpiece that seems so bare now without the elephants. My mother and sister look down on me from their oak frames. Without the elephants and Jack's pictures, it's hard to look away from their dark eyes.

'Anjali?'

Mum's shriek brings me back to the conversation.

'I'm learning to sail.' I'm stumped for any other excuse.

'You've started sailing?'

'Yes. At the harbour. On a Sunday.'

I close my eyes, waiting for an interrogation.

Nothing.

I open my eyes.

'Mum?'

Nothing.

I look at the pictures on the mantelpiece again, wondering why I don't have one of my father. I think about Mum's flat and how little there is of him in there too: just the Buddhas that have crept in over the years, and the trinkets Mum has picked up from car-boot sales. But somehow you still feel his absence. No matter how you crowd over the spaces, fill in the silence, the things that make you hurt don't go away.

'Mum? Are you OK?' I'm getting worried now. Maybe she *was* leaning out of the window, and fell out.

'I'm here,' she says, after a while. Then, 'So you will come next week?'

The summer has quietly slipped away, the children on the street outside already playing with tiny conkers, the edges of the seasons blurred with every passing year. Perhaps one day the leaves won't fall; the quieter flowers won't blossom. I touch the blue iris petals, delicate veins fanning out from brief yellow spines. I haven't been at Mum's for weeks. I can't really blame her for shrieking.

'Next Sunday,' I promise.

The following Sunday, there's a sailing event in the Isles of Scilly, so the club is all but deserted. Maybe the rowing sisters have gone too, as they are nowhere to be seen either. The Sailor's dinghy seems to move more freely through the water; it feels a little easier to breathe. Not that my sailing's improved any.

'How come you didn't go to the Scilly Isles too?' I ask the Sailor, at the end of the session. The boat's moored and I'm waiting to jump out. But he hasn't moved.

'Work,' he says.

'Oh, right. Are you busy with a project or something?' He really isn't good at small talk, but then Mum always said Dad was a quiet man, too. I wonder if we should just type out the history of our lives, in Comic Sans, to read at home with a glass of whisky.

'No, just work,' he says.

'Oh, right.' I start to get to my feet.

'Do you want to come back to my place?' he asks.

I'm startled.

It's late in the afternoon. I've got a couple of hours before I'm due at Mum's. But all I want to do is lie down. It feels like I've not been sleeping for weeks. And the thought of going back to the Sailor's place terrifies me. At least on the boat, the act of sailing distracts us. Without a tiller, it's not clear how we'd manage.

'I've sort of got plans,' I lie.

The Sailor turns his dark-lashed grey eyes on me. The fact is, his, like my dad's, are particularly pretty eyes. They have a canine quality, in that they fill you with an urge to stroke his neck and tickle his ears.

'And you're probably busy,' I inform him. 'Don't you have club duties?'

At that moment, Red Beard comes out of the shed and unlocks his Toyota. He gives me a wink, and I get the sense that he maybe sees me as some kind of nautical prostitute. I give him a smile and a nod to convey that I always use my buoyancy aid. Red Beard drives away.

'Not especially.' The Sailor shrugs his heavy shoulders. 'It's quiet today.'

Slate-grey clouds have crept in, darkening the sky. Spots of rain are starting to fall; it's forecast to get heavier. The harbour is deserted, our only company the ducks and swans and seagulls. Nobody else is sailing, no one walking along the banks.

'We'd best be heading off.' I start to get up.

'Stay. Please?' the Sailor asks. Looking at his sad, pretty eyes, I sit back in the boat.

This man really doesn't say *anything*. And yet there's something he wants to talk about. I can feel the need nudging at my skin, as palpable as the raindrops.

'What are you thinking?' I ask, finally.

The Sailor turns to me and looks surprised, as if he forgot I was sitting there.

'I was married once,' he says.

'Oh.' It's not quite what I was expecting. 'What happened?'

'She left me,' the Sailor says. 'She said I needed to lighten up.'

I sort of see her point. I'm about to ask whether he has any kids, thinking of the rowing sisters, when he says, 'And the fact is, she was right. Look at me.'

I look at him. 'You seem OK to me. The company, the flat. Nice car. Mercedes, you said?'

'Then why am I sitting here surrounded by emptiness?'

'Thanks a lot.'

'I don't mean it like that.' He faces me, his words very carefully enunciated. 'You could be the best thing that's ever happened to me.'

'What?'

'I mean, look at you. You're so full of life. You decided to learn how to sail, and that was it, you just walked into the club and here you are.'

'Unable to afford lessons and bumming rides with you.'

'And you're funny!'

'With no concept of wind resource assessment.'

'Hilarious!'

'And a shocking incomprehension of the compass.'

'Brilliant!'

There's something disturbing about the Sailor's ability to get more and more excited by my negative qualities.

'You see, when I met her, my ex, this was all I wanted to do.' He looks out at the water. 'Sailing was my life. Then I got focused on the money. Now look at me. More at home in a boardroom than a . . .'

'Bulwark?' I suggest.

He blinks. So do I. The truth is, I've no idea what a bulwark is, except that it features in *Moby Dick*.

'But listen.' I move the conversation quickly on. 'Sailing still is your life. Just because you're not doing it all the time doesn't make it any less important.'

'I wanted to sail in the Olympics,' he says.

'Did you try?'

He shakes his head. 'My parents told me to give it all up; they said there was no stability in it. They used to run a boatyard, but they lost everything. They didn't want me to suffer the same fate. For a while there, I thought I was doing all right for myself. But lately . . . I suppose I did all of this for them. And now I don't know what I'm doing.' He looks up at the sky. The rain is coming down in a thick, heavy sheet, his pale blue waterproof steadily darkening. He looks back at me. 'The truth is, I've become somewhat lost.'

It's a kind of heartening revelation, realising that I'm not the only one. Gazing around the damp, deserted harbour, I picture all the people tucked inside their houses, or in offices, bars, libraries, soft play centres, trying to do the things someone else thought they should do. I wonder how many of us are just trying to live up to our parents' hopes for us.

I see the Architect, working through the night to take his mother to San Francisco. I see myself, coming out here every Sunday, trying to live my dead father's dream. I see my sister's degree certificate on the wall, which would gather dust if not for Mum's fastidious housework. I see that image again of my sister as a little girl, five years old, sitting on the carpet of our bedroom, tracing circles with her fingers. *Why are you lonely, Anjali?* The Saxophonist's question echoes through my mind. I think of Mum's missed calls, how much I'm staying away from her place, how lately every time I go over there, I'm reminded of the day I left.

'Listen,' I say, 'you're not the only one who feels lost.'

'You too?' he says.

'Why else do you think I'm here?'

'I don't know, split up with your boyfriend or something?'

It's a funny thing then. For the first time in a long time, I realise I haven't been thinking about Jack. My family are the ones who have lately been on my mind.

The rain isn't letting up. I take hold of the Sailor's damp hands. They're big and warm and parental. If they weren't so pale and long-fingered, it would be in the bag, this whole Dad business. 'You're only having a midlife crisis, you know,' I tell him.

'Is that what this is?'

'Yep.' I lean on his shoulder, liking the feel of our wet heads together.

'So what's going on with you then?' he asks me.

'A quarter-to-midlife crisis. It's the new thing.'

He turns my face towards his and kisses me. For a midlife crisis, it's a good kiss, unexpectedly decisive. But it kind of takes me by surprise.

'Sleep with me,' he says, when I break off.

'What?'

'I want to harness your energy.'

'I'm not the wind.'

'Sleep with me.'

For a moment, I actually consider it. He does have this air of authority about him. And maybe, all things considered, I wouldn't mind being a nautical prostitute (which would make my fee £425 plus on-board counselling). Or maybe in these few minutes I am feeling a connection with the Sailor that I never thought possible. He's offering me a ticket, as well as a tiller. Another way out from this maze of lost feeling. But then I'm seeing the hurt again in the Architect's eyes as he stood at my door; experiencing once more that coldness when the Saxophonist eventually withdrew his arms.

There's something else I need right now, although as much as I've searched in sex and saxophones and sailing boats, it's remaining pretty elusive.

It's also possible that sex on a dinghy might not be as easy as it sounds. Plus, there's that outside chance that the Sailor is my father.

'I'm OK for the moment,' I say, a little awkwardly. 'I mean, sex-wise.'

The Sailor slumps in the boat. His chestnut hair is flattened by the rain. 'I don't have anything to offer anyone,' he sighs.

'Yes you do,' I say, alarmed.

'I can't make it work with anyone.'

'Yes you can!' Now I'm starting to sound like a cover band for A Tribe Called Quest.

'I wanted you to like me.'

'But I do like you.'

And here I'm not really clear what occurs. I'm standing up and he's standing up, and I'm trying to reach out to provide some comfort, although at the same time thinking we are in an actual storm and we really should be making tracks, and I don't know exactly how the next thing happens, unless he's trying to kill me, but then why would my dad be trying to kill me, but basically, my head somehow makes contact with the boom and I find myself being propelled out of the boat. It all happens in a kind of slow motion, with the sky and the sailing club and a couple of approaching figures sort of turning on their sides as my body touches, then plummets into, the freezing depths below.

As I fall through the murky water, there are glimpses of dahlias, lavender, roses, irises drifting in the darkness surrounding me. I'm seeing my sister again as a child, sitting in our bedroom, head in her hands.

I'm going to die here. And maybe that's just what I deserve.

Thankfully, as I previously indicated to Red Beard, I always wear my buoyancy aid.

I bounce back up.

'Take my hand,' the Sailor is shouting. The approaching figures are closer now, and they aren't passers-by. It's the rowing sisters, not on the Isles of Scilly after all, but standing right here on the bank, in shining black anoraks, their expressions struck between amusement and curiosity.

'Now!' shouts the Sailor, his face entirely pink, stretching out his arm.

Like a da Vinci portrait, our fingers are almost touching, then clasp together. I feel something tear in my shoulder as he pulls me up, slithering, back into the boat.

The rowing sisters nod their heads. They look barely twenty years old, yet poised in a way I'll never be able to achieve. Their dark eyes bore into me. Is the Sailor really their father? Was this part of an elaborate plot? Were they all trying to kill me?

My shoulder is burning.

'Sorry.' The Sailor looks stunned. 'I'm not sure . . .'

'It's fine,' I say. 'I was wet anyway.'

The rain's stopped, or at least it's not so heavy now, only a little drizzle on our faces.

I pick up my bag. 'It's been great,' I say, as cheerfully as I can. 'I'll see you.'

'Next Sunday?' the Sailor asks.

'Oh, I'm back to working Sundays again from next week.'

'Saturday?'

'I'm down to work the whole weekend.'

'You will come back, won't you?'

I step dripping onto the jetty. There is a relief at being on solid ground. There's something too shifting about water, something too unstable about boats.

'You're going to be fine,' I tell him.

'I am?' His voice is breaking and there is a tension in his jaw.

I stop. Whatever happens, I cannot let this man cry.

'Yes, you are.' I lift my voice so that it has never sounded more confident. 'And anyway, there's still time to do the things you want to do. There's always time.' I take off my buoyancy aid and set it down on the jetty. I sling my bag over my hot shoulder, the soggy weight dragging it down. I squeeze water out of my hoodie.

'There is?' he asks.

'Of course there is. You just need to start. You're going to be fine,' I repeat. 'I know it.'

'Come sailing again,' he says.

I pause. The bump to the skull might be affecting my thought processes. But I know there's something else I'm looking for, even if I don't know what it is yet.

'No.' I shake my head. 'I've got to follow my own advice. And I can't actually sail.'

For a moment, the Sailor doesn't speak. Then, 'Thank you,' he says.

I tip an imaginary hat to him. 'So long.'

He sits back in the boat, looking a little dazed. I glance towards the sailing school, still silent, the boats locked up in an orange line. I turn to the women, who have been watching me for all of these Sundays, in their striking black costumes. It's time to confront my demons.

'Can I help you?' I ask.

They look surprised. Then the taller one steps forward. She towers over me, a vision of black hair and ivory skin.

91

'Our crews are down. We're hoping to recruit.' She has an unexpectedly rich West Country accent.

'To recruit?'

She nods. 'To our rowing team.' Her sister comes forward, enthusiastically.

I stand there looking from one to the other, trying to take this in.

'But I've never rowed,' I tell them.

'You look resilient,' the taller one says.

'Resolute,' the second urges.

I blink.

'So what do you say?' they ask, in unison. Close up, I can see their foundation doesn't quite cover their acne, and there is a line of light brown at the roots of their hair. I recognise their water-proofs; there's a whole range at Tesco. They're smiling hopefully, like children. But they probably don't belong to the Sailor. There's a giddy feeling inside me, perhaps the start of concussion.

I hesitate. 'I'm flattered. It's so kind of you. But you know, rowing's really not my dream.'

They raise their hands in understanding.

I make my way down the harbour, wet trainers squeaking.

I head to Mum's, my clothes and hair still wet, my shoulder still sore. The thought of her interrogation makes me want to bail and go home, but my flat is getting harder and harder to face. I'm not too sure why that is. It's supposed to get easier, isn't it? That's all anybody ever says when I tell them about breaking up with Jack. And now there are three men between the two of us. You'd think that would do it.

'So you have decided to stop gallivanting and spend time with us?' Mum screeches almost as soon as I open the door.

'Please, Mum.' I'm so weary, I go straight through into the

lounge without giving her a kiss, and slump on the settee. Ordie tries to jump onto my lap, but her old legs can't make it. Leaning down, I lift her up and nuzzle my nose into her fur. She's losing weight; I can feel her little ribs.

'Why are you so wet?' Mum asks. 'And what is this mark on your face?'

'What?' I touch my temple and feel the beginnings of a bruise where the boom made contact. 'Oh. I fell out of the boat.'

'You fell out of the boat?' It's not clear why Mum always needs to repeat everything.

'Yes, and before you start, I won't be sailing again. Where's Shanthi?'

'She has gone to lie down.'

I wait for Mum's long list of tribulations to start, already very much regretting my decision to visit. But no words come. Instead, I'm surprised when the cushion shifts and I feel her perch beside me on the arm of the sofa. She touches my aching shoulder. It feels soothing.

'Your father wanted to sail.'

'I know.'

'He liked to watch the fishermen at night,' she says. 'In Sri Lanka. When he could not sleep, he would go down to the beach to watch them, far away in the sea. That was why I was always up, waiting for him.'

I stay quiet. It's the first time Mum has told me this.

'I was frightened, not knowing where he was when I woke up.' I can feel her smiling. 'But he always came back.'

Her voice drifts away for a time.

I think about these last few weeks with the Sailor, how it was kind of nice to feel closer to Dad. Even though it wasn't real. 'I wasn't very good at sailing, Mum.'

She leans down and puts a kiss on the top of my head. 'He would say that does not matter, *duwa*.'

We sit like that for a while, Mum holding my shoulder, and me holding Ordie. I would like to have a photograph of this moment. I would like to stay with them both for a little bit longer.

After a shower and supper, I go into Shanthi's room and find her asleep on her bed.

On the windowsill is a new clay vase. I'm touched to see bright yellow irises peeking from the top. Lowering my head, I breathe in their earthy scent. I wonder if my sister remembers the story I once told her about these flowers, about how they are named for Iris the rainbow goddess. I see Shanthi sitting cross-legged on the brown settee in her stained and fraying jeans, eyes closed, listening to my tale of Iris and her rainbow, the bridge between heaven and earth.

She's curled up now on top of the duvet. The hollow has deepened beneath her collarbones, and for a moment a prickle of worry runs down my spine. If I touched her, I might feel her ribs, like Ordie's. Her face is in the pillow, her hair fanned out all around her. Thick, curly and unmanageable, like Dad's, like mine. We've all of us been stricken with it. There are two time periods for me: pre- and post-GHDs. But I once tried to blow-dry Shanthi's hair straight, when we were teenagers, and afterwards it looked wrong. Her curls are a place to tuck her pencil or her pen; without them she didn't seem herself.

I gaze at a tiny streak of deep blue paint on the back of her hand. Somewhere in my mind is the image that won't go away, of seeing her in this room, just a child, wearing the huge jumper, tracing the red circles on the carpet.

She got sick the year she finished her degree, the year I met Jack. It was an illness that affected her mind, not her body, although the weight fell off her then too, and the chain-smoking did nothing good for her chest. I'd just finished my first year, coming home from friends' places to find my sister in our room, as if she hadn't left it for days. A packet of cigarettes, then a second, then a third, butt ends piled up in saucers on the floor, spilling onto the carpet. My sister sitting beside the serpent screen or standing at the window. The hollows growing in her cheeks, the fusty smell of the clothes she'd stopped changing. The odd things she was starting to say to me.

There's someone watching, Anjali.

'What's the matter with her?' I asked Mum, a throbbing in my head and in my chest, wanting her to say something that might make it all go away. But she couldn't.

The strange words kept building; the tiny branches of red veins kept growing in my mother's eyes. I was shrinking away from home, staying at friends', unable to sleep beside my sister. Slipping back in the morning, tiptoeing around gathering my things, then leaving for the shop again, the tea Mum had made turning cold on the kitchen counter.

By the time Shanthi recovered, I was no longer living in the flat. Maybe the gaps had already crept in by then, the distance between us too far to bridge. It's hard to believe that at one time I could have been standing behind my sister, hairdryer and brush in hand, giggling at her dubious face in the mirror as her locks grew sleeker.

Shanthi stirs and turns over. I unfold the blue blanket at the foot of the bed. My heart thumps as I cover her thin body, trying to cover over these memories too.

I can't let myself think about them now.

Quietly, I get into my own bed. The serpents meet my stare, their tails twisting on the screen. An old school painting of Shanthi's flashes into my mind. Grey snakes on a soot-black canvas, thick bodies coiled round and round into an ashen cloud. I close my eyes, but the image is still there in the darkness. I pull up the covers and concentrate on the deep rhythm of my sister's breathing until my own begins to settle. So many hours I used to spend in this bed listening to her sleep. Then her steady breath was replaced with Jack's.

It's been odd recently, sleeping alone. I've been more aware of the sounds that can be concealed by another person: the creak of a radiator, the rustling of a tree, the waking of the robins.

My eyelids are closing, the snakes slowly fading. For the first time in many days, in the faint fragrance of Benson & Hedges and the hint of irises, I sleep.

In the morning, it takes me a while to work out where I am. Before I've opened my eyes, I can sense the light coming into the room at a different angle, can feel the edges of the bed instead of the double mattress that my body is used to. There is a dull ache in my shoulder. With my eyes still closed, flashes of yesterday fall into place. The shock of the harbour water, the wrench back into the dinghy. The downcast heavy fringe of the Sailor's eyes, his straight, narrow nose, the thin lips of his mouth. The last glimpse of him on the boat, drenched, but with something like peace settling into his features. He isn't my father. And he isn't trapped for ever. Maybe he is opening his eyes at the same time as me, blinking in a shining apartment, ready to start the second half of his life. And maybe it's time to figure out what I'm looking for, too.

Mum will already have left for her early Tesco shift. I'll have to head to the shop soon, but there will be time for a coffee with my sister. I wonder if we can talk, really talk. Whether it might be possible to confide in each other again.

Sitting up, I peer around the corner of the serpent screen. Shanthi's bed is empty. There's a note on the chest of drawers in her careful script. *Went to the studio early. Didn't want to wake you.*

The flowers are gone too. Just the grey vase left on the windowsill, sculpted by unknown hands.

Five

September blurs into October, into November. Pumpkins glow on doorsteps, fireworks bathe the sky, the red and golden leaves do fall. The irises wilt, the roses hold out, our shop flushes scarlet with poinsettias. By mid November, we've given in and the windows are strung with fairy lights and the flowers glitter with threads of silver tinsel. I hang mistletoe over the front door, gazing at the cluster of shining berries, little white orbs. Somehow the days keep passing. November will soon slip away and Christmas will have to be faced.

The pain of Jack is subsiding a little. Sometimes I even wonder if I'm over him, although his absence is still palpable when my eyes close at night. But the encounter with the Sailor has made me aware of other absences too. Of a gap that my father might once have filled; of the empty place so often at the dinner table when I force myself to go over to Mum's. My sister is rarely there. At least she'll have no excuse at Christmas, although I don't exactly want to subject her to that. Mum's pretty excited that the three of us might be together for a change; she's gathering enough energy for a whole lot of fresh cross-examinations. I'm not entirely sure how I'll get through them.

'What do you think?' I finish putting up the mistletoe and call out to Clara.

She peers out from the back, wiping her hands on her yellow apron, and gives me a thumbs-up.

Just as I'm climbing down from the stepladder, the door opens. As my last meet-up with the Sailor has confirmed, health and safety was never my strong point. I do a strange kind of leap off the ladder to get away from the door, and manage to embrace the customer walking in.

Under the mistletoe.

'Hi,' he says.

Oh God, it would have to be a man. A strong-armed, six-foot-something, smiling-faced man.

'Ernie!' Clara comes running out from the flower arrangements as I back away, embarrassed. She gives him a hug. 'You're home!'

The two of them start chatting away, while I stay hidden in the background, trying to work out who the stranger is. Midway through their conversation, I've surmised that he is Ernest, a friend of Clara's family, who has recently moved back to Bristol after a few years spent travelling. Whenever I think of travelling, I picture vibrant city bars, maybe a vodka cocktail mixed with lychees or rainbows. But I learn that Ernie has been out in the sticks, building houses, schools, furniture, teaching English and practical skills to younger generations. He's an engineer by trade, but many other things besides – guitarist, nature writer, dreamer; liking nothing more than a big field and a makeshift barbecue and the smell of woodsmoke tinged with fairy tales.

You can kind of tell all of these things by looking at him. Sort of.

'We haven't met.' He breaks away from his catch-up with Clara and turns to me. His face is shining; he's still under the mistletoe. It's disconcerting. After the Sailor, I'm pretty certain that I should be avoiding any kind of male at all costs.

Although I can't just stand here.

'Anjali,' I say, holding out my hand.

'An-ja-li.' He speaks my name as if it's music. Taking my hand, he considers my palm. 'Strong lines,' he informs me, and I can't help feeling proud that my body has cultivated these for him. 'Where are you from? I mean, your family?'

'Sri Lanka,' I tell him.

He knows more about Sri Lanka than I do. After a few minutes, and a couple of ignored customers, I'm learning all about Vipassana meditation and Theravada Buddhism.

I'm feeling enlightened, like the Buddha.

Well, not like the Buddha at all, because his enlightenment consisted of forty days of meditation beneath the Bodhi tree, after which he was able to see his past lives and the past lives of other people. He understood suffering. He saw in his mind the life of the world and the other planets and comprehended the meaning of existence.

Meanwhile I'm just having an interesting chat.

'You should come along to the Buddhist Centre.' Ernie fishes in his pocket for a crumpled leaflet. We've moved towards the counter now, and he spreads it out on the surface. *Urban retreat. Living the meaning of life – going beyond the self in daily existence.*

'Oh, right.' I stare at the words. Is this what I've been looking for? Maybe Ernie is actually here for a reason. Maybe he's come to deliver the real answer to my problems.

'What do you think?'

'I've never done anything like this before.'

'This might be a good beginning if you're curious. It's just across the road. A lunchtime thing. Not a silent retreat or anything.'

'A silent retreat?' I look back at him.

He touches a flaming red leaf on the cash till poinsettia and smiles. There's a deep cleft at the base of his chin, which is also fairly disconcerting. 'You interested? I know of a Christmas one coming up. Three weeks, no words.'

I close my eyes and breathe in an image of bliss.

'D'you know him well?' I ask Clara later, after Ernie has departed, in just his T-shirt, oblivious to the chill outside, sauntering off into the world.

'Ernie?' Clara has finished serving the customers I've ignored and is now frowning over an awkward eucalyptus. 'Oh, for years. He was a regular part of the Sunday roast.' She pulls off a dying leaf and inspects it. 'I don't mean we ate him; he just used to come round a lot. Well, until he turned vegetarian, I suppose.'

Another notch in his perfect post.

Clara looks up.

'Oh, I see,' she says. 'You've fallen for him.'

'No, I haven't.'

'I heard you pretending to be Buddhist.'

'I am Buddhist.'

'My arse.'

'My mother.'

'What?'

'My mother would correct you.'

'Well good on you.' Clara returns to the eucalyptus. 'He's a kind one, Ernie. I used to fancy him as well.'

'And now?'

'He just wasn't someone you could shag.' Clara's dreadlocks are falling over the succulent. 'He's not that sort.'

'What sort is he?' I imagine Ernie in monkish robes, studying ancient Sanskrit texts by (Fairtrade) candlelight.

'He makes love, of course.'

I'm just interested in meditation. I'm not falling for him. I'm really not.

I decide to visit the Buddhist Centre the following Saturday lunchtime, when the earnest of Bristol gather for meditation and reflection. We are then supposed to go off and live our lives in as meditative and reflective a way as possible. This is what Ernie's leaflet clutched between my frozen hands is telling me as I rush along Gloucester Road towards the centre. I'm late. My fault for getting over-involved in a debate about thistles (invasive weed or misunderstood?). Once again I'm unprepared for the stab of approaching winter; I've forgotten how the cold physically touches you, stretching sharp claws over your skin. The forecast next month is for snow. I remember the one time Jack and I woke up to a world blanketed in white; how we made a sledge out of one of the shop's cardboard crates, tramping through the slushy roads to find a hill. But the last thing I need right now is to be thinking of Jack. I hate snow.

I'm late.

I think I said that.

I burst into the centre, the windows informing me that my hair is wild (GHDs never help for long), my eyes are red (near-equatorial genes struggle with the arctic climate) and I'm looking somewhat inflatable in layers of outdoor gear. The term 'retreat' has been classified in my mind in the same category as walking, so I'm hoping multiple fleeces are suitable attire.

Except everyone else is wearing floaty dresses or loose pyjama-like trousers. They all look up at me from the floor of the hall.

'Welcome.' A pyjama-clad gentleman sitting cross-legged at the front smiles at me. 'Join us.'

I clunk into the room in my heavy boots, find a corner on the floor and try to peel off some of my layers, whereupon I discover that zips actually make the loudest sound in the world.

Meanwhile, the pyjama man is telling everyone how to breathe, which turns out to be a bit more complex than I've always believed. I scour the room for Ernie. I'm startled to find him sitting right there next to me. 'Hey,' he whispers.

Ernie's origins are mixed, his mother Nigerian, his father Irish. His skin tone is a deep brown, much darker than mine. In the shop, he had a clean-shaven face with that disconcerting cleft; I look for the cleft now but find it shaded by dark stubble, stippled with grey. His thick charcoal hair is cropped close to his scalp, dancing with flecks of caramel. And a little grey, too. He's mid thirties perhaps.

Breathe. This is what I should have been doing.

Everyone is cross-legged with their eyes now closed. Pyjama man is guiding us into the meditation. 'Try to find a spot where the breath is more noticeable.' I concentrate on the back of my throat, which is starting to feel clogged up. 'If you want, you can count your breaths. Breathe in, breathe out, count one. Breathe in, breathe out, count two. Go up to ten and then go back to one again.'

Breathe in, breathe out, one. Breathe in, breathe out, two. Breathe in, breathe out, three. Breathing is nice. I can smell

Ernie's aftershave, something lemony, spicy. *Breathe in, breathe out, five.* There's a little urge inside me to put my nose to Ernie's neck, to investigate for other scents. *Breathe in, breathe out, seven.* Is that his breath I can feel against my right arm? I wonder if he's counting; I wonder what number he's on. *Breathe in, breathe out, nine.* I like meditating, I decide. Although it's a bit uncomfortable, sitting cross-legged on the hard floor. And it's bloody cold. *Breathe in, breathe out, twelve.* Yikes, I'm supposed to stop at ten.

Breathe in, breathe out, one. If Jack could see me now, maybe he'd be impressed by how far I've come. *Breathe in, breathe out, two.* Although this is only my first meditation. It isn't like I've come that far. *Breathe in, breathe out, four.* And besides this, what else have I done, except have a couple of interactions with inappropriate men? It's not like Jack would think much of that. *Breathe in, breathe out, eight.* But then, who is he to judge? When he was sleeping with the burlesque dancer for over a year? When he was lying to me every single day, even on my birthday? How could he do that to me, after all our time together? *Breathe in, breathe out, thirty-two.* Yikes. Start again.

Breathe in, breathe out, one. Hard to believe that our relationship ended this way. *Breathe in, breathe out, two.* Not just with one infidelity, but a whole series of them, hundreds of times over whole weekends, when I'd just pictured him out with friends or alone in a hotel room, preparing for an assignment. *Breathe in, breathe out, eight.* Would I ever know how many of those hotel rooms Julia visited? Whether he thought about her when he was with me, while we cooked spaghetti together or sat curled up on the sofa, watching *The Sopranos* with its numerous infidelities unfolding before us on the screen? Whether he thought about me at all, once, during any of those times with her? And why is there always this constant voice in my head asking me what I did to make him go? Asking me why I found it hard to be intimate, I mean, really intimate with Jack? Asking me why I ran away? Yikes, I've stopped counting altogether.

Breathe in, breathe out, one. But then, isn't that what I always do – run away? Look at my sister, look how she uses her paintings to face what she's been through. Those blocks and lines, they mean something. They mean something about her experiences, about what she's facing now, about how the world is for her. And I don't understand them. She's seeing a guy now and I don't know him, and she won't talk about him or introduce us. But why should she? Did I bother to introduce her or Mum to Jack when I met him? Have I ever thought about anyone but myself? Shit, I've stopped breathing altogether.

Breathe, just breathe! I start coughing. The noise reverberates around the hall. A couple of people open their eyes. *Stop coughing and concentrate on the breath!* But it's no use. My throat is exploding.

There's a hand on my arm, and turning, I see Ernie looking at me, concerned. 'OK?' he whispers.

'Fine,' I mouth, but the coughing won't stop. More people start shifting on their perches as I hack away at their peace.

Get out of the hall!

I try to escape quietly, but my throat won't allow it, and then I tread on a woman's toe-ringed foot and she shrieks out in startled, non-meditative pain. *Oh God.* But we're all of us Buddhists here, there's no point turning to Him.

Outside, I find a kitchen and down a glass of water, my face hot. Brilliant. What a way to ingratiate myself with the urban retreaters.

'It can be really hard, the first time.'

'What?' I turn around and see that Ernie has followed me out. The coughing starts again. He waits for me to stop and then says, 'Lots of things can come up when you first try.'

'Really?'

'Sure.' When he smiles, I can make out the cleft in his chin again, drawing me through the layer of stubble. 'You can get a strong physical reaction, or you can find yourself having to face up to all kinds of things that you've been trying to keep out of your mind.'

Can he actually see right into me? How does he know how I feel?

'Everyone feels the same way,' he says. 'To some degree.'

'Why do it then?' I ask him. 'I mean, why do something that's so painful?'

'I don't know.' Ernie shrugs his broad shoulders, and I have an intense longing for some mistletoe so that I can be held once more inside his strong arms. 'But I suppose that's what it's all about, isn't it? Being aware of what's going on for you. That's the first step towards moving beyond the self.'

'And what happens when we move beyond the self?'

I really like Ernie's smile. It lights up his warm eyes, reaches into every corner of his face so that you can't help but mirror it. 'Then we find out there's a whole lot of other shit out there.'

He asks to come with me to the traders' market. If it's a date, it's the oddest one I've ever had. The two of us in Clara's van, driving through town at four at the morning, our eyes still narrow with lost sleep, our conversation for some reason whispered, as if to not to wake up the rest of the world. The dark early hours illuminated by sodium lamps, the occasional passing car. We lower the windows to catch the call of the first robins, to breathe in the River Avon, to raise goose bumps on our arms. A fox stops for a moment, startled in the glow of the van's headlights, its rough red fur glimmering. We stop too, meeting the fire in its orange eyes. Then it darts away, a bristling tail vanishing into a garden. I glance over at Ernie, see the deepened crease in his forehead, the slight parting of his full lips. There's a stirring in my chest and something clogging up my throat once more. How good it is to notice the wild again. It feels as if I'm waking up.

At St Philip's Market, Ernie pulls on the obligatory hi-vis jacket and gazes beneath the strip lighting at the stalls with their thousands of flowers on display, buckets filled with delicate pink camellias, deeply scented purple freesias, scarlet winter roses.

I rush around gathering our order from the sellers and catching his eye every so often. He looks out of place, too tall for the low stool he's sitting on, too quiet in the midst of shouts and rushing feet, yet he doesn't seem to mind. He seems pretty content. Kind of how I always imagined my dad would look, if I'd ever been able to bring him here. It feels strange to share this part of my world with someone. I wonder why I never brought Jack.

'I like this life,' Ernie says, when we're sitting in the van outside the market, eating warm bread from a just-opened baker. 'I like your flowers.'

'Do you like your work?'

He considers. 'Sometimes. It's absorbing.'

'Was it what you always wanted to do?'

He shakes his head. 'Parents.'

Ah, another one.

'I get it.' I smile.

'My mum would have had a fit if she knew I'd sacked it off and gone travelling.'

'Would have . . . ?'

He tells me that both of his parents were older; they had long-term health problems – his mother with multiple sclerosis, his father with heart disease. They died within a short space of each other a few years ago.

'I'm sorry.' I wonder how alone it makes someone feel, when both of their parents are gone, and for a moment I experience a fierce sense of protection for my own mother, a sense I haven't felt since a child, despite the threats to her life she has frequently laid at my doorstep.

'What about yours?' Ernie asks me.

I tell him about my parents, the dad I never really knew.

'Although I've kind of made him up,' I say. 'I talk to him a lot, in my head. He's very supportive.'

It occurs to me I've never told anyone this before, not even Jack.

Ernie laughs. 'But you're not making him up,' he says. 'Because you're a part of him.' He pauses. 'I talk to my parents all the time too. It's incredible how much better Mum is at listening.'

'And your dad?'

'Still the same. Half an eye on the rugby.'

'Did you ever believe in heaven?'

'Nope. Did you?'

'I kind of wanted to. It seemed easier than reincarnation.'

'There's the downside of hell,' he points out.

'So where do you think our parents are?' I ask him.

He swallows a mouthful of bread and passes the loaf to me. The light is slowly making its way into the day, shadows clearing from his square face. I want to touch the deep lines around his mouth, the dip in his chin, to press my lips to the soft part of his cheeks.

'They're everywhere, Anjali,' he says.

My name still sounds like music.

'Does meditation actually help?' Clara asks me, in the shop a couple of Saturdays later.

I think about it as we set out our fresh batch of poinsettias. 'I'm not really sure.'

'Because you haven't been doing it long enough?'

'Because it sort of feels like a chest infection. D'you think that could be a good thing?'

Clara gets out the price gun. 'If it's helping you forget Jack, then I'd say it's OK to sacrifice your lungs.'

I muse over this. Meditation doesn't make me forget Jack, not exactly. Not unless you count forgetting someone as thinking about them with every mark of your breath. And there's the other things about my family it seems to bring up. But maybe Ernie's right when he says that if you block out the bad, you could also be blocking out the good stuff too.

'He's wise, isn't he?'

'Jack?' Clara turns to me, gun pointed in my face.

'Ernie, you dork.'

Clara smiles, turning back to price up the poinsettias.

'What?' I walk round to stand in front of her.

'You.'

'Me what?'

'You're so rubbish at hiding your feelings. You've so fallen for the Ernster.'

I'm about to protest, then decide against it. Ernie's due to pick me up in a few minutes to go over to the Buddhist Centre. I can't

109

deny the way my palms tingle when he's about to arrive, how much I look forward to the two of us having a drink in the local café. Even if we do only have peppermint tea.

'Nothing's happened,' I tell Clara.

'Not yet.'

'He's different to me, Clar.'

'That's no bad thing.'

'I'm not sure what I think of meditating.'

'Does that matter?'

'It's important to him.'

'He hasn't always been into this stuff.'

'Hasn't he? What made him get into it?' I ask.

We're interrupted as the door opens. Ernie comes in, wearing a T-shirt as usual because he never feels the cold, satchel slung over his back. It's strange, this dizzy feeling I get when I see him.

'I'm early,' he apologises.

'Perfect, you can help us with these,' Clara tells him.

'I was going to sit in the corner and have a quiet read.' He points at his satchel.

'Here you go.' She hands him a poinsettia.

Ernie looks at me and raises his free hand in protest. It's helpful that Clara's given him work, because as always when I first see him, my voice is stuck somewhere deep in my windpipe. And the poinsettias are large enough to hide behind.

I listen to Clara and Ernie banter as they set out the stock, laughing away, comfortable, like brother and sister. It's kind of nice being on the outside, getting to see this other side of him. He helps Clara to bring in the rest of the poinsettias, running his broad fingers over the furry red leaves. They reminisce about a Christmas their families once spent together, all of them crammed around a tiny table, the two of them, their parents, his older brother and sister and Clara's younger brother, and I find myself wishing that I could have been there too. I think about those early Christmases with Mum and Shanthi, how Mum cooked curry in a frenzy and dressed us up in matching frilly frocks, the worst of Sri Lankan fashion. We always played Monopoly, and Mum always lost. There were always presents too, and a tree, but I'd go to bed wondering why it felt like there was something missing. Wondering if Mum felt it too, as she lay in the big bed by herself.

'Hey,' Ernie says.

I look up, realising I've just been standing there staring at the same poinsettia. Clara's now out the back, rummaging through the drawers. There's a deep cleft between Ernie's eyebrows and he's gazing at me, a little concerned. 'We lost you,' he says.

It's time to leave for the meditation centre. I slip on my coat and we wave goodbye to Clara. As we start walking, our hands touch for just a moment before they move apart, uncertain. A wave of warm feeling passes along my spine. There's something about being with Ernie that makes me feel like maybe I've been found.

Days later, I take Mum a poinsettia. Christmas is still three weeks away, but she's brought out the old tree, which has shed half its plastic needles in the box, leaving it a little lopsided. Mum hasn't noticed, whirling around the flat with the squashed paper-chains we once made at school. It's the first Christmas I'll have been home in ten years. Mum might keel over with excitement.

'Here? Or here?' She pulls a purple tinsel angel out of the decorations bag and puts it on the sideboard, then on the windowsill.

'Do you believe in angels?' I ask her.

She considers this. 'We must use this one, it cost money,' she decides. She passes me the tangled lights for the tree. Most of the decorations are jumbled up. It occurs to me that she and Shanthi stopped decorating the past few years.

'You are working on Christmas Eve?' Mum asks me for the hundredth time.

'Yes.'

'And then you will come here afterwards?'

'Yes.'

'You must lock up your flat.'

'Yes.'

'You must leave a light on.'

'OK, Mum.'

'You must be security conscious, Anjali. You do not know who might come in and kill you.'

'They can't kill me if I'm here.'

'How long will the shop be closed?'

'We open again on the twenty-seventh.'

'Another year.' Mum stops for a moment, putting a plastic Santa on the table. 'And what are you going to do next year?'

I finish the lights, groaning inwardly. It wasn't worth hoping the decorating would make her forget to ask. There's never any sidetracking my mother.

'The same, Mum. I'll go to work, I'll come home.'

'You must think about the future, Anjali. You cannot stay in that shop for ever.'

I start hanging the red and green baubles.

'And what about that flat? Are you just going to live there by yourself? You will not find yourself a good husband if you are hiding in there.'

Mum keeps wittering away and I control the urge in my

hand to bounce a bauble off her forehead. And at the same time to shout, 'I have met someone! I think you might love him!' I wonder what she'd say if she did meet Ernie, if he'd be able to win her round with his kindness and that smile that lights up his entire face, and everyone's around him. Maybe he is someone I can actually tell my mother about.

'. . . and she does not tell me where she is, I am never knowing,' Mum is saying now. Frowning, I realise she's moved on to Shanthi. She continues to berate my sister's absences while separating out the tinsel, and I decide I won't mention Ernie yet. Anyway, our hands might have brushed past each other's a couple more times, but it's not like anything else has happened. I need to hold fire, even with myself.

I finish putting up the baubles and stand back to look at the tree. It's a sorry sight, gaunt and gaudy. I glance round at all the little trinkets in the flat: the faded royal family plates, the glass cabinet filled with second-hand porcelain ballerinas. The Buddhas sit in their quiet places, observing the decorations. I think about what a different kind of Buddhist Mum is to the people I meet at the centre. She doesn't talk about mindfulness, she doesn't talk about the noble truths or enlightenment. As far as I know, she never counts her breaths. Buddhism growing up for me was something that was always there; something that was just part of our lives and that I didn't fully understand or question. I only thought about it as a kid when Mum tried to teach me about reincarnation, usually in the context of something bad I'd done. 'In your next life, you will be a cow,' she would shriek.

I pull on my coat and get ready to go home. The poinsettia is where it was left on the dining table, looking a little out of place amidst all the tack. I give Mum a kiss; she's still midway through a tirade. It's dark outside, the evenings getting shorter and shorter. My phone rings, Ernie's name flashing up. My hands start tingling again.

'Hey, you,' he says.

'Hey.'

'Are you still at your mum's?'

'Walking back now.'

'On your own?'

'Yes.'

'I'll keep you company.'

'How are you? Did you call for a reason?'

He pauses. 'Not really. I just felt like talking to you.'

He just felt like talking to me.

In the days that follow, I hang out with Ernie all I can, learning more about meditation, learning more about him. With this comes a sort of happiness that I cannot remember in a long time. There's a lightness in my body that I've never felt before. It's the kind of feeling that makes me want a montage. You know the kind, right? An *A-Team*, *Rocky*, *Dirty Dancing* kind of montage. Where scenes of creation or fitness or just very diligent dancing are pasted together in a way that can make a person, should they have been a victim of infidelity, or any another unfortunate circumstance, truly appreciate the lack of creation or fitness or acceptable dance moves in their lives.

In my montage, we're walking down St Marks Road in Easton, where Ernie lives, my arm linked through his, the two of us noticing the soft shapes of the clouds, the changing shades of grey in the feathers of the wood pigeons, the chicory in the trays outside the Sweet Mart. Hell, maybe Ernie even grabs three giant bulbs of chicory and starts to juggle them high into the air, causing us to dissolve into fits of montage laughter.

Then, cut to the local Sugar Loaf pub, where we're sitting outside in T-shirts in an improbable December sunshine, while Ernie talks to me (earnestly) about his meditation practice (of course you can't catch his actual words, but you can guess them from the inflexion of his forehead and the reception of my eyebrows), and I nod and take in his wisdom, becoming progressively enlightened with each tilt of my head.

Then a road carpeted in white, scored with the tracks of the makeshift cardboard sledge that we're dragging along behind us. I'm smiling at Ernie the whole time, not gazing at the sledge and remembering the way Jack and I crammed ourselves into the cardboard crate, cracking our heads together on the way down the hill, laughing through the pain. Not at all. Not one bit.

Quickly moving on to Ernie trying to meditate in his living room, the room with the wooden warrior carving and the woven rug and the box of second-hand vinyl and one small, shining Buddha, and me coming up beside him and putting my hands over his eyes.

And as the soundtrack of our montage (I haven't fully decided yet, but maybe something by The Cat Empire, mine and Clara's current favourite band) draws to a close, there are the two of us, still in his living room, our expressions altered, not laughing so much, but more serious now, and this is it. The kiss.

It's as good as the montage. Some bits are different. The Sweet Mart is battling austerity and has run out of chicory, and we can't drag a sledge across the road because it turns out there's no snow. And there's barely any sunshine this December either. Also, Ernie hasn't heard of The Cat Empire. But otherwise, it's perfect. It feels as if my eyes have fully opened. I don't have to stay trapped in the darkness of the past few months; I can walk out and be a part of the world.

'How did you come across meditation, anyway?' I ask Ernie the day we're sitting on cushions in his living room, beside the warrior and the box of second-hand vinyl. I'm thinking about what Clara said, that meditation wasn't always something he was into.

The top window is open a crack, fresh December breeze pouring right in. We're two days away from Christmas, the whole world smelling of cloves and oranges and good deeds. Between us is the poinsettia I brought over from the shop. Ernie touches a drooping velvety leaf. 'Oh, you know. It's the kind of thing everyone does when they're travelling.'

The tiny caramel beams shimmer in his charcoal hair. There's something here he isn't telling me. 'Clara didn't,' I say.

'Clara's so laid-back, she doesn't need to.'

'So you weren't always laid-back too?'

'I'm an engineer. I can dream about spreadsheets.'

'But you drink peppermint tea.'

'My mum told me to. She made me promise on her deathbed.' I look at him.

'All right, she didn't. But she bought it in bulk. My cupboards are full.'

'Do you miss her a lot?'

Ernie rubs the long, faded scar running across the back of his upper arm.

'How did you get that?'

When he smiles, I glimpse a crooked lower tooth. 'You ask a lot of questions, has anybody told you that?'

'It's a vice,' I admit.

'Broke my arm.' He touches the scar. 'When I was eight, looking for a sparrow's nest. Next question?'

A sudden desire fills me, to be a child once more, exploring in the trees. A buried memory surfaces, of Shanthi and me clambering over branches in the woods beyond the suspension bridge, smearing our frilly frocks with mud and bark, Mum shouting at us both to come down.

I turn back to Ernie. 'You were telling me about your parents,' I say.

'Was I?' That crooked lower tooth again.

'And how you found meditation.'

'All right, Anjali, I'll give you everything.' He holds up his hands. 'But not without the peppermint.'

Two steaming mugs warming our palms later, and he is studying his tea, as if not sure exactly how much to divulge. 'I started taking drugs after my parents died.' He doesn't look at me. 'Mainly coke to begin with.' He tells me it was just a temporary way to escape, until things started to escalate. The darkness in his life lasted for two years, only it wasn't a darkness he was fully aware of; he'd thought everything was all right, even though the drugs spread from the weekends into full weeks, and he lost his job. 'I told you my brother and sister live abroad.' He takes a sip of tea, and the cleft deepens between his eyebrows. 'They're a lot older than me. My friends were whittled down to the ones with my lifestyle. I didn't care about what I was doing.'

Then one day he overdosed. It wasn't something he'd planned, but high on drugs, he wanted to end his loneliness. He can't remember who found him. He woke up in a hospital bed, attached to a heart monitor.

I steal a glance at his warm brown eyes, the deep lines of his square face. I picture him opening those eyes alone on a ward, a drip feeding into his arm. I study the branch of thick veins in his hand, wanting to trace them with my fingers.

'Was that when you went travelling?'

'To get away.' He nods.

'And that's when you found meditation?'

'Well, I found an international bar crawl first,' he admits.

'The peppermint tea is making a lot of sense.'

He laughs. I like his laugh, deep and warm and echoing. He tells me that it was in India that things started to change for him. He ended up staying a lot longer than planned. It was why he returned to the country later and got involved in building and teaching, wanting to give something back to the people who'd helped him.

He touches the poinsettia leaf again. We're side by side on the cushions and I wonder how it would feel to take both his hands, to press my lips to his palms. When he looks up, there is something searching in his expression that reminds me of my sister.

'Were you close to your parents?' I ask.

'You've had all your questions,' he protests.

'Last one, I promise.'

He tells me that oddly he got to know them better when they became unwell, when he moved back into the family home to look after them when he wasn't at work. After his dad died, he took unpaid leave to look after his mum full-time. Having smoked occasionally in his university days, he got hold of some cannabis again in his mother's last months, before she became bed-bound, hoping it could help her. He didn't know then it was going to set him on a downward path. He and his mum smoked it together on the back step, gazing at a shining sliver of moon and listening to the hoot of tawny owls.

He's glad he had that moment.

'You know it was my mum who first tried to get me to

118

meditate,' he tells me. 'It helped her with her pain. But I wasn't ready for it then.' He falls silent, studying his mug. Then he lifts his head. 'Does it bother you?'

'What?'

'All this stuff I've told you?'

'Why should it?' I think about where I was a few years ago, settling into the flat with Jack. Burying myself in that life, staying away from my mum and sister. It's odd to think of Ernie and me existing in the same city, with our separate lives and problems.

'It's not something I talk about,' he says. 'I haven't thought about all of this for a while.' He falls silent again. Then he puts aside our mugs. 'So you've had your questions. It's time for you to tell me something.'

His living room smells of wood and the faint animal scent of the kilim rug on his wall. The bright shapes on the rug remind me of Mum's dresses, and although that could be disturbing, it isn't. I like how at home I feel in his flat, how at home I feel in Easton in general. It's inner-city Bristol, full of all kinds of people who come from all over the world. There are Polish, Jamaican and Moroccan restaurants a few yards away, another place dedicated to vegetarian food; people dress in bright colours, different languages flow from one end of a street to the other. It feels possible to talk about anything here.

I tell him about Jack.

In the last few weeks, it's started to feel as if I could be getting over what happened. But it's hard to get used to Jack's absence. Sadness still waits there in all the places where he isn't. When I realise that I'm losing the sound of his voice.

'I'm sorry,' I say to Ernie. 'This is in every rule book, isn't it? Don't talk about your ex.'

He runs a hand through the tiny curls of his hair. 'We're not teenagers. Ten years is a long time. I suppose we both have a lot of history.'

I wonder again where Jack might be now. Whether he might be sitting cross-legged on the floor of someone else's lounge, telling that person about the decade with me.

'So you were living together for ten years as well?' Ernie asks.

'It's how I met him. Through a house share. We got our own place a couple of months later.'

'Sounds like it happened quickly. Was that why you didn't finish uni?'

'No, not really.' I pause. 'There was a lot going on.'

I see Ernie about to ask me more. I put my finger to his lips.

'I'll tell you all of this, I promise. Just not right now.'

'What do you want to do now?' he asks.

I hesitate, my finger still touching his mouth.

He leans over the poinsettia and kisses me.

I've never experienced the sort of kissing that we do. Even his lips feel wise. As if they know they are the most sensitive part of the body, the opening for our breath, our speech, our nourishment. I keep hunting out new places on his lips to touch, wanting them to open so that I can reach further into the wisdom that is Ernie's entire mouth. I consider, for one brief moment during the kissing, that I wouldn't mind being swallowed by him, so that I could be consumed into his knowledge. And then he could excrete me into the toilet bowl tomorrow morning while reading the *Guardian*. This last thought comes a bit unbidden, I have to admit.

Ernie pulls away. I hope he can't actually read my mind. 'What are you thinking about, Anjali?'

I'm about to brush the question aside. He might not even get the *Guardian*.

'Or trying to stop yourself thinking about?'

His irises are deep pools of brown. I can see my reflection in the ink of his pupils. There is anxiety growing in my own eyes.

'Is that why you ask a lot of questions?' he asks, quietly. 'So you don't have to talk about you?'

With the other guys, it was easier to hide in their stories. But it's harder to do that with Ernie. It's hard to look at the kindness in his eyes; the more I stare at it, the more I can't bear it. Because it isn't something I deserve.

I swallow. The images flowing into my mind now won't be held back. Ten years ago, the summer, the warmth and fresh green grass and a shop full of flowers. Wanting to work every day, every hour, every minute, to focus on something beautiful, to stay away from home.

'What was going on at home?' he asks.

There's someone watching, Anjali. There's always someone watching.

I feel again the sharpness in my spine, because back then, Shanthi never called me by my full name. I see once more her pictures strewn across her bed, over the floor. Serpents. Like they had slipped off the screen and were starting to crawl towards me.

I see my mother, her tears building, refusing to admit that anything was wrong. *She is tired, Anjali. She has been working so hard. She is so tired.*

I went away. Back to the shop, out every night with friends, drinking until I could block it all out.

'But one day I came back and our bedroom door was locked,' I tell Ernie. 'Mum was standing outside, begging my sister to let her in. She'd been standing there for hours.'

I'm not sure how I persuaded Shanthi to open the door for me.

Ernie waits for me to speak. Then, gently, 'What did you find?'

I close my eyes. I see again our bedroom; not the plain green walls and two canvases that are there now. But the old floral wallpaper, where Shanthi used to tack her pictures. Now covered with serpents. Every inch of the wallpaper filled with tiny snakes, thousands and thousands of them, not just pencil on paper, but inked onto the walls themselves. Shanthi standing on a chair in a room stinking of smoke, pen in her hand, drawing on and on.

I don't know how I made her stop, how I was able to remove the pen. How I was able to look into the wild, bright eyes that were somehow more alive than I had ever seen them.

I stop. Looking down, I see that Ernie is holding my hands, rubbing the base of my thumbs with the tips of his own.

'Schizophrenia,' I say. It's a word I haven't used in a long time. It sounds odd, flat on my tongue, like it doesn't want to come out.

'That's what the doctors told you?'

'Not at first. A bit later.'

'Did it help? To know what it was?'

I think of the almost-relief on my mother's face when she gave me the diagnosis, across the dining table at home, because I hadn't been on the hospital ward to hear it for myself. *They will be able to help her, Anjali. They will know what medicine she needs.*

'It helped my mother,' I say. 'Maybe it helped my sister.'

'And you?'

'Why do they use that word, Ernie? People hear it and they think split mind. As if my sister is Jekyll and Hyde. She isn't. She's the same person. She just goes to a place where it's hard to reach her. I wish they would call it something else.'

Ernie moves closer to me, his arms tight around my shoulders. I look at the tiny bend in his nose, the smooth curve of his ears, the crooked lower tooth in his parted mouth, see the vein standing out in his neck, the veins branching in his forearms.

I think of our first meeting, underneath the mistletoe, only a few weeks ago. There's a strong yearning inside me to return there, to when meditation seemed like a fun thing to try, just a distraction, like with everything else, like with the Architect, the Saxophonist, the Sailor.

I kiss him again. I kiss him harder now, opening my mouth, wanting more than ever to creep away inside him. I feel him resisting at first, as if he isn't sure whether this is the right thing to do, and then when I refuse to pull away, I feel my body lift as he gathers me up and takes me to his bed.

Sex with him is not like it was with the Architect. Not like it was with Jack.

My eyes are closed, but when I open them for a moment, I see that his are open too. His kisses, his caresses are slow; fine, electrical sensations run up and down my body. He gazes upon me in a way I never gaze upon myself, looks right at all the places I always tried to shield from Jack, my less-than-perfect waist, the soft flab around my hips.

I come. It's the first time in a long time. Maybe that's why I start to cry. I haven't really cried since the afternoon Jack left. I'm burying my head in Ernie's broad shoulder and I can't stop the tears from falling, and I know that I'm not crying about Jack, but for my sister, for my mother, most of all for the person that I was, leaving them all those years ago. For never really going back.

'I'm sorry.' I untangle myself from Ernie's firm limbs and scramble for my clothes, pulling them on quickly.

'Hey, where are you going?' Ernie's face is clouded in confusion; he moves to touch my arm but I'm too far away from him.

'It's nothing, not much.' I'm trying to talk properly, but the tears won't stop.

'Anjali, what's wrong?'

In ten years together, I never told Jack about running away from home. He knew how hard I found my mum, he knew about my sister's diagnosis. But he didn't know that it was my fear of schizophrenia that made me pack my bags.

Ernie is sitting up, his strong body against the headboard.

'Anjali, please talk to me.'

But I've told him too much. I blink. Around me are shelves and shelves of books on ecology, philosophy, meditation and Buddhism. The cloth-covered drum, the ukulele, the guitar. I don't know this room. I don't know this man.

'I've got to go.'

Once I'm outside his flat, I run.

I met Jack not long after my first year of uni ended. There were still piles of unfinished notes on mine and Shanthi's shared desk, the texts from the year stacked on my bedside table, only briefly scanned. I'd continued to live at home while at uni, scrabbling work together the whole time. It wasn't like the English classes at school, my books grown fat with scribbled notes in every margin, when I couldn't wait for the lesson to talk about them.

I was lost that year, staring out of the window at the sloping lawn, unable to concentrate on the seminar discussions. *Anjali, what do you think?* The tutor's voice, rousing me away from the late roses along the border, then the snowdrops, the hyacinths, the daffodils.

It was hard to concentrate. Shanthi was away at Goldsmith's. I'd missed her so much those first couple of years, the flat with Mum seeming too big, Mum's wittering too much to take alone. I'd noticed my sister was growing quieter on her visits home, spending whole weekends almost entirely in her room, and by her third year she was smoking. But so many students smoked and Shanthi had always been a loner. In that final year, it became harder and harder to pretend there wasn't a problem. Visits home reduced from fortnightly to monthly and then more rarely, the phone calls dropping off too, till Mum was at her wits' end, phoning the shared student house every night and confusing the poor person who'd picked up the receiver.

We must go there, she told me one Saturday in March.

London with Mum was no good thing, crammed beside her on the train while her agitated fingers drummed the top of the table and her restless legs shook beneath. She took the Tube like it was a house of horror, bag clutched heavily to her Persian-rug-clad bosom, jolting every time we passed through a station: *Is this the one, Anjali?* New Cross was crowded, the roads packed with pedestrians, cars, double-decker buses.

Outside the red-brick terraced student house, Mum bent double over the wall, heaving, getting her breath back. A young woman came to the door with her hair wrapped in a towel. *She's not here*, she told us. She called over her shoulder – *Does anyone know when Shanthi's back?* – but it was like they all had to think who she meant. These were clearly not friends, not proper housemates, not people who were looking out for my sister. *Can we wait in her room?* I asked. *It's probably locked*, the woman said. But it wasn't.

Is this how's she living? For once I wasn't annoyed by Mum's rhetorical question, because it was the one on my mind too. The tiny room was filthy, clogged with smoke, ash on the carpets, the windowsills, smeared into the desk. Books and papers scattered on the floor, stained clothes on the bed. Curtains half pulled off the grimy window. No artwork.

We stayed there for hours, Mum hoovering and scrubbing and going out to find washing powder, barely letting me help. Shanthi finally got back. She was thinner, too thin, her clothes hanging off her and covered in paint, her nails rimmed with black, fingers stained with nicotine, curls falling loose and lank. Her eyes bloodshot, heavy circles beneath. *My baby*, Mum said, but Shanthi shrugged her off.

Where have you been?

Working.

Why are you back so late?

Working.

We caught the train back the same day, leaving London in the night. There was nowhere for us to stay and we couldn't afford a hotel.

Then the year ended and Shanthi came home with her certificate. We took the first-class degree as an answer to it all. It was why she'd been away so much, why she'd let everything else go. It was how we were determined to see it.

But it didn't get better. Shanthi didn't look for work like Mum expected her to, did not leave the house. She stayed in our room, smoking out of the window and drawing at the desk. Neither Mum nor I sought help then. Neither one of us could voice the problem. Mum cooked and cooked, the table always overladen with curry. She burned more sandalwood so as not to smell the cigarettes, sprayed air freshener, scrubbed every surface until her hands started to crack and bleed. She made up the camp bed for me in the lounge. *I think Shanthi is needing some space of her own, Anjali, now she is back home for the first time.*

I was going out a lot, staying over at new friends' flats whose walls did not reek of curry. They cooked for me, simple meals: pasta and pesto, beans on toast, pizza. I often woke up in a

126

sleeping bag on their bare floors, my back aching from the hard surface, but not caring, because for once sandalwood was not drifting through the gap under the door, just the warm aroma of toast, bacon, eggs. I ate every slice of bacon that was offered to me, even though it made me a bit nauseous, feeling an urge to defy my mother. When I got home, I'd find my sister sitting beside the serpent screen, or staring out of the window. Sometimes when I approached the bedroom door there was a distinct sense she was talking to someone, but when I went inside, there was nobody there but her.

Are you OK, Shanthi?

Fine, fine.

I wanted to leave home.

The desire was so intense, it was almost as if I could reach out and touch it. Friends' places offered me a glimpse of a different life, of laughing talk, relaxed routines, plates piled high in the kitchen. My days became filled with shifts in bars and the local chippy, trying to pull together as much money as I could to afford to get out of the family flat.

In July, I was scanning adverts for house shares; a flat came up with a slightly lower rent and no deposit, a temporary place filling in for someone who was going travelling. I'd be sharing with two other guys; their advert sounded relaxed and happy.

When I knocked on the door of the flat, it was Jack who answered. Tall and slim, fine hair coming down to just below his ears, a rich auburn brown. Eyes deep blue. A dimple in each cheek when he smiled.

'Was it bad sex?' Clara asks.

It's the following morning in the shop. I'm at the door, looking up at the mistletoe.

I shake my head. 'It was great.'

'You're still hung up on Jack.'

'It's been five months.' I don't tell Clara that it isn't Jack. That the thoughts about my family won't stop going round and round my head. About how telling Ernie has freaked me out.

'Five months isn't such a long time.' Clara is walking round with the price gun, discounting the holly wreaths. It's Christmas Eve. For the last ten years, I've spent Christmas with Jack, the two of us staying at home without much fanfare, just a turkey crown and a couple of crackers, and later in the afternoon a drink at his dad's flat. His dad might bring out oven chips, maybe the Trivial Pursuit cards, and settle back in his armchair with a glass of beer, cardigan loosened over his belly. The game itself, the board and the counters, stayed in the box. It was how we wanted it; none of us fussed about festivities.

Clara puts down the last wreath and comes to stand next to me. I'm staring out onto the street, at people going about their last-minute shopping, cloth bags stuffed with pre-wrapped gifts. I wonder where Ernie spends Christmas.

'Has he contacted you?'

'Ernie? He sent a text. I didn't answer.'

'I meant Jack,' Clara says. 'I thought he might be in touch again before Christmas.' She waits, as if about to say something else, then dismisses it. 'Why didn't you reply to Ernie?'

I glance down at my phone, tucked into my jeans pocket. Because I'm a coward? Because I never can face it when things get tough? 'I don't know.'

'Too early for whisky?'

I smile at Clara's twinkling green eyes and reach out to hug her, glad of her freckled arms, her earthy scent. 'Probably.'

'Hot chocolate coming right up then.'

Later in the afternoon, Clara heads out to do some last-minute Christmas shopping herself. I wander the shop, breathing in its peppery fragrance, straightening a dislodged fern, running a finger over the lazy leaves of a poinsettia. I glance at the door from time to time. Light is draining from the day, the shadow of the mistletoe a dark puddle at the entrance. It would have been better for Ernie if I hadn't managed to fall right into his arms.

At the counter, I study his text. *Please talk to me, Anjali.* I want to reply, to say something to justify why I ran out. But I don't know how to make sense of the shame that has engulfed me since I spoke to him. I don't know how to explain the fear that lodges inside me when I get close to someone, the fear that didn't allow me to be honest even with Jack, in all of our years together. I close my eyes. *Is that why you ask a lot of questions?* I think about how much I've tried to keep hidden, even from myself. But Ernie seemed to offer me a bridge back out into the world. His presence made me feel warmer somehow, that little cleft in the scoop of his chin, the kindness in his eyes, the way he held me.

A moment later, I hear the push of the door and the thud of footsteps. It's funny how you can come to recognise the tread of a person's shoe in just a short space of time.

'I didn't know whether to come,' Ernie says.

He's shaved again, the cleft standing out clearly. There are darker shadows beneath his eyes, deep creases in his forehead. I think about how it feels to let the soft fuzz of his hair run through my fingers, to touch his shining cheeks.

'You can tell me to go if you want.' Ernie looks back at the Christmas shoppers brushing past the window, and smiles. 'Although, man, it's brutal out there.'

Then I'm walking to him, wrapping myself again in the comfort of his arms, breathing once more lemon scent, the warm musk of his sweat, feeling his breath against my neck.

'I'm sorry,' I tell him.

'Why didn't you answer my text?'

'I didn't know what to say. I'm sorry.'

'Don't apologise. Just keep talking to me.'

He pulls me closer into him. I lift my head to his, our mouths almost touching.

The door opens again, then closes.

Breaking away, swinging around, I see the back of a person, returning onto the street. Someone who was about to come in and then changed their mind.

I realise the person is Jack.

I dash to the door. He's walking away fast, hunched over, hands shoved in pockets. I can't doubt the glimpse of rich hair, the slight outward turn of his feet. He's always walked that way, since he was a child. His parents took him to the doctor's when he was little; they said he would just grow out of it, but he never did. Usually he concentrates hard when he walks, says he doesn't want to look like a penguin.

The memory of him saying that makes me smile. Then my eyes are filling and I'm blinking hard because I can't start crying again.

Ernie comes to stand next to me. Jack has disappeared, replaced by the crowd of Christmas shoppers, people standing outside bars, smoking cigarettes, starting their celebrations early. I feel sorry that Jack had to see me like this with another man. Even if what he did was worse. The familiar ache is back in my head.

'Anjali, please tell me what's wrong.'

Some other shoppers come in. Ernie carries their flowers and talks to them so that I only have to wrap up their bunches and take the money. When they've left, we go out the back. There's an old box of peppermint tea in the kitchenette cupboard. We sit with our mugs, side by side on wooden chairs, our feet resting on crates. Clara and I keep meaning to sort this space out; it's crammed with containers and brown wrapping, yards of ribbon, tissue paper, old Easter bunting, leftover tinsel.

'That was Jack at the door,' I say.

Ernie nods. He studies his mug for a while. 'I think I came into your life at the wrong time.'

I shake my head. 'You didn't.'

'Maybe you need to speak to him.'

I shake my head again, more fervently this time. 'No. I'm not sure what there is to say.'

He looks across at me, as if to check I really mean it. 'You told me a lot of stuff at my place.'

'So did you.'

'I didn't mean to say so much. I'm guessing you didn't either.'

I look down at a stray piece of blue ribbon on the floor. 'I didn't tell you everything. I didn't tell you that my sister's illness was the only reason I left home. That I left because I couldn't handle it.'

I stare at the ribbon, waiting for his answer.

'I sort of figured that out,' he says.

'That's the kind of person I am.'

'You were so young, Anjali. And moving out isn't so strange at that age.'

'It's not just when I was younger.' I pick up the ribbon and twist it around my fingers. 'That was the first time she got sick. But there have been other times. A few times. She's been in hospital twice; the second time I wasn't even in the country.' I think about the day Jack gave me the elephants in Sri Lanka, to keep me safe, when it was my sister who needed them most, back home, on a mental health ward.

Ernie faces me. 'I ran away too. That's what the drugs were about.'

'But you were there for your family,' I say quietly. 'You were running from your grief.'

He reaches up to touch my cheek, wipes away a tear that I didn't realise had fallen. 'You were grieving too. You thought you were losing your sister.'

'And because I left, I did.'

He leans his head into mine. His voice comes softly. 'You haven't. She's still here.'

'It's different now, Ernie. We hardly talk.'

'It can change. You're changing. She will be too.'

'She's got a boyfriend. I don't know a thing about it.'

'My sister never tells me anything. First I heard of *her* boyfriend was a wedding invitation. In Seattle. And then she moved there. I mean, come on, sis.'

I smile. I gaze at his fingers curved over his mug, the pale half-moons of his nails. I think of those hands stroking my body, cupping my face. Hands that once bathed his father, carried his mother. This man would never cheat on me, I know this with a certainty that lies deep in the pit of my belly.

He puts our mugs down. Then his hand reaches out for mine and our fingers lace together. The paler shade of my brown skin against the deeper shade that is his.

He puts a kiss on my temple.

'What are you doing for Christmas tomorrow?' I ask him. And then, out of nowhere, I say: 'You could come round to my mum's if you're free. I know she'll cook way too much food for the three of us. You could meet Shanthi. I'd like you to.' As soon as the words are out of my mouth, I'm seeing the image of my mother's shocked face on opening the door to me and six-foot-two Ernie, her panic at not having enough food or the right food, then whirling around Ernie's bemused face until she reaches something like eighty-eight miles per hour and sends herself back to the future.

'Hey, that's really kind of you,' he says. 'But I'm going to be at my aunt's in Bath.'

'You could bring your aunt?' Again, my mum's stricken face.

'She's a bit infirm. I don't think she'd survive the move.'

'OK,' I say. 'But can we see each other again, after Christmas?'

He doesn't reply for a while. I pick up my cup and drink some more of the hot green liquid. I've been trying to like peppermint tea these past few weeks, although sometimes I worry it might be disgusting.

'Anjali, there's another reason why I came to the shop.'

My chest starts to thud. I notice again the heavy shadows beneath Ernie's eyes.

'I was up thinking about it most of the night. I'm going to take on a work assignment. In Vancouver.'

I swallow. For a moment I can't speak.

'Vancouver? As in Vancouver, Canada? Not Vancouver, just down the road, round the corner from Easton?'

'Is there such a Vancouver?'

'I want there to be such a Vancouver.'

'It's the one in Canada.'

There's a dull ringing in my ears.

'Why?'

'My brother lives there. He's got a couple of kids, I've hardly seen them. And then there's my sister and her family, they're not that far off. This opportunity came up a while ago, and I said no. But talking to you about family. Well. It got me thinking.'

I look at his hands, resting in his lap, far apart from mine now. There's a sense of something slipping too fast out of my grasp, like trying to catch water with my fingers. It's the sense I have whenever I try to recall memories of my dad. When Ernie turns to me, the deep crease is back in his brow and I know that there are memories he might be trying to keep hold of too.

'You said assignment? For what, like two weeks? Ten days?'

But I'm kidding, and he knows it.

'Eight months.'

Eight months. Long enough to forget a person, if you wanted to.

I focus on a crack in the laminate flooring. 'You were right. We did meet each other at the wrong time.'

He hesitates. 'I thought about staying. I haven't felt this way about someone since ... since a long time.' There's a tiny lift in my heart, although I know there will be a *but*. 'But I don't think it's me you need at the moment.'

The scenes of my daydream montage are drifting apart. I think about how it might feel to lie next to Ernie in bed at night, our bodies entwined, pale brown skin on dark, the morning light streaming through his bare windows onto the poinsettia on the bedside table. But looking into his eyes, I see everything that has been stirred in me recently, the awareness of the gap in my life ever since I left my family.

'I think I should go,' he says.

I'm blinking hard.

It's past closing time. Clara will be back soon to help shut up. Darkness has seeped into the shop, the flowers shadows in their buckets. Ernie pauses at the door, beneath the mistletoe. His eyes look almost black, the lines in his square face deepened with sadness.

I feel scared to think about not seeing him next week, or the week after. About this kind and gentle man slipping through my fingers.

'Take care,' he says.

The next day, Mum cooks enough food for twenty. The table is crammed with curry – spicy potatoes, green beans, mushrooms, aubergines in spinach, lentils bright with turmeric. And on the side, a defrosted supermarket nut roast. She thought she should mark the occasion.

The crackers got left behind in Tesco. Shanthi's sitting on my left, folding bright pieces of paper into crowns. She's washed all the paint and pen off her hands and shampooed her hair, though Mum still comments on the holes in her jeans. I find myself wondering at Shanthi's ability to let the steady rain of Mum's criticisms fall, gently stepping out of the way.

'Seconds? Who wants seconds?' Mum races back to the kitchen to fetch more food, even though we've barely made a dent in what's already on the table. Shanthi and I look at each other and roll our eyes. It's not just Mum, it's probably every Sri Lankan mother. There's no point in asking them to sit still. And especially this Christmas. Mum tried to play it down this morning, telling us that Christmas isn't our tradition, but she can't quite believe we're all three together for the holiday. You can't miss the spark in her eyes.

'Here you are Shanthi, keep on eating now.' Mum piles more aubergines, swimming in oil, onto my sister's plate.

I notice that Shanthi is even thinner than when I last saw her.

'I'm stuffed, Mum,' she protests.

'You cannot be stuffed. You are skin and bone.'

'I can't help that.'

'Until you are fat, you will keep eating.'

Mum's not so good at talking to us about the deeper things. So food is her emotional currency. I guess that's true for a lot of people.

'And what about you, Anjali?' Mum asks. 'You are getting thin also, I see.'

'I'm fine, Mum,' I say, irritated when she ignores me and ladles more aubergine curry onto my plate too.

'You are not looking very good.' Mum puts her hand on my chin and surveys my face. 'How do you expect to find a husband when you are in this state? Eat up.'

'Mum, for God's sake. I don't want to find a husband.'

'You want to be alone for the rest of your life?'

'And what if I do?'

'Pull yourself together and keep eating. Remember we are going to Sri Lanka in February. Do you want the family to think I starve my children?'

I'd kind of forgotten about that holiday, booked months before. I swallow the aubergine.

Later, when we've eaten about four more servings and Mum's gone for a lie-down, Shanthi and I sit in front of the TV and watch *Top of the Pops*.

My sister has a piece of paper on her lap, as always. She's sketching the little Buddha that sits beside our television. This Buddha travelled from Sri Lanka, starting off in Dad's parents' home, Mum told us. All of our grandparents are dead now.

I watch Shanthi's hand move over the page, the Buddha's face coming to life. His eyes somehow conveying wisdom, peace, kindness. I wonder how she is able to do that.

'You've been out a lot,' I say, after a while.

'Have I?' She looks up. 'I suppose so.'

I study my sister, the frown in her forehead as she draws. Her hair is clean but already tumbling from its bun; every so often she absent-mindedly tugs a loose thread on her jeans with the tip of her pencil.

'Is it just the one friend you meet?'

'Sometimes the others.'

'Where do you go?'

She picks up the paper and tilts her head. 'Sometimes just the studio. Sometimes we go for food or drink.'

'What do you drink?' Shanthi doesn't like tea or coffee. She never touches alcohol.

She laughs. 'Hot chocolate. Orange juice. Water. Anjali, you ask so many questions.'

I hold my hands up in concession.

'Well, I'm glad you're getting out. Beats staying in with Mum all the time.' I think of the jobs Shanthi started over the years, in the longer stretches when she was well – I picture her in the tailored suit on her first day of work at Marks & Spencer, smart until you reached her ankles and saw the scuffed Doc Martens; the time she even donned a navy uniform and stacked shelves in Tesco alongside Mum. She worked hard at those jobs; there were no issues as far as I know. Then, after a while, she would end up drifting, until sickness would make the cycle start over again. Mum used to wonder if things would have been different if Dad had still been around. My sister was five when he died. In the way you sometimes pick up things without ever being told, I understood that this was a point where Mum recognised she'd changed, that afterwards my sister had started to retreat further into herself.

'How are things at the studio, anyway?' I ask.

Shanthi puts down her pencil. Her collarbones jut sharply above the neckline of her T-shirt. Another prickle of worry runs along my spine. The images of ten years ago are so close to the surface now, bobbing about like a cork on the sea. The saucer beside my sister's bed, overflowing with ash and butt ends; Shanthi standing at the open window in the same grey T-shirt, the material thin and damp with sweat, stained with ash. The words I couldn't always understand, muttered under her breath, floating out onto the wind.

'We're going to do an exhibition,' she says.

'What?' The words are so at odds with the pictures in my mind that I feel as if I've been woken from sleep.

'The four of us. We've been talking about it for a while.'

'Where?'

'We've been offered a space at Ashton Court.'

'That's bloody amazing.'

'We haven't done it yet.'

'It's so cool.'

'Hold your horses. It'll be a lot of work, Anjie.'

Anjie. She hasn't called me that in years. A soft feeling comes with this pet name, coursing along my spine. Shanthi is smiling, a spread of little lines from the corners of her eyes.

I'm smiling too. It's not from illness that my sister is thinner; she's just working hard. She never finished those carrot and beet-root sandwiches at school; she never has time for food when her mind is full of art.

She's been OK now for almost two years. The pictures in my head should be of my sister in her good jeans and T-shirt that she wears to the community café, serving the customers their veggie soups and falafels, meeting the artists there who told her about the space in the studio, that desk by the window, the place where she's met the person she gives yellow irises to, where she's planning a showcase of her work; the place where we all thought she would be at the end of Goldsmith's.

I lean back against the settee, snuggling Ordie to my chest.

It isn't such a bad Christmas, all things considered. When *EastEnders* is over, we play Monopoly. Mum doesn't say that there's no need for me to buy any hotels, seeing as I treat our home like one. Maybe she's trying. Maybe I'm trying too.

Shanthi and I go to bed, on opposite sides of the serpent screen.

'You should get rid of this thing,' I say, after we turn our lights off. 'I hate the snakes.'

The shiny reptiles with their wide-open mouths are still faintly visible, peeking out of the stand. Sometimes I still wake in the night to the image of thousands of serpents, their bodies crammed and twisted together.

I hear my sister's pause. 'I don't mind them.'

For a while we don't speak, and I wonder if she's drifted off to sleep.

I pull up the covers against the chill coming through the gap in the window frame. I think of Christmases in this flat when we were children. Hoping for a Santa Claus none of us believed in, looking out for a sleigh in the sky before we went to bed. I think of the one Christmas Eve Shanthi made me stay up all night, when she was seven and I was five, just to check that he didn't really come, how I fell asleep in my curry the next day and Mum chided my sister. We thought we'd proved his lack of existence, but the following year we were still hopeful, just in case.

My mobile flashes on the bedside table. A hope stirs inside me that it might be Ernie.

It's Clara. **Mum's drunk and singing Tom Jones. Next year we're opening the shop.**

I peer out through the crack in the curtains at the night sky. It's too cloudy for stars. I wonder whether there are stars where Ernie is, whether he might be lying in the spare bedroom at his aunt's house, looking out at the night, thinking of me.

I'm about to close my eyes when I think I hear Shanthi tap on the serpent screen. I hesitate, and then another light thud comes. I reach out my arm and tap back. We do it three more times. The cobra code, that was our name for it when we were kids. I always choose the same serpent. Maybe she does too.

Six

I knew it would come to this. I just didn't know it would come so soon. It's almost the end of January. Several Sundays have passed, and I've made sure to be in attendance at Mum's for each one. My sister's made a point of being there too, although she has often gone off to the studio afterwards. Mum said Shanthi's started to paint through the night, getting ready for the exhibition. Perhaps some of this time has also been spent in the relationship I've decided she's in, although I give no hint of this to Mum.

But getting back to the point: these last few weeks, Mum has accepted her weekly bunch of flowers without question, without interrogation, without cupping my chin and commenting on the state of my appearance. Maybe because since Christmas I've discovered my appetite again, and could probably do with losing weight rather than gaining any. Maybe she's finally given up on me, and knows that I'm now in a place that no salvation can reach. Maybe she's actually seen some kind of distant, very faint light, and realises that twenty-nine is not so close to the end of my life after all, and is leaving me alone to sort out my personal affairs at my own pace.

Or maybe she's been biding her time.

'He is a good boy, this one,' she says as soon as she opens the door to me on the last Sunday in January. She takes my snowdrops – I've created a beautiful arrangement in a tiny green bottle – without even setting eyes on them. 'You will like him, I am sure.' She hurries me into the flat, casting the snowdrops on the table (again without one backward glance).

'Where's Shanthi?' I look around.

'She's gallivanting,' Mum says, almost merrily. She takes my hand and swings me into the kitchen, where she flips the switch on the kettle and brings down the chipped mugs in one swift movement. She turns to face me, and only then does the excitement etched into the little lines around her eyes make me appreciate the words she spoke on opening the door.

'What boy, Mum?'

'I have found you an excellent husband, Anjali, of this I am sure.'

She turns back to finish the tea, and I bang my head against the door frame. Then I do it once more.

'Stop doing that, Anjali, you will damage the wood.'

Mum's been trying to set me up with people for as long as I can remember. Literally for as long as I can remember. When I was four, we happened once upon a brown woman and her five-year-old son in St Andrew's Park, and Mum stayed in touch with her for years, for the sheer hope, I know, of future nuptials between the boy and me. When the boy eventually did get married (to an English girl, would you believe), she threw up her hands and wailed.

Don't get me wrong, Mum doesn't try to fix me up with any old random. The mother and boy in the park were Sri Lankan, and at first, all suitable candidates had to be from our home country, that went without saying. But over the years, Mum's Sri Lankan contacts have dwindled and she was reluctant to move the family to London, despite the better prospects there. So with limited options, she had to loosen her eligibility criteria somewhat. A general South Asian origin would suffice, it appeared, so long as the person in question was a doctor/accountant/lawyer. Over time, however, her despair of me led to further modifications. Anyone brown seemed to be the next concession. Even that diminished over the years. A slight brownish hue in skin tone would probably sum things up at the present time.

OK, Mum *is* trying to fix me up with any old random.

'Why don't you just let her?' Clara asks me a couple of days later in the shop. We are sorting out the delivery and I bury my face in the latest snowdrops to avoid further persuasion.

'Anj?'

'You don't understand.' I withdraw my head and wipe a spot of soil from the tip of my nose.

'But, I mean, what could be so bad? It's like meeting men without making any effort.'

'It'll be like meeting male incarnations of my mother, without any effort.'

'You never know . . .'

'And I don't want to meet anyone anyway.' I think of Ernie. There's been no message between us since Christmas Eve in the shop. Nothing to say he might be missing me too. *I don't think it's me you need at the moment.* His words keep playing in my head. I knew he was right. In all these months, it isn't a man I've been searching for. Even when I was happy, or thought I was, with Jack, there was always something missing. Ever since I ran away from home.

'Come on, they won't actually be like your mum.'

I unpack more snowdrops and breathe in their sympathetic fragrance. 'Maybe not. But every time I look at them, I'll hear Mum's voice: "I'm telling you, he will make an excellent husband, Anjali." I can't live with that for the rest of my life.'

'It doesn't have to be for the rest of your life,' Clara suggests. 'Shag them and leave them. That will make your mother stop trying to set you up.'

'I don't want to shag anybody.'

'But you're miserable.'

'I'm not.' I set some of the pots on the counter and turn to face her. 'I'm getting better, Clar. You must see that.'

She crosses her arms and studies me.

I'm aware my girth has expanded a bit, I know my hair is flattened for once by grease and tied up with an elastic band I found on the floor of the shop, I know the circles beneath my eyes have deepened and there's grime in my nails.

I know I listen to the clock at night, counting four hours back to Vancouver.

I know that every time my phone beeps, I still hope it might be Ernie.

'You could do with some fun, Anj.'

'Then let's go out dancing.'

'I'm just saying.' Clara bends down and starts arranging the buckets. 'Maybe give this guy your mum's found a chance.'

'But I know what he'll be like.'

'What will he be like?'

'Try dull, fastidious, narrow-minded ...'

'Come on, your mum wants better for you than that.'

'Are you kidding? That's her perfect man.'

'Was your dad like that?'

144

I frown. 'No, not at all.'

It's funny. Aside from being an upstanding member of the medical community, it hasn't occurred to me to wonder what kind of person Mum would want me to be with. It's never occurred to me to ask her advice about any of my life choices. Including leaving home.

'There's my argument then,' Clara carries on. 'You should give this guy a go. And I'm too skint to go dancing.'

She swings back round to the snowdrops. I study the brown and blonde threads of her dreadlocks, wondering what difference it might make if I stopped fighting against Mum. Just once.

'OK, well just tell me a bit about him then.'

It's Wednesday evening and I can't go on ignoring Mum's calls. Well, actually I have been ignoring all of her calls, not quite ready to take any sort of plunge, and it's only her arrival on my doorstep that has interfered with this effective strategy.

Mum hasn't been to my flat in years; only that one time when we'd just moved in. It was the first time she'd ever met Jack. She sat on our Freecycle faux-leather sofa (mistrustfully, having to be reminded the leather was fake), surrounded by all Jack's boxes and bags and the one chest I had alongside my small case. She looked around at the shabby IKEA furniture, at the ceiling furred with mould, at the patches of dirt on the carpet. She placed the plastic containers of curry she'd brought onto a coffee table sticky with ring stains.

But Jack was good with her. He made her a cappuccino and asked about her work and offered more frothed milk and sugar and agreed that Lionel Richie would always be remembered. Tapping his feet and twitching his fingers, he waited until she'd gone before hurrying out to the garden for a cigarette.

I scrubbed and scrubbed the flat after that and Jack got out his guitar and learnt to play 'Dancing on the Ceiling' with a straight face, but Mum didn't come back.

So finding her on the doorstep earlier this evening was fairly startling.

We're outside now, sitting at the wooden table on the little square of concrete. I wanted her to see what I've done with the garden. My snowdrops have just lifted their heads above the soil. The story goes that when Adam and Eve were evicted from the Garden of Eden, and Eve thought that winter was going to last forever, an angel came along. The angel transformed some of the snowflakes into tiny white flowers, and then Eve knew she was on the home straight. I always think of this story when I look at snowdrops, little heads of hope waiting for spring.

Although it's still bloody freezing.

And the outdoor light's stopped working. You can't really see the flowers.

And I don't know how long I'm going to have this garden. On my wage, I'm either going to have to hand in my notice or get evicted too. Ain't no angels in Bristol. None that transform snowflakes, in any case.

'Shall we go back in?' I ask Mum. In truth, it's pitch black; I can't even make out her face.

We go inside. I know she's taking in the dust on the mantelpiece and the IKEA bookcase, on the large concertina shade of the corner lamp. She'll have clocked the tiny kitchen, no longer sticky with grease, but with a sink full of dirty dishes, unwashed laundry abandoned in a pile in front of the washing machine. She won't notice that I replaced the gaudy curtains with white muslin, that I removed the ring stains from the coffee table with vinegar; she won't see the shiny green leaves of my rubber plant.

I wash out two mugs and make tea. There's only one way to distract her from my poor housekeeping. She's hovering behind me, waiting to give me the details about this guy she's found, and maybe, just maybe, if I gave in to her, just this once . . .

'So how do you know of this man, then?'

Might it turn back the clock a little, welcome me back into her gigantic bosom, do something positive for our relationship? More than this, do something positive for our whole family?

She gives me the particulars.

So it starts with Aunty Arie, who isn't really an aunty, but someone Mum knew from the temple who is now dead. Turns out Aunty had a sister, who is also dead. This dead sister had a cousin, who is similarly deceased. The deceased cousin had a niece, who once again has now expired. The expired niece had a daughter who, thankfully, is still living. The living daughter has a cousin, with a regular pulse. The pulsing cousin has a nephew, who is also going strong. The strong nephew got married, to an equally robust woman. The robust woman has a similarly animate sister. The animate sister has a friend. Who is alive, a man, a British-born Indian, a Hindu (which can be overlooked), but more importantly than anything else, a DOCTOR.

Ka-ching.

'And he is single.' Mum's eyes cannot get any wider. This is more than winning the lottery for her, this is like the final round of *The Great British Bake Off.*

'But how have you been able to set us up?'

That has involved a complicated series of phone calls, of which the robust woman seems to be at the centre.

'And why does he need to be set up anyway? Surely he can find his own partner if he's so eligible? An Indian one too, if he wants. How old is he?'

But Mum's wittering on and misses my question. In my mind I'm picturing a very old, frail medic who is, by dint of lifelong incompetence with the opposing sex, still a virgin, and who has arthritically leapt at the opportunity to procreate and spread his failing seed.

'His mother does not want him running off with any of these English girls,' my mum finishes proudly. And this is as exciting to her as the prospect of a medical son: a like-minded woman with whom she can share stories about her struggles with this country (while consuming numerous cups of PG Tips and copious quantities of Victoria sponge or other quintessentially English cake).

'And has this guy ... this doctor ... does he know anything about me?'

'I have told [the robust woman] all about you. And she thinks you are very suitable.'

Suitable in what way? I wonder. I glance down at my abdomen, imagining it filled with a series of ailing doctors.

'But what about the guy himself? What does he think?'

I'm picturing the dying, stooped doctor picking his few remaining brown teeth, happy to meet whatever woman he is supplied with, so long as she is young and nubile and keen to massage his hairy toes.

'He has said he will meet you.'

To be honest, when you see it through the medium of my mind, you can understand why I'm terrified.

'So, I shall organise the meeting,' Mum says. 'I will ask them all over to dinner on Sunday.'

'No!' I'm shocked by my own vehemence. Mum puts down her

148

mug, surprised. 'No way,' I reaffirm, in case I wasn't clear. 'That would be too embarrassing.'

'Anjali, you are no longer a teenager. This is a serious matter. You should not be worrying about embarrassment.'

'Mum, I just can't sit at yours with a group of strangers staring at me.'

My heart's thumping. I picture being watched by the decrepit doctor and his entourage of Asian pimps, their notebooks poised, gold-plated pens ticking off every time a piece of spinach lands between my teeth. Then they disappear to be replaced by Ernie, standing beneath the mistletoe again, eyes glistening. The ache in my chest grows stronger. Going from one guy to another didn't help with Jack. It won't make this emptiness go away either.

'So you won't meet him then?' Mum's face has fallen. She looks tired, her skin dry. It seems every week the line deepens across her forehead.

The ache in my chest is for her, too.

'All of this work I have done in finding him, Anjali. All of this effort I have always made for you.'

I swallow. 'Mum, I'm grateful, I just don't know if now's the right—'

'You won't even give this boy a chance?' Her voice grows ever more plaintive. 'He is a doctor, Anjali! You know what this means.'

'Yes, yes, he's rich and—'

'No, it is much more important than that.' Mum looks wounded. 'It means he will look after you, Anjali.'

'Mum, I just don't think—'

'You would rather sit here, looking at your garden, doing nothing?'

149

'OK!' I say. 'OK, OK, I'll meet him.' I sigh. 'Just not at our place, all right? Somewhere neutral, outside, where it's just me and him.'

'That's fine.' A brief flicker of fire is back in her dark irises.

'But if I don't like him, then you have to be cool with that, OK?'

She holds up her hands. 'It is your decision. I will not force you to do anything you do not wish to do, I only wish for you to meet him.'

I sigh again, the tightness in my chest loosened a little.

My phone beeps.

That hope flashes once more, a frisson along my spine. But it's not Ernie, just Google, asking if I want to back up my content. I glance at Mum, in her own world, probably planning the Sri Lankan bridal ceremony, officiated by a circle of orange-robed monks. Ernie's not going to contact me now; I have to let him go. I wonder what Shanthi would say, if we could talk about any of this. But where to start? It would be hard to explain how much I want to make up for how I was all those years ago. Even if I could, I'm not sure she'd want to hear it.

Oh well. Maybe just doing this is the surest way to back up my content. A brief date with a guy who doesn't know anything about me or my issues. My mother will stop being disappointed in me, for a couple of minutes anyway, and it will relieve my weary spine of the weight of her persistence. And it doesn't matter if he does turn out to be a dying brown-toothed virgin with hairy toes and a mild hope of procreation.

It's not like I'm going to sleep with him or anything.

His tongue is pulsing away at my nipples and I can't stop enjoying it. I hold up my breasts for him, to make enjoyment even easier. He returns to kissing my neck in the way that first made me offer said breasts to him, then he keeps moving up the bed until he can lower his dark cock into my mouth. My hands are attached to his buttocks and I push him into me until I am gagging. He pulls himself out and starts working his way down my body again.

'Now?' I ask. (Translation: Fuck me at once?)

'Wait,' he tells me.

When he goes down on me, his tongue moves in the same way it did on my nipples, a firm, regular circular movement until I have to cup my hands over my mouth to stop myself from crying out.

'Now!' I cry out. (Translation: Fuck me at once!)

'Wait!' He lifts his head to command me, and I moan from the loss of his tongue. Fortunately, it returns. I'm going to come. And this time I'm not going to cry.

'NOW!' I shriek. (Translation: FUCK ME AT ONCE!)

He relents, slips on his condom and fucks me at once. In the mirror is the reflection of his pumping brown bottom, our tangled limbs, almost exactly the same milky-coffee shade of brown, difficult to tell apart. There's an odd sense that I have fallen into a derivative and contrived sex scene, and one that's far removed from the sex I had with Ernie; but then it's not like Ernie has contacted me or means to contact me or has even been thinking about me or wants to see me when the eight months is up, and anyway at least Mum would be pleased, kind of, proud even, maybe, that I'm making a go of things here and . . . *Stop it, Anjali! Stop thinking about your mother and concentrate on the derivative sex!*

This guy works away for maybe as long as the Architect, but the prolonged experience is welcome this time. If he keeps going, I might come again. I've never had a multiple orgasm. I've only heard of them, whispered, like Greek myths. Not that Greek myths tend to be whispered, *but never mind that, Anjali, forget about the myth thing and get back to the sex!*

I don't come again. But it's a close one.

'Ah,' he mutters with his orgasm.

Then he collapses, and his ample, toned body falls on top of me.

We lie like this, him above me, me suffocating, both of us struggling to get our breath back, for a fair while.

Then I manage to extricate myself.

I turn my head to look at the Western Brown Man.

'Hi,' I say.

I mean, there are benefits to being with a doctor. They have more money than the guys I'm accustomed to seeing, for one thing. It means they can afford to meet you in grand hotels and then pay for a bed if, within seconds of looking at each other, you decide to have sex. It means that they can order room service.

'Meat,' I say, looking at the menu. 'A big piece of meat.'

'Steak?' he interpolates, the telephone receiver clasped to his ear.

'Yes.' I close the menu. 'A huge rare steak. The bloodier the better.'

'I thought you were a vegetarian?'

'Yes, that's right.' I pull the covers over myself, sighing with happiness. Mum will forgive me the meat. She'll just be so glad I'm embracing this whole situation. I can't quite believe I'm embracing this whole situation. But I actually fancy someone Mum approves of. This could be the start of my entire family's contentment. It's possible I'm delirious.

'You're brilliant,' the Western Brown Man says, and I sigh even more.

I break away from the meat-related praise being heaped upon me to ground myself a little. We are in the Hotel du Vin, in the centre of town. Maybe Ernie might have known what my earlier Wikipedia search revealed: that this is actually a restored Sugar House, which was once the main destination for the sugar arriving from the British colonies. Perhaps he would have told me it's a collection of Grade II listed warehouses dating back to the 1700s. Maybe he would have repeated: 'The seventeen hundreds,' before putting his warm lips on mine, *but stop it right there, Anjali! You've got to stop thinking about Ernie now. And anyway, Grade II listed buildings are more up the Architect's street, surely.*

Our room is small but plush. Soft chequered carpet, and a heavy mahogany bed with a thick, firm mattress. A real leather armchair reclines beside folds of scarlet velvet curtains. There's a drop-leaf table at the foot of the bed on which rests the bottle of champagne and two glasses (not even flutes; these are saucers, actual crystal saucers) that the Western Brown Man hastily obtained before leading the two of us up to this room.

He pours me a saucer now, and I pull myself up to pillow height and stretch out my body like a cat. Yes, a cat. It's the kind of room that makes you feel like a furry, domesticated and carnivorous animal.

'For you, beautiful lady.' The Western Brown Man passes me the glass.

He is rather beautiful too, all things considered, and not remotely frail. In the foyer I noticed his designer black-rimmed spectacles straight away. I have a weakness for glasses. They make a person look like they're fond of poetry. To be fair, glasses are more likely to indicate myopia than Mayakovsky, *but never mind about refractive errors, Anjali, just focus your 20/20 vision on the Western Brown Man!*

Aside from the glasses, he has a youthful, and symmetrical, face. A steady dark gaze, and incredible white teeth. No hint of plaque; this man is in regular attendance with his dental hygienist.

Thick, curly black hair, a shortened version of my own. If we have a baby girl, she'll need to borrow my GHDs.

A baby girl?

Where did that come from, Anjali?

OK, so children are far from my mind, but the thing is, I'm starting to wonder if my doubts about my mother's intentions have all this time been unfounded. I mean, why have I dismissed as crazy the idea of her setting me up with a well-spoken, well-dressed (he isn't wearing any clothes at the moment, but I can see an Armani label on his jeans) and well-educated man? And why have I been dismissive of doctors all this time? I don't know what kind of doctor the Western Brown Man is, as the conversation part of our meeting has yet to begin, but Mum is probably right – doctors are generally good people, as far as our knowledge of the profession, bar the occasional Shipman, goes. It's likely that the Western Brown Man (who shall hitherto be known as WBM) could be the very person to treat my encumbered spine when it is crippled with the weight of Mum's accusations.

Except maybe there will be no further accusations now.

I picture Mum's face when she hears the date went well. The happy things we can talk about during Sunday dinners from now on, the years of accusations just drifting away with the curry fumes through the open windows, way out into the Bristol skies.

My sister, being eager to know more, maybe even opening up about this possible relationship of hers, too. Ernie somehow slips into the image, sitting at the end of Mum's dining room table, but I try to ignore him. He's almost five thousand miles away. He made me no promises. The WBM is right here, right now, and he has my mother's backing. Maybe this is it: the end of all of these years of fighting and cross-examinations and stumbling and tripping, of not being able to find my way.

'What kind of doctor are you?' I finish my saucer and hold it out for a refill.

'I'm a psychiatrist,' he says, leaning over for the bottle.

OK, so he can't treat my spine, but his profession at least raises the possibility of a comfortable couch. There's a little rise in my chest. Maybe one day I could even talk to him about my sister.

'How old are you?' I ask.

'Thirty-five.'

'Oh good.'

'Why good?'

'Oh.' I realise I've been speaking out loud while mentally ticking off his points against my list of criteria. 'I mean, it's a good age, isn't it, thirty-five? A good, solid age.'

'It's a young age,' he says.

'Yes, a good, solid young age.' I don't know when I became an advert for this particular milestone, but there you are. These roles can sometimes be thrust upon you.

'I've got a lot of life to lead yet,' he says.

'Yes.'

'How old are *you*?' he asks.

'Twenty-nine,' I say.

'Brilliant.'

'Why?'

He shakes his thick, curly head as if sharing a joke with himself.

My confusion is interrupted by the arrival of our steaks.

The WBM reveals his body to me again briefly before covering it up in the thick hotel robe. A waiter brings our dinner in beneath gleaming silver covers and arranges it on our folding table. I smile at him demurely, as if being naked at 5 p.m. on a Saturday (Clara gave me the afternoon off) is an acceptably decadent way of living. The waiter smiles back.

We eat on the bed, plates on our laps. The steak is fantastic. I want to grab hold of it with my hands and gnaw away at it, but force myself to use the cutlery.

'It's brilliant that you eat meat.' I notice the WBM watching me with a kind of fascination.

'Um,' I respond, my mouth full of beef.

'We're a strictly vegetarian family,' he tells me.

I swallow. 'So are we.'

For a moment, we pause, looking at the bloody juices of our meat pooling on our plates.

'Brilliant,' the WBM repeats, getting stuck into his fillet.

We eat in silence for a while, and then he says to me, in an offhand way, 'So remind me what you do for a living again?'

'No need to remind you,' I say. 'I haven't told you yet. I'm an assistant florist.'

'That's right!' He puts down his fork with gusto. 'Prema told me that!' (Prema, I remember, is the animate sister, thinking back to Mum's explanation of the link between us.) 'That's brilliant!'

Now I put my fork down. 'Why is that brilliant?'

But the WBM only laughs, slapping his thigh. I've never

known someone to actually slap their thigh when they laugh. It makes the bed vibrate and my peas roll.

'I don't understand,' I say.

'It's just fantastic,' the WBM says.

'Do you like flowers or something?' I look at the arrangement of fake lilies on the sideboard.

'Love them,' the WBM declares.

Well, that's good, I suppose. But there's something about the WBM's reactions to everything I say that feels a little disconcerting. Still, it's not like I've ever been with a psychiatrist before. Maybe they are always this warm about a person's basic credentials.

'Listen, beautiful lady, I'm on call tonight.' The WBM suddenly thrusts his plate to one side and leaps out of the bed, bulky muscles flexing beneath the parchment-coloured robe. He starts pulling up his Calvin Klein boxers and Armani jeans.

'Haven't you had ...' *too much to drink?* Then I notice that he's still only on his first glass of champagne, barely touched. I must have drunk the rest. My head starts feeling fuzzy. It occurs to me I've kind of rushed things a little. 'Are you going now?'

He's buttoning up a shirt so white it makes my eyes hurt. Wait, is he seriously about to walk out and leave me naked on the bed? Being mistaken for a nautical prostitute was one thing, but this feels like proper sex work. What if that waiter's still pushing his trolley in the corridor? I'll never be able to face him.

'Here you go.' He slams something down on the bedside table and my heart turns cold. It can't be money.

No, it's not money. It's his card. This man has a card.

'Call me,' he says. 'Let's do this again.'

'You mean the ...' *Sex? Steak? Slightly strange conversation?*

'All of it,' he says. 'And I've got the bill.'

He swings on his leather boots, slings his black cashmere coat over his shoulder and, giving me one last shot of his fantastic teeth, waltzes out of the room.

'It went well, Mum. I think.'

She's back in my flat. She's not even focused on the dust or the sink or the pile of clothes beside the washing machine. I'm not sure she's looking at anything. Her fiery eyes are darting gleefully around the room; in a moment I think she might dance.

'Steady on, Mum.' Going through to the kitchen, I start shoving the clothes into the machine. It's time to sort myself out. And I need my best knickers. I throw yesterday's jeans into the drum, then hastily retrieve them, pulling the WBM's card out of the back pocket.

'Tell me about his family.' Mum throws herself on the fake leather.

'Oh – I don't really know about his family.'

'You didn't talk about your families?' She looks crushed. I swear that all arranged marriages must occur because our parents never had Facebook or Snapchat or whatever. They need some way to feel connected.

'Tea?'

'Coffee,' Mum says, glumly. 'The nice coffee that boy made me.'

Jack will always be 'that boy'.

'The machine's gone. It was Jack's.'

'He was selfish, that one.'

'Tea?'

'Tea.'

I open a new box and fetch the mugs. Listening to the hiss of the kettle, I glance around at the tiny space, the wonky cupboard, the old electric cooker, at my mother on the sofa, which has sagged to one side with the weight of her, flicking through one of my floral magazines. She looks quite at home. I peek out of the window; there are my snowdrops, bright green shoots pushed up fully through the soil, my little heads of hope. It feels easier to be here somehow. Jack is still about, his shadow lingering around the flat. And Ernie is always somewhere in my mind, no matter how much I try to avoid him. But that brief chapter of my life needs to be closed now. And the WBM's card is waiting on the counter.

I pick it up. Yesterday was a whirlwind. I'm still not entirely sure what got into me. And I didn't really get my conversation with the WBM. But there's something appealing about his energy, his enthusiasm, his bouncy buttocks. Butterflies are dancing in the pit of my belly, and there's this hope that keeps tingling. What will happen if I phone this man? What if we do fall into a relationship, become my mum's real-life Facebook page, updating her home feed regularly with our meetings? What if we even one day marry, have kids, have a house full of brown people, competing to serve each other food, to wear the worst dresses, to buy the gaudiest car-boot trinket? There's an image in my mind of my mum and his mum locked in deep, brown conversation, slices of Victoria sponge squashed into their mouths, happiness decorating their faces.

I look back at Mum, her heavy legs tucked underneath her now on the sofa, absorbed in an article on white forsythia, star-shaped, flushed pink, the kind of flower for a winter wedding.

The WBM and I meet again. And again. Each time he answers the phone, 'Beautiful lady,' and suggests a hotel I can't afford, The Royal Marriott, the Berkeley Square. Each time I try to pay my share, he waves my overdrawn card aside and tells me that in a couple of years he'll be a consultant, and not to worry about the money. I think about telling him that I *do* worry about money, not just about not having any, but about taking it from someone else. Jack and I split everything down the middle; we were equals. But by that point the WBM has usually bounced out of the room, and there's just me, naked in the bed, talking to myself.

The third phone call, before he has a chance to speak, I say, 'Handsome man. Tonight we're meeting in St Werburghs.'

'But where—?'

'My flat.'

'Your flat?'

'My flat.'

For a second it seems this could go on, but there's a pause.

'Your flat,' he confirms.

He looks out of place in my flat. He's large, for one thing, not particularly tall, but with bulky arms and legs, the kind you earn by regular attendance at the gym, not by signing up in January then realising in August that you've paid £250 for one session. We try to sit together on the fake leather couch, but the sag of his side means I just fall straight into him. Which he doesn't seem to mind.

He never kisses my mouth. Or hardly. He always goes straight to my neck and presses his lips softly down one side. Up until this point I'll have been asking questions, determined that we will actually talk this time, but as soon as the electrical sensations start to drift down my body, my words are shuttered. He rubs his hands down my arms, reaches my abdomen, and this is the point with Jack where I would have breathed in or shifted away, but my soft midriff is not an issue here. It's like our outward appearances are entirely incidental and we are simply a mass of sensation.

Not today, though.

No, today I am going to talk to this man. Not a hasty few minutes snatched with a steak (always steak); today we are going to have a proper conversation.

'I'm making dinner,' I tell him.

Maybe I haven't said it out loud. He is starting to pull up my skirt and ahhh . . .

'Paella,' I say.

'With prawns?' He breaks away for a moment.

'Peppers.'

But vegetables do not interest this vegetarian man. He slides his hand underneath my skirt and I think, *Sod it. We can eat afterwards.* The sex is too good. Although there is the uncomfortable memory that is lately bothering me more and more, of the tender way that Ernie held me, the way our lips kept touching, how he looked at me, properly looked at me. I glance at the WBM, still wearing his designer spectacles, but with his eyes tightly closed.

'Right.' Gathering all the strength I have, I manage to push myself off the WBM.

He blinks. 'What happened?'

'Dinner,' I tell him.

He kisses my neck at the cooker. But I steadily stir the rice, add the fine gold strands of saffron, ignore all bodily sensations, think about how much saffron costs, tip in the non-prawn peppers and finally dish up onto the plain plates Mum got discounted from Tesco.

We eat on our laps (there's no table).

'So tell me about your work.' The WBM flicks through a floral magazine while he eats.

I tell him about driving to the traders' market, the blue light of early morning filtering through the clouds. About the mini garden centre Clara and I have been working on this month in the corner of the shop, snowdrops one of our first additions. About our love of the old myths behind each flower, how our best customers stay for coffee to listen to them.

'Even Mum, once.' I remember how she popped in, and Clara fastened her to a stool while fetching her a drink. Mum pretends to be frightened of Clara's facial piercings and glued hair, but there's a secret soft spot within her vast chest, I can almost see it.

'Does your mum work?'

'At Tesco.'

'Ha, that's right!' If his plate wasn't resting on his thigh, I'm sure he would have slapped it.

'Does *your* mum work?' I ask, confusion creeping back into my mind.

'Nope.' He downs another spoonful of rice and goes back to the magazine, skipping past the forsythia.

I study the inky black almost-curls of his hair and the jagged curve of his hairline. The pale light of the dusty concertina lamp is reflecting from his glasses; I can't make out his eyes. No matter the number of times I sleep with this man, I don't know him, have no idea what is behind the things he says.

'You were born here, right?' I ask.

'Here?' He glances around my flat like it was the site of his home birth, a square of plastic spread over the small living room floor, his non-working mother praying on her haunches before the WBM was pushed out, slapping his little thigh.

I blink away the frightening image. 'The UK.'

He grins. 'Hackney. But we moved to Bristol when I was nine.' There are still faint touches of an east London accent.

'Did you always know you wanted to be a psychiatrist?'

'Goddammit.' he nods. 'First book I ever read was *The Psychopathology of Everyday Life*.'

I raise my eyebrows.

He puts his plate on the floor – and slaps his thigh. 'No, of course I fucking didn't. Sorry, excuse my French. My dad's a psychiatrist. There was nothing else I was going to be.'

He pushes his glasses up the bridge of his nose. I know all about parental pressure, of course. But there is a slight waver in his forefinger; his eyes close a fraction longer after a blink than they should do. He's feeling something here that I can't quite put my finger on and that I can't quite understand.

'Where do you live?' I wonder, also wondering how I can have slept with this man so many times without knowing. 'Where do your parents live?'

'Clifton and Clifton.' He sounds almost bored. Then he suddenly leaps up, yanking me from my cross-legged position on the floor.

'Come on.' He is pulling on the black cashmere coat, slipping on his boots. 'Get your jacket.'

I look at the oily little mounds of yellow rice still left on our plates, the peppers pushed to one side on his. 'What? Where are we going?'

'My mother's,' he says.

'Your mother's? Now?'

'Why not? I want to introduce you.'

'You do?' As strange as the WBM is, there's something about his enthusiasm that sweeps you up with him. And it occurs to me that it's promising he does want me to meet his family. It's not like we can have sex in front of them (I banish another terrifying image). We'll *have* to talk. A quick flash in the mirror confirms my hair is about as wild as it ever gets, but at least I've put on my best jeans and a brush of mascara.

'Come on, my car's outside.' He holds up his key with the shining silver Mercedes symbol.

His parents live in the heart of Clifton Village. We drive past buildings over a century old, the boutique shops, the fancy wine cellar, the pastel-coloured cake parlour. I glance at the charity shop with elegant floaty dresses and suede boots in the window. He keeps driving, towards Sion Hill, then left and further on, pulling up to a stop at Royal York Crescent. I gaze upwards at the white-painted facades of the Grade II listed terraces. The Architect could be beside me, pointing out the pedimented doorways and segmented stone window arches. Though to be honest, he probably wouldn't be saying anything; would just be staring in awe as I am, at the fact that somebody we know actually owns a place here. It's probably the most expensive street in the city.

The WBM gets out of the car. I'm kind of rooted, glancing down at a yellow saffron stain on the thigh of my jeans. Maybe he thinks I'm waiting for him, because he's heading up a flight of stone steps to the elevated entrance of the building, and then stops and dashes back down to open my door.

I climb out. 'So they've got a flat here?'

'*I've* got a flat here,' he says. 'They're number four.'

'The whole house?'

He's looking at me a bit impatiently.

'Right, I'm coming.'

There's a hanging basket at their door, trailing ivy and creeping thyme, a mini fir and little violas, buttercup yellow and fringed in purple. I look down at the drooping snowdrops in the tiny pot I'm carrying. I swallow.

Before the WBM can put his key in the lock, it's opened.

'You're here,' says a woman who can only be his mother.

Thank God his dad isn't home. I'm not sure I could bear more than one set of eyes boring into me from across the polished oak table. I was expecting another large Persian-rug-clothed woman, but this lady is willowy, elegant, skin glowing and the colour of rich soil, long nails painted deep burgundy, wearing a lavender chiffon dress with wide sleeves. Her hair is long, unnaturally straight, gathered in a French pleat, not a wisp of grey in there. Except I bet she doesn't use Tesco hair dye.

There's a chandelier bathing the table in yellow light, crystal diamonds sparkling. There are huge gold-plated mirrors, shining occasional tables. There's a colossal brass statue of the Hindu god Ganesh, his elephant head staring right at me. There's not a single royal family plate, dancing china figurine or other car-boot trinket.

On the table are dishes of Punjabi kadhi pakora, a traditional curry, the mother tells someone, possibly me, made of gram flour and buttermilk, onion pakoras floating in the sauce. Somehow this has been produced without fanfare, without chopping boards and saucepans littering surfaces. The mother smells of nothing but Chanel.

I can't eat anything. I'm not hungry, for one thing, because of the paella. I'm also somewhat terrified.

Fortunately, the mother says very little to me, just kind of stares while ladling extra curry onto my barely touched Wedgwood plate from time to time. Something in common with my mum, at least. Most of the conversation takes place with her son.

'I thought you were working,' she says.

'No, no, I was at Anjali's flat.'

'Her flat?' Her gaze flows from my forehead down to where my body disappears beneath the table.

'Yeah, you're renting, aren't you, Anjali?' The WBM is tucking into his pakoras. 'Cool tiny place off the motorway.'

'The motorway?' the mother asks.

'St Werburghs,' I try to say.

'But not quite.' The WBM's voice is cheerful. 'All the drunks and the litter but not much of the name.'

I stare at him.

'I love it,' he says. 'It's brilliant.'

'And what does Anjali do?' The way the question's worded, I'm not sure it's really intended for me.

'She works in a shop,' the WBM says. 'Assistant florist, right Anjali? D'you like the snowdrops, Mum?'

The mother doesn't really answer.

'She can get you some for a discount, couldn't you, Anjali? You've been working there for years. Since you ditched university.'

I don't really remember telling him about that, but maybe it was whispered between orgasms, along with the Greek myths.

'And will Anjali continue to work in the ... shop?' This conversation about me, but not involving me, is making me feel a little disorientated, like I'm walking through a thick fog.

'Oh, you don't know what you're planning, do you, Anjali?' The WBM's large hand is squeezing my thigh, and I'm pretty certain his mother spots him doing it. 'You just see where the wind takes you.'

I'm not sure this is too accurate a description of me, but the WBM seems fairly convinced. He asks for more curry, downing spoon after spoon without taking his eyes off the tight-lipped woman across the table.

'And Anjali's mum works in Tesco,' the WBM informs his mother. 'But I think you knew that, didn't you, Ma?'

I get the impression he's not supposed to call her Ma, and I wonder what the Punjabi word for mother is.

'I did know that,' the mother says. Unlike my mum, who still sounds as if she is currently living in Sri Lanka, this woman's accent is only faint, the rest a kind of received pronunciation, no hint of Bristolian.

'It's brilliant,' the WBM says. 'Maybe her mum can get us some cheap frozen curries. Save the cooking.'

'I do not think we would be so rude as to ask Anjali's mother for food.' There are brief gaps between each of his mother's words. I get the feeling she might communicate in subtext too, just like my mum.

We eat in silence for a while. Ganesh looks on at me while I do my best to clear my plate, and maybe the mother is aware of Him too, for she says, 'And Anjali is Buddhist, I believe.'

'Yep.' The WBM pushes his plate to one side, finally finished. 'Doesn't give a crap about all our gods.'

I'm startled. There's a sensation sharp as cut glass shooting along my spine.

'No,' I say. 'I've got no problem with—'

'But it's not your thing, is it, hey?' he says.

'It is getting late,' the mother interjects. I look up at the clock. It's nine. I imagine this woman has a lengthy cleansing routine. 'Perhaps you will take Anjali home now.'

'Oh, she's staying over at my flat,' the WBM tells her.

I am?

'I'm not,' I say, hastily. 'I work Sundays. I've got to be up early . . . I don't need to . . . I'd better go home.'

The mother is not looking at me, but Ganesh is. I could swear that his elephant trunk has shifted ever so slightly. A very old memory from an RE lesson at school suddenly comes into my mind. Ganesh, remover of obstacles.

Which one of us is the obstacle here?

'It was really nice to meet you,' I tell the mother.

She says absolutely nothing. She is glaring at the WBM with an intensity that I would never be able to face, but he is meeting it with an unbreakably cheerful expression.

'Um, shall we go?' I put my hand on his shoulder, see the mother's eye muscles twitch, and remove it again.

'Yeah, let's toodle-pip.'

Did he really just say that?

'Maybe Anjali would like to get a taxi,' the mother suddenly says. She really does need to stop talking about me in the third person. In fact, chandeliers, Wedgwood and Hindu gods aside, she and Mum are really not so different. Except when my mum's finished with her ranting and her whirlwinds, the lines soften around her mouth and a kindness comes into her eyes. 'You will pay for it, of course.'

'I like having Anjali in my Merc,' the WBM informs her.

As I get out onto the street, the cold evening air floods my skin. I take in deep breaths, releasing small clouds of white mist, gazing down at the twinkling lights of the harbour and the fixed glow of the buildings and the street lamps way below us.

We descend the stone steps, and he fishes out the key to his Mercedes.

168

'Hang on a minute.' I face him. 'What was I missing in there? Wasn't it our parents who wanted us to meet?'

The WBM shifts a little on his leather boots.

'Well, not exactly,' he says.

'I mean, my mum wanted me to meet you,' my mum sounding more than ever like my very own Asian pimp, 'through some aunty or other. I assumed your mum was involved in the arrangement too.'

'Well, not exactly,' the WBM repeats, slipping his keys from one hand to the other. He still seems oddly excited. 'Well, sort of. My mother did come to me and tell me that there was this girl she wanted me to meet.'

'And . . . ?'

'And I got uptight as usual, asking her why she couldn't leave me the fuck alone.' He grins. 'Well, maybe I didn't say fuck. Maybe it was crap. I said I couldn't stand the fact that she doesn't understand my life and keeps trying to set me up with every goddam Asian woman who comes my way.'

'Oh. And . . . ?'

'And to get her off my back, I finally agreed that I would meet you.'

Up until this point, although I'd understood the two of us to be a set-up, I'd kind of thought it was only me who had been forced into it. I'd never have assumed that my male counterpart would have resisted. I mean, who wouldn't want to meet me?

'Right. So your mum did set you up, like mine, then?'

He shakes his head. 'But then, you see, she found out a bit more about you.'

'What?' I can see where this is going and I want to stop it, but can only watch his mouth moving, stunned.

'You know, she found out your mum works at Tesco, and that you were working in a grocer's . . .'

'In a florist's.'

'Yeah, sorry, don't know why I said that,' he nods, 'and she said, don't worry, it's fine, you don't have to meet her.'

'What?' My stomach is starting to feel uneasy. I think of the three steaks that have made their way through its passage these past couple of weeks. All of those horrible ounces of poor animal flesh.

'But then I said to her: well, fuck you!' He grins again. 'Well, maybe not fuck. Maybe sod. I said: you wanted me to meet her, so I'm going to meet her. And now I've met you. And you're everything that she was worried you would be and ...'

'And?'

'And so much worse!' He's laughing as if this is the happiest discovery since Prozac. 'I mean, your age, for a start.'

'Twenty-nine?'

'Exactly, plus you can't stick to a vegetarian diet, plus you—'

'I ...?'

'You shag guys on the first date without even talking to them!' He slaps his thigh again. 'You're worse than all the English girls Mum tries to keep me away from!'

Something sharp passes through my abdomen, as if he's kicked me in the guts with the solid inch heel of his leather boot. Nausea rises in my throat. Maybe the animal flesh didn't pass through my stomach; maybe it stayed right there and is now working its way back up my oesóphagus, the poor cow (whose life is to be my destiny if karma has its way) desperately trying to get out.

'You shagged me too,' I say quietly.

'I know,' he says. 'And it was great.'

'You're *six* years older than me.'

'I didn't mean—'

'You didn't even touch your peppers.'

The last is perhaps a weaker point, but my head is spinning and the words are coming out unchecked.

'Listen, it's not that I meant to offend you. I think you're—'

'Brilliant?'

'Exactly. I really do. I'm just fed up of doing everything my mum wants. This will teach her.'

'You're with me – to teach her?'

And now there's a different look on the WBM's face. The cheerfulness has faded. He's taken off his glasses to rub his eyes, and when they look back at me, they seem smaller, the irises blending into the pupils in one solid colour, as dark as the surrounding sky. He is still passing his keys from one hand to the other, and both hands are shaking and his feet are jittery, and I realise that whatever I feel about my mum messing around in my life, the expectations she has always put on me, it has never been this anger that is coursing through the WBM's entire body right now.

'I've shown her.' There's a gap between each word; he is almost spitting.

I stare at his trembling hands, overwhelmed by a sense of protection for my own mother, working her supermarket shifts day in, day out; for my sister, who could one day walk into an outpatient appointment and find herself opposite this narcissistic man; for myself, wanting so much to get to know the WBM over the past couple of weeks, daring to dream that this relationship would put both of our families to rights.

'Anyway.' He swallows hard and rubs his nose. 'It's getting on. Why don't you come up to my flat and—'

'Are you serious? I'm not going anywhere with you.' I take a step backwards.

'Anjali, come on, don't let my mother—'

'Your mother's not the problem.' I stare at my Hush Puppies boots, the ones I picked up from the charity shop near work, someone else's sweaty feet once wearing out the heel, scuffing the toe.

'What?'

'She's obviously got her issues, but you're the one who's treated me like this.' I raise my head and look straight at him.

He puts his glasses back on, lenses briefly shimmering in the lamplight. 'I'm sorry, Anjali. Look, come up to my place and we can talk.'

I glance around the street, the dark shadows of garages at street level, the lights of the elevated terraces above, the iron railings stopping people falling off the edge. I mean, this place is grand. But it's just somewhere to live at the end of the day. Just walls to keep you warm, a roof to escape the rain.

'I can't afford my flat near the motorway, you know,' I tell him, taking another step back.

He frowns, confused.

'And we'll always live off discounted meals.'

He starts to speak, but I hold up my hands.

'And you know what? I love the flowers.'

I'm starting to walk away now, turning back to see him gazing at me, shoulders hunched, looking smaller, eyes shrunken behind the dark rims of his spectacles. If he's ever read any Mayakovsky, he's never said.

'And you're thirty-five years old,' I tell him. 'One of these days you'll have to stop blaming your mother.'

I'm walking faster, feeling my feet get lighter.

Maybe I deserved it. I was so desperate to convince myself that this relationship could miraculously fix my family that I ignored every warning sign and just ploughed right on in there. Why did I ever think I could confide in a man like this about my sister? And did I really think I could put Ernie out of my mind just like that? Why was I always looking for an easy way out?

And looking back now, I can't quite believe I started off so superior about the whole blind date thing. Frail, arthritic doctor indeed.

I'm walking past the smart Georgian buildings, the tree-lined avenues, the boutiques, past the taxis I can't afford and the drunken students lining up at the rank, playing with their autumn-coloured pashminas.

It's started to rain, heavy drops seeping into my hair and beneath the collar of my jacket, dripping through to my top underneath.

I'm thinking about my age, and his. About shagging people on first sight. Why is it OK for him, and not for me? I'm wondering how things can still be so different for men and for women. My fists are shoved in my pockets, tightly clenched.

I assume I'm going home, and when my feet start trudging up the path to Mum's flat, I hesitate. It's gone ten o'clock. She'll be getting ready for bed, or watching something mindless on telly. As soon as I step through the door, she'll know something is wrong.

'Anjali, what is wrong?'

How does she do it? There's Mum, leaning out of the upstairs window. Maybe she fitted us with chips when we were kids and covertly monitors us on the computer she pretends she can't use. It's all part of that top-secret project.

'Nothing. I'm coming up.' I open the main door and sigh.

After the WBM's family home, there is something nice about

173

the familiarity of Mum's flat. Something comforting about the spice aroma. The saggy couch, the second-hand furniture. It was all high quality once.

'What has happened?'

Mum's in her grey Tesco dressing gown, towel wrapped around her head. Her feet are bare, toenails a little yellowed. I notice her painful bunions, swollen ankles from being on her feet all day. I notice the dry cracks in her hands, the gold bands tight on her fingers.

'You were seeing the boy you said, no? You made him dinner?'

'It didn't go well.'

'*Anay*, Anjali, you must get a rice cooker.'

'Not the dinner, Mum. The whole thing. It didn't work out.'

'*Anay*, Anjali, you must give the boy a chance.'

'It wasn't my fault. We met his mum. She hates me.'

'What?'

'Because I'm old, because I'm poor, because . . .' I stop myself coming clean about the steaks.

'What?' With the towel stretching her temples, Mum's eyes can't get any wider.

'He was just using me to disappoint her.'

I'm not quite sure why I am telling Mum all of these things. Her swollen ankles aren't just her job, they're heart disease. This is probably going to kill her.

'Oh.' This is one of the few times she's been lost for words. She sits down at the dining table. 'Oh no.'

Her daydream is slipping away too.

The touch of the WBM is still on my skin; I need to rinse this whole thing off me.

'You finished in the shower?' I ask. 'Can I go?'

'You haven't fixed yours yet?' she says, absent-mindedly.

'Um – they're waiting for a part,' I'm not too sure why this has become a complex lie. Then, 'Where's Shanthi?'

'She is sleeping,' Mum says.

When I come out of the bathroom, Mum is still sitting there. The snowdrops are beside her in their little green bottle, petals wilted, heads drooped out.

'So no more set-ups, OK, Mum?' I join her at the table.

She considers this. 'Well, this one family were obviously no good.'

'Mum . . .'

'This one family were not the nicest of people perhaps. But there are lots of nice people out there, *duwa*.'

'I know that.' I go through my checklist of recent men. Pausing as always on Ernie's dancing eyes, the warmth and safety of his arms. 'But I'm not ready for them, Mum. Not yet.'

'All right, *duwa*.'

'Promise? No more set-ups?'

She hesitates. 'Well, we will be going to Sri Lanka soon . . .'

Next month now. The holiday's been booked for almost a year. It's been so long since we were away as a family, I'm not sure whether to look forward to it or not. And with hints like this . . .

'No more set-ups,' I insist.

She sighs. 'Well, we can talk about it another time.'

'Mum! I know you like these bloody rich doctors with bloody huge houses and expensive cars and—'

'Do not swear, Anjali. And that is not true.' The fires are all out in Mum's eyes, the colour dull and flat.

'Isn't it?'

'Not in the way you are saying.' She rubs her face. The towel

175

falls, and I notice she hasn't dyed her hair recently, the grey creeping back. It is thinning, too, pale patches of scalp visible beneath. 'It is not the money I care about. It is just what it means.'

'What does it mean?'

'That someone will take care of you, Anjali.'

I look at my mother's worn and tired face. Wishing once more I could have made things work for her. For us.

'I don't need someone to take care of me,' I say gently. I think of my flat, dusted for the WBM, smelling of furniture polish and Windolene and abandoned paella. The creaking boiler is ineffectual; my home is always cold. But that's what my jumpers are for, and my tatty hot-water bottle. 'I'm fine.'

Then she says something that surprises me. 'I know you are.' She touches the bottle of wilting snowdrops, picks up the tiny white petals that have fallen on the checked tablecloth. 'You always have been, Anjali.'

Ordie jumps onto my lap, purring gently. I stroke her little head and snuggle into her bony body. My eyelids are heavy. I think about creeping into Shanthi's room and getting into bed. There's an odd sensation inside me, of wanting to return to my childhood, to be a little girl again, closing my eyes while Shanthi stays up reading in the bed beside me, until Mum comes in and chides her softly, giving us both kisses and turning off Shanthi's light.

And underneath this wish, there's a deeper yearning, that wants to go back to a different childhood altogether. One I've never known but have dreamed about for many years. Where I'm falling asleep but can hear my mum and dad talking out in the lounge. My dad with a small glass of whisky; he and Mum hashing out the events of the day. His laughter, deep and rumbling, echoing into our room. As I drift away, he will be putting down his whisky, coming to massage my mother's swollen feet. Soothing the bunions, rubbing away the pain.

In Shanthi's room, a few canvases are stacked against the wall. I lift them out carefully. The top one I recognise from the studio, a set of bold blocks and lines that stirred something so strong in me the first time I saw it. I think it will be something I can ask her about on holiday, find out what these pictures mean to her. But the ones after this are different. Masses of colour on a grey surface, streaks of violet, red, dirty orange, scores of heavy black. Up close, it's difficult to work these out, to make sense of the erratic brushstrokes.

My sister is fast asleep, eyes twitching. I wonder what she is dreaming about. The clay ashtray is overflowing with butts. Her right hand is on top of the covers, a yellow nicotine stain on the middle finger.

I undress and look for a T-shirt in the small pile of clothes I keep in the bedside cabinet. That's all the stuff I have in here; everything else is Shanthi's. I've often told her to get rid of my bed and make the room hers. There's the single camp bed in the hallway cupboard that'll do for my sleepovers. She says maybe she will, but each time I come, nothing has changed.

Getting into bed, I notice a piece of paper caught at the bottom of the serpent screen. I pick it up; there are serpents on this as well, pencilled in Shanthi's hand, hundreds of them, tiny wriggling bodies and heads, staring eyes, a couple open-mouthed with sharp teeth. They are clogging up the paper until no white space is left.

I go back over to her side, looking around at her clothes folded on the chair, a couple of books on painting stacked neatly on her bedside table. Everything seems in order. On our old shared desk, just pencils and pens in a wooden tidy, a dirty cup, a notebook.

Shanthi turns over in bed and settles back into sleep.

I open the notebook. There are thousands of tiny serpents in here too, filling every page.

A headache is starting, stabs of little hammers inside my skull.

Seven

This holiday to Sri Lanka has kind of crept up on me. It's something we would normally talk about for months beforehand and that Mum would plan meticulously. Although maybe Mum has been planning away while it's been at the back of mine and Shanthi's minds.

We tend to go to Sri Lanka every few years, which is about as long as it takes Mum to pack the suitcases. There are a lot of presents that need to accompany us home.

Home is a word that makes me think. Its definition includes the physical structure in which you live or the place where you reside permanently. But it's also a valued place of origin, and the place that offers you security and happiness. That place for Mum will always be Sri Lanka. I'm not sure that she has ever, despite all her years in this country, felt secure and happy here. When I was younger, I would put my hands over my ears and shout at her to stop moaning and just try to fit in.

But she would reply (and I could always hear, as hands are no barrier for my mother's words) that it didn't matter how hard she tried, 'they' would never want us here.

Go home, Paki.

The truth is that when my parents first came to this country, phrases like this were often called out to them across the street, hissed in bus stops, one time even sprayed on the side of our building. The words stayed there for six days and nights, until Mum and Dad were able to paint them over, their hands stiff with cold, my two-year-old sister trying to help. Meanwhile I'd stayed curled up inside my mother's swollen abdomen, protected from the neighbours' watching eyes.

It wasn't until I was five years old that I got to see how my parents might have felt. A group of teenage boys with dirty T-shirts had surrounded Mum, my sister and me on our walk home from school one day, spitting insults. I don't remember wondering why *Paki* appeared to include everyone from South Asia. I don't remember wondering if the boys' pointing fingers would even be able to locate Pakistan (or Asia) on a map. I can only remember the shame that started with the drop of saliva that landed on my forearm, that went on to sink into every crevice of my body. Alongside a wish that our skin would turn white and my mum would stop wearing saris. Not long afterwards, she did.

I didn't want to think about any of this when I was younger. And maybe it was easier for me. At school, I got to hang out with a mix of white, black and brown friends who didn't care what colour my skin was. I was welcomed into their homes and found they wanted to share my vegetable patties and were weirdly jealous of the bright orange and red sandwiches in my lunchbox. I'm not sure exactly when I was able to start feeling proud of my differences. Maybe it was around the time I went to sixth-form college and noticed that there were people of many colours gazing up at the Georgian architecture.

Yet lately I wonder how much the country has changed. I wonder about the negative attitudes to European migrants, to refugees fleeing from a horror that I can never imagine. I know it's something Mum thinks about too. *First it was us, now it's them.* It's hard to fit yourself into a place that doesn't want you. Reading the papers, you might be forgiven for thinking that it's the Polish or the Romanians or the Syrians or the Somalis or small Persian-rugged women like my mother who are responsible for the lack of jobs and the country's deficit.

So Mum lives a cobbled kind of life. The obvious racial abuse has subsided, but it lurks there in the immigration headlines. She questions 'English people' and 'their' ways of potentially destroying her, but has a set of colleagues at Tesco who are close to being her buddies. She is scared of the government and its treatment of the vulnerable, but thinks highly of the NHS that looked after Dad and continues to care for us.

She doesn't feel happy and secure here, but she has a physical structure in which she lives permanently.

I'm kind of thinking about all of this while crouched over the fat suitcase blocking the hallway of the flat. It's supposed to be for my stuff but is crammed with the gifts that Mum has packed for the hordes of aunties, uncles and cousins in Sri Lanka: Union Jack flasks, Marmite, and Sindy dolls.

'Seriously, Mum, do we really need all of this?'

'What? You want us to go back empty-handed?' Mum stands in the doorway of the kitchen, aghast.

'D'you know how expensive excess baggage is?'

'It will be fine.' Mum drops her wooden spoon and waddles into the lounge for the scales. It takes our combined might to lift up the suitcase. Mum stares at the reading.

'Seriously, Mum, do we really need all of this?'

'Take out some of your clothes then.' She waves away the problem.

'But I need clothes on holiday!'

'You have so much. And you would deny your aunty this?' She holds up a jar of Marmite fiercely.

This isn't the time to enter into a discussion on the pros and cons of yeast extract. I pull a pair of linen trousers out of the case.

'Shanthi, if you don't talk to her soon, our suitcases will explode.' I go into my sister's bedroom. 'And if that happens at the airport, it will be terrorism.'

Shanthi is sitting cross-legged on her bed, a book on her lap. Her own case is already packed, so light that Mum was able to sneak in plenty of extra bits. If she's reading that book, I can't tell. I look at the old scar just beneath her left eyebrow, a brief indented line. It's midday on Saturday and we're due to catch the bus to London in two hours.

'Shanthi?' I say, when she doesn't acknowledge me. 'Are you OK?'

Her eyes are bloodshot, too bright, lined underneath with crescent-shaped shadows. 'What?' she asks, rubbing her face.

'Are you OK?'

'Fine. Sorry. Spaced out.'

She gets herself up and makes her way to the bathroom. Her frame is so slight inside her nightgown, she barely makes a sound when she moves. I think of the notebook of serpents. The tension is growing inside my head.

'You're working too hard,' I tell her.

'Exhibition soon.' There's something vacant about her words, almost like she's bored.

I look at the empty box of cigarettes on her dresser. The butts have continued to collect in her ashtray, now spilling over the

182

edges. The bedroom stinks. Normally she smokes out of the window.

I touch a spot of fallen ash, smearing a grey patch on the pine. She's often working through the night, Mum says. Sometimes with the others, sometimes alone. The exhibition is a huge thing for her; it's the first time anything like this has happened in her life.

No wonder she isn't sleeping, no wonder she's losing weight. She always forgets to eat when she's in the middle of a painting.

Her notebook's gone. Apart from the cigarettes, everything's tidy.

I go back to my packing.

Sometimes you want things to be all right, and you look the other way.

It's bloody hot. That's the first thing you notice about Sri Lanka, unless you arrive in the middle of a monsoon. I'm sitting on the veranda of my aunty Mala's house, green cotton dress pasted to my skin, a bead of sweat trickling like a tear down my cheek. I'm in a bit of a daze, gazing at the thick, twisting branches of the frangipani in the dusty front yard, its buds opening into the deep pink and white flowers that are offered at temples. Beyond this, a leaning palm tree, spiky green fronds hanging still in the humidity. The air is filled with the sharp scent of foliage, the drift of fish and spices. A sweet fragrance beckons from the bowl of jasmine flowers lying at my bare feet.

We arrived a few days ago. My uncle Garmony picked us up from the airport and ushered us onto the cracked and dusty seats of his Ford estate. He steered us through the Sri Lankan landscape while talking at the same speed as his driving (to clarify: fast) to Mum in Sinhala.

A word about language here. I was never taught my mother tongue; Mum said they made that decision because of Shanthi. Shanthi came to the UK when she was two. She was slow to learn English and continued to struggle when she went to school. The teachers were impatient, the children name-called. My parents were worried. Well, Dad was sick at that time, but Mum was anxious enough for the both of them. She took Shanthi aside and went through the alphabet with her, over and over for hours.

After that, it was English all the way in our house. The private Sinhala words between Mum and Dad would have floated above my head, never quite making contact. After Dad died, a short while later, there would have been less reason for there to be any Sinhala in the house at all. Sometimes I lay on my side of the serpent screen and listened to Mum in the hallway, making one of the rare phone calls to Aunty Mala. The language was like a code. If I listened hard enough, I might uncover it.

'D'you ever think about a longer trip to Sri Lanka?' Clara asked me on the eve of this holiday as she sat at the counter, going over the books.

'Are the accounts that bad?'

Clara smiled and closed her laptop. 'I just wondered if you fancied living there for a bit.'

Truth is, I *have* considered living in Sri Lanka. It was three years ago that I made the trip here with Jack. It was one leg of a travel writing piece he was covering in Sri Lanka, India and Nepal. We spent three weeks in cheap guest houses, seeing places I'd never visited with Mum or Shanthi, finding the ebony elephants. I didn't know my sister was unwell at home, was able to distance myself from the worry that was always there somewhere, in the back of my mind. Seeing the country through Jack's eyes, it was somehow easier to imagine that one day I could belong.

It's odd to think of Jack now. We spent a decade of our lives together and yet sometimes, looking back, it feels like a dream.

So, first of all, Aunty Mala and Uncle Garmony's place. We are in Dehiwala, which is just south of Colombo city centre. This is the town where Mum grew up. Wandering along its dusty streets in the afternoon, shaded by the high-rise buildings, the air heavy with heat and salt and petrol and fish, you can see groups of schoolgirls with braided hair waiting for the bus, all dressed in white. It's difficult to imagine my mum as one of these girls, giggling, clutching her satchel of books, turning away as she catches a tourist's eye.

But if I must accept what Mum tells me, then this sprawling bungalow, on whose veranda I am now sitting, is the same place where she grew up, white-dressed and hair-plaited, with her own mum and dad, her brother Garmony and her three sisters, Deepthi, Lakmini and Kalani.

Uncle Garmony married Aunty Mala and they stayed on in the house with their daughter and two sons, my cousins, Helani, Deshan and Mahesh. My three cousins have since got married and moved away, but are presently right here on the veranda, having come over to see us. Helani's little twin girls, Samani and Sithara, are running around the front yard, waving their new Sindy dolls.

As for my aunties: Deepthi got married and moved far south. But Lakmini and Kalani remain unwed so are right here with Aunty Mala, fussing about with the tea tray.

As for Mum's parents, my grandparents, they aren't here to add to the confusion, as they died in a car accident when I was five years old. The first time I met them was after they were dead and their bodies were laid out in the front room of this house. It was a disturbing meeting for me, all things considered, which for some reason my Sri Lankan family find hilarious.

'Oh, Anjali was so scared to see their bodies!' Aunty Kalani weeps with laughter as she pours tea from the fine bone-china pot.

'I remember, she was asking us if we could all go outside and sleep in the yard!' Aunty Mala cackles, holding onto Mum's arm and spilling some of her tea in her exuberance.

I should say at this point that my extended family all laugh at everything. I'm not kidding, everything. The size of Uncle Garmony's shirts (XXL), the barren avocado tree in the driveway, the exploded jars of Marmite in Mum's suitcase. They are the most jovial people I have ever met, which I would enjoy an awful lot more if most of their mirth wasn't directed at me.

I wish Shanthi was here for solidarity, but she's in her room. Since we arrived I've been making excuses for her, trying to ignore the anxiety growing at the back of my mind.

'So, *duwa*, why are you not married yet?' Aunty Mala asks, as the laughter dies down.

I look up at a sea of peering faces. Aunty Kalani and Aunty Lakmini are standing beside Mum – Mum's face fat and dimpled, Aunty Kalani's papery and creased, Aunty Lakmini's somewhere in between. Aunty Mala and Uncle Garmony consider me with slightly cocked heads. Helani, Deshan and Mahesh lean forward with their drinks. All foreheads carry exaggerated expressions of interest. I'm startled. I knew questions like these were coming and thought I had prepared myself for them, but I hadn't counted on the power of the interrogation. I'd kind of forgotten that coming to Sri Lanka was like having a thousand Sunday dinners with my mother, all at once.

'Well, I'm too young for marriage, Aunty,' I say.

This turns out to be just as hilarious as my grandparents' dead bodies and sends them all off again, Mum included, tears pouring down fat, dimpled, papery, creased, cocked and leaning faces.

I steady myself for the challenge.

'Twenty-nine is not so old in England,' I tell them.

Aunties Lakmini and Kalani rattle their cups as their respective hefty and wiry bodies wobble, tiny puddles of tea forming on the red concrete floor of the veranda.

It's going to be a long visit.

I always have such high hopes for Sri Lanka. I always think that the older I get, the easier it will be, and the less I will have to sit on the outskirts of family conversations, listening to judgements about my life. But no matter the ageing process, I will always be a little girl at the mercy of the grown-ups. It will probably be no different when I am eighty. Although by then I guess a few of this lot will be dead. (Even in death I can't imagine the aunties and Uncle Garmony not laughing: their souls will be incontinent as they watch me contemplating their deceased bodies.)

'And what about work, *duwa*?' Uncle Garmony booms. He is a little bit deaf, with a voice like a foghorn to compensate. 'What is it you are doing now?'

'The same, Uncle. I am working in a flower shop.'

Florists being the last word in comedy, the family clutch their sides.

Come on, Shanthi. I will my sister to come out from wherever she is and take the pressure off me. Nobody else seems to notice that she isn't here.

'I keep asking if Anjali will get another job.' Mum shakes her

187

head, and my throat starts to feel sore with all the things I want to shout at her. 'But she says she is happy with the flowers.'

'I *am* happy with the flowers,' I say.

A fresh round of guffaws.

I look over at my cousins. Helani and Deshan have high positions in the Bank of Ceylon, and Mahesh is a doctor. I ruefully recall the days when we were younger and careers were an unimportant, distant prospect. I look with envy at little Samani and Sithara, wondering if I can go and seek security with them behind the fruitless avocado tree.

'Well, maybe we do not need to worry about Anjali now, nay, *nangi*?' Aunty Mala winks at Mum. *Nangi* is Sinhala for younger sister.

'*Ow*, maybe,' Mum says.

They begin talking in Sinhala and I eye them with suspicion. The corners of their mouths are lifted up into half-smiles, there's an excited tone in their voices, and that was definitely a wink that Aunty Mala just gave Mum.

I want to ask them what they are plotting, but am afraid this will spark off a conversation about how I don't speak Sinhala, which would also be a matter for high entertainment. For some reason, although it was Mum's choice not to teach me, I still get hounded for it, as though I pushed away some kind of innate ability to understand the squiggly letters of their alphabet.

I'm soon going to understand the nature of their winking, however. As the sun continues to burn down on the yard, Deshan, Mahesh, Helani and her kids say their farewells and set off in their cars, and Mum and her sisters go off to respective corners of the house to have a lie-down. Aunty Mala starts clearing up, stacking the gilt-rimmed teapot and cups on a tray. Uncle Garmony sleeps on the veranda with his mouth open and intermittent twitches in his immense limbs (dreaming no doubt about deceased grandparents, elderly unmarried daughters and avocado crumble). I get up and wander out of the yard and down the path into the wider world, red dust on my flip-flops.

I still feel a bit jet-lagged, and my senses are taking a while to wake up. But now, with the heat beating against my back, I look up to the song of a mynah bird, then back down to a slender green gecko flicking past my toes. At the top of the path, Sri Lankans come and go in bright-patterned saris and dusty sarongs; a single pushbike swerves by, overloaded with passengers. Beside me, fingers of pink bougainvillea creep over a wall. The actual flowers of the bougainvillea are white, but each cluster is surrounded by colourful bracts or leaves, as papery thin as sweet peas.

'Beautiful, no?' a quiet voice says.

I look up, surprised. There is a young, slim man in front of me (definitely young because he is about the same age as me), dressed in loose blue jeans and a long-sleeved white shirt. He's squinting against the sun, eyes narrowed in crinkled folds of skin.

'They are beautiful,' I say. 'I could stand here and look at them for hours.'

'Then you would become very tired.' He smiles. 'After flying so many miles to arrive here.'

'What?' I'm surprised again. 'How do you know that?'

'Anjali?' he asks me.

'How do you know my name?'

It occurs to me that this might be the reincarnation of my father, come to rescue me from the exuberance of my mother and extended family.

'I saw you walk up the path,' the man says. 'And I was coming to walk down the path. To Aunty Mala's house.'

189

Possibly not my father then.

'Who are you?'

'I am Roshan,' the man says. 'I am friends with your cousin, Mahesh. Do you not remember me? We have met a few times.'

And then I do remember him – we met briefly on my last holiday with Mum, and the holiday before that. Apart from greetings, we didn't actually speak; both times he stayed in a corner with Mahesh, chatting about cricket.

'Oh, you've missed Mahesh,' I tell him. 'He left just a few minutes ago.'

'That does not matter.' Roshan shrugs his narrow shoulders and shakes his head in a familiar Sri Lankan gesture. 'I can see him another time. Aunty Mala asked me to come and see you.'

'She asked you to come and see me?' I say, slowly.

'Oh yes, she said it would be nice for me to come.' His voice is still quiet, but each word is stabbing.

No, Roshan is not my father. (I resist the urge to call this out in the manner of Luke Skywalker.)

He's a set-up.

'I'm sorry, I've just remembered ...' Trailing off, unable to finish my excuse, I start walking away from the bougainvillea, from Roshan, rushing down the path, my flip-flops scuffed with red dust. My head is spinning. *I don't bloody believe it. I told Mum! I told her! I told her to leave me alone!*

As I listen to Roshan's hurried steps behind me, I'm seeing it all: my mother in the hallway in England, screeching down the phone to Aunty Mala, telling her that I have no decent job, no decent man, and they need to *do something*.

'You will never guess: I have the man!' I can imagine Aunty Mala hiccoughing with laughter. 'Roshan! I will place him next to the bougainvillea until we have broken Anjali down!'

'Anjali, are you well?' Roshan is asking as he follows me into the yard.

I turn around. He has an unusual diamond-shaped face, orange glints in his eyes, bee-stung lips. In another life, I'd be quite happy if he was enquiring after my health.

'Yes,' I say. 'Well, no. I mean . . .'

'Anjali?'

'I think you've been brought here under false pretences.'

'Under . . . ?' Roshan squints.

'I'm not looking to meet anyone.' I feel damp cotton against my skin, curls slick against my forehead, and wonder whether Roshan can actually be interested in me anyway, now that I'm here in the sweaty flesh. 'Mum and Aunty Mala made a mistake.'

'I . . .' begins Roshan.

'I have to go now.' My voice is so urgent that it jerks Uncle Garmony awake. 'So long!'

I run into the house and into my room. I throw myself on the narrow single bed, springs creaking in protest beneath me. My phone's on the bedside cabinet; I pick it up to message Clara, to tell her that I can't cope, that coming here is just as bad as I feared. That's when I see there's a message there already.

From Jack.

When Jack and I came to Sri Lanka three years ago, I didn't tell anyone except Clara. We didn't visit a single relative, despite Jack's requests, and although it killed me to lie, I told Mum we'd gone to Tenerife. Coming back alone on the plane, Jack having continued on to India, I hugged the ebony elephants to myself. My mind was full of the wonders of my home country, unfettered by criticisms. People had observed me as just another tourist, the glances we'd received were those reserved for strangers: a brief glimpse and then a look away, our presence of no significance at all.

What's your problem? Jack wondered. *Why do you let your family get to you so much?*

It was difficult to explain how their words managed to touch the raw part inside me, the part that housed my deepest worries and fears.

I stare at the message on the screen of my phone.

Come back to me, Anj.

After that day he almost walked into the shop, the missed calls and messages from Jack stopped. I knew they would. Seeing me with Ernie would have felt as unreal to him as it had been for me, all those months ago, picturing him and Julia.

I'd stopped missing those calls and messages, had started thinking about Ernie every time there was an alert on my phone. But now, stuck here, with all the judgements and the criticisms and the family who don't know me, now that's it been so long there's less and less chance Ernie will make contact, seeing Jack's words is stirring something inside me I don't quite understand.

The tall fan in the corner is creaking, dust caught in its blade. I look up at the mosquito net coiled around its hook, full of tiny holes that scupper its purpose. This was Mum's old bedroom when she was a child. This was her old narrow bed. This was her grey concrete floor, her tall *almari*, once full of her clothes. Over on the wall is the long gold-framed mirror, not quite straight, in front of which her teenage self would have posed.

I gaze at my reflection. Here is my sweaty body in its green cotton dress. Here is the scoop of my neck, the curve of my belly. Here are my eyes, dark as cinnamon, just like Mum's.

Did Mum ever stand here and think about Dad, before they married? Did she think about the way he might hold her, the way he might steady her face with the palm of his hand? Did she ever wish that she might wake up one day in the curve of his back, finding a mole, a resting place that would be hers to watch over for always?

Come back to me, Anj.

For a moment I want to call him. I want to go back to the time before the burlesque dancer, before I ever had to type her name into the search engine of my laptop and watch her spread her beautiful body over my screen. To go back to the time when it was just days at the flower shop, evenings with Jack, or on my own, flicking through my florists' manual, reading about violas, hyacinth, lemon-yellow mimosa; studying the texts I never got round to at university, losing myself in Morrison or Angelou or Shakespeare's sonnets, filling the hours so there wasn't time to think about my family, to worry about how they were doing, even if that worry was still there, somewhere, lingering. To a time when I was just Jack's girlfriend, when I could brush aside thoughts about what I should be doing with the rest of my life, when I didn't have to open up to him in the way I hadn't been able to hold back from with Ernie.

I hover over Jack's number.

'Anjali, what is the matter with you?' The door crashes open and Mum hurries in, rubbing sleep out of her eyes, a crusted patch of dried drool at one corner of her mouth.

I drop my phone.

'What is the matter with you?' she repeats.

For a second, I think she's staging an intervention. My mouth is open and I'm about to confess that yes, I was thinking of calling Jack, when she clarifies her meaning.

'Roshan is a nice boy. He came to visit us. Uncle Garmony said you were rude.'

I sigh.

'Mum, I told you back home, I don't want another set-up.'

'How do you know that I arranged this?'

'Come on, Mum. It's obvious, the way you and Aunty Mala were winking at each other.'

'We were not—'

'You need to stop sticking your oar in.' My voice is louder than I intend, but it's infuriating the way her eyes dart to the door to make sure nobody can hear us. I think about how Mum sends Shanthi down the road to smoke her cigarettes, how my sister has spent most of the last few days in her room and her absence has been barely noticed. I think about how little the family here, living in this sprawling bungalow with fine bone china and frangipani trees, know about our lives in north Bristol, our tiny shabby homes and the long hours we work to keep them. I think about how we hide our true selves from the people here instead of coming clean about who we are. I raise my voice even more. 'You need to stop trying to set me up with any old person you come across just because you're worried—'

'He is not any old person. Your horosocopes, Anjali, they are matching.'

I stop.

'Our what?'

'Your horoscopes.'

I know the deal about horoscopes. It's a tradition for Sri Lankans to consult astrologers about marriage proposals and proceed only if the couple's horoscopes match against set guidelines. To work them out you need birthdays, birth times and birth places. Some kind of mathematical calculation is involved. You also need money.

I stare at Mum, imagining the international phone calls that will have taken place about me and a boy I don't know, alongside the passing-on of her credit card details. The extra few hours that she will have stacked shelves, chosen fruit and vegetables for richer people's online shopping, with ever-increasing swelling in her feet and pain in her bunions, to pay for this horoscope. For an official piece of paper that might allow her to hold her head up high amongst her family. Because I, her twenty-nine-year-old spinster daughter Anjali Chandana, am just not good enough as I am.

Of course, it's impossible to explain to Mum the complexity of my thoughts. Instead I come out with, 'What does a bloody horoscope tell us?'

She winces.

'Where's Shanthi, anyway?' I ask. 'Why is it always me? Why are you always focusing on me and my miserable life?'

'Shh, your sister's sleeping,' Mum hisses, like our fighting will wake her up in a bedroom on the other side of the bungalow. 'And Roshan is outside.'

'He's what? What's he still doing here?'

'I told him to wait for you. I told him you were suffering from the flight.'

'You did what?'

'*Anay*, Anjali, do not pass up this chance. Not after the last man.'

'The last man? The last man who didn't give two hoots about me and was probably some kind of medical psychopath?'

'Anjali, keep your voice down. You are making a scene.'

'What would Dad say, if he was here?' I don't know why I'm bringing my dad into it – it seems a bit unfair given that he's deceased – but he does participate in my internal monologues

195

and maybe he wouldn't mind being given a voice. 'Don't you think he would just tell you to leave us alone?'

Of course, I've got no idea what my dad would think, having only the idealised version of him inside my head.

'No, he would not say that,' Mum says, the cleft deepening between her eyebrows, her voice lowered.

'What would he say?'

'He would say he was ashamed of you.'

I swallow. There's a weight in my chest heavy as a brick. For a moment I can see my dad, with his Burgher-blue eyes and long sideburns, sitting in the corner of this room, shaking his head.

'I need to get out of here.' I push past Mum and hurry out of the door.

'Anjali . . .'

I dash through the open-plan space beyond, dimly aware of the long table, the bodies sitting in wicker chairs beneath the family portraits and the pictures of the Buddha. I push through the white muslin curtains onto the red-floored veranda, past the bowl of jasmine flowers and into the dusty front yard.

'Anjali!'

Footsteps are following me, but I don't stop.

Go away, I'm saying in my head. *Just leave me alone.*

'Anjali?' A male voice.

I turn around. It's Roshan. His squinting, diamond-shaped face is etched with concern.

'I'm sorry.' I look away from his eyes, wishing that he hadn't been brought into this mess created by my mother. 'I'm just . . . I'm just going out now.'

Credit to Roshan, his two encounters with me thus far must have been pretty confusing. He should really have turned around and walked away, horoscopes or not. But instead he comes closer and puts a hand on my shoulder.

'Are you going for a walk?' he asks.

I raise my hands in the air hopelessly. I'm not so much going on a walk as throwing a tantrum.

'May I join you?' he says.

At the doorway, I catch the movement of Mum's waddling body, heading out to the veranda.

A walk it is, then.

We go to Mount Lavinia beach. I'm always so keen to see the water when I first get to Sri Lanka. I love the first glimpse of it you get when you turn down the beach road, that glistening ribbon of blue. My chest swells whenever I sink my feet into the burning white sand. The waves are thunderous. If you go into the water, you'll get sucked into holes and never come out.

That's not exactly true. It's what Mum used to say to stop me and Shanthi from getting our feet wet.

'Anjali! Be careful!'

That isn't my mum, just Roshan calling to me as I lift up my dress and crash into the waves. The spray goes above my calves, my knees, turning green cotton into a second skin, plastered to my body. I lick my lips and taste salt.

'Be careful!' Roshan calls again.

I'm remembering my five-year-old and Shanthi's seven-year-old selves, running into the water when Mum's back was turned, giving ourselves away by our shouts of laughter. I think of Mum's stricken face as she called the two of us back out, chiding Shanthi afterwards for not being more responsible. *You are the older one.* I think of Shanthi now with her bloodshot eyes and nicotine-stained fingers. The last couple of days she's barely even joined us at the table for dinner. *She has been working so hard, she is so tired*, Mum explained to the family, the conversation then quickly passing on. The uncomfortable feeling that has been growing at the back of my mind for days is working its way to the forefront, and I'm trying not to let it.

'There's nothing to be afraid of!' I lift my arms out to Roshan before a wave knocks me down, slamming me onto the firm bed beneath. Seawater fills my mouth as I splutter.

'Anjali, you must come back,' Roshan shouts. 'Your mother has asked me to look after you. Can you please come back?'

'I'm staying right here!' I cough.

I watch him hesitate. He pulls off his shirt, rolling it into a ball and tossing it behind him, further back from the shoreline. He takes off his jeans. Then he and his thin, dark torso and legs are crossing the waves towards me.

'You must be careful,' he says again when he is next to me. 'There are very strong currents in here.'

I'm laughing, maybe a bit hysterically. I wouldn't blame him if he doesn't know what's more dangerous at the moment, the ocean or me.

'Don't be so serious, Roshan,' I tell him.

'I must be serious, I am trying to look after you,' he says.

'You're doing a swell job.' I turn towards him. 'Swell. Geddit?' Then another wave comes, from a side angle, and in a moment my face is pressed against his.

What would it be like to kiss him? In that split second, I see Mum's smiling face, her relaxed shoulders, the international phone calls she would make to her sisters planning the wedding: the saris, the flower girls, the guest list of five hundred aunties I've never met before but who swear they have a picture of my baby bottom in their family album. I see myself no longer having to prove myself to the extended family, turning instead into a demure Sri Lankan housewife serving tea in gilt-rimmed cups, ladling out meals of rice and curry that I have become famous for, all with my signature white jasmine flower tucked into my hair. And my hair itself – well, it's no longer the sad, frizzy mop of its UK existence, but a glorious mass of curls floating down to my waist, liberated in the humidity of its natural habitat.

I'm holding onto Roshan to steady myself; his hands are supporting the small of my back. He is looking at me carefully, as if making a study. This is all set up to be a Kodak moment. Except Roshan is a tall Sri Lankan (which in itself is a bit of a paradox) and it's a bit tricky trying to get the right standing alignment. I'm having to rise on tiptoe, then back on my heels to manage the pounding of the ocean. It kind of feels like trotting.

A wave knocks us to our knees, tiny shells pressed into our shins. I swallow a mouthful of seawater, and as I come up to the surface, that alternative vision of my life is ebbing away, carrying itself back to the horizon. Mum's happiness isn't going to be secured by me kissing this man with the bee-stung lips and the matching horoscope any more than it was by my shagging a narcissistic brown psychiatrist. Hooking up with Roshan won't make Jack's text go away, or the hopes that idle, wishing Ernie would come back. It isn't going to make my dead father any less ashamed. It won't make Shanthi better.

Roshan leads us out of the water onto the shore. The sun has begun its descent, trailing in silvery orange lines across a pastel pink and blue sky. The water glistens like a wash of diamonds. I gaze at the drenched body of this man and think of Ernie on the other side of the Indian and Pacific oceans, the crinkle of his kind eyes. The ache settles once more in my chest and my head.

'I have always loved you,' Roshan says.

I'm startled. We sit dripping on the sand, me in my drenched green dress, he with glistening naked torso and limbs, the break of the waves catching our toes. It turns out I've met Roshan more than a couple of times; he's seen me on every one of my holidays here, starting with that first evening when I was five years old and my eyes were wet with the sight of my dead grandparents. I don't remember him from back then. There were so many people to meet at that time, so many names I wasn't used to pronouncing. He tells me that he always stood at a distance, waiting for his chance to speak to me.

'We were always shy of you. You were the beautiful English cousin.' He smiles.

It's funny to hear myself described in that way. I've always felt so awkward amongst my peer group here, so out of it when they were laughing away in Sinhala, then correcting themselves and continuing in English for my benefit. The jokes never seemed to translate that well, language being so much more than simply the letters of an alphabet. It's the cadence, the emphasis, the pauses, the history, the culture that gives words so much of their meaning. I found myself standing apart, wanting to connect with the people of my home country but not knowing how.

It's kind of nice to know that in all that time, I was loved. Or that someone thought they loved me.

'You can't love me,' I say, after a while. 'You don't even know me.'

'I do.' Roshan is firm.

'If you knew half the things about me that I know about me, you'd soon change your mind.'

'I do not believe that.'

'You know I'm not a doctor or anything, right? I work in a flower shop.'

'I like flowers.'

'I sometimes eat meat.'

'I always eat meat.'

'I get drunk a lot.'

'I like lager.'

This isn't going to plan.

'Aunty Mala has told me a lot about you,' Roshan says. 'I know you, Anjali.'

'No.' There's a sudden rush in my chest as forceful as the pounding waves in the sea. My cheeks are hot with the thought of what my aunties might have told him about me, about my lack of career and my advancing age, maybe the fact that it wouldn't matter because once I was his wife I could wash his lentils and cut his toenails as well as anyone. 'You don't know me!'

He swallows and wipes the drops of water from his forehead.

'All of you Sri Lankans,' I say, suddenly glad to distance myself from the group, 'think you know everything about me. And Mum. And Shanthi. And our lives in England. But you don't know us at all. Nobody does.'

'I do not think that we—'

'We don't make much money.' I hear my voice starting to crack and I clench my fists. 'Mum stacks shelves in a supermarket. My sister chain-smokes in her bedroom. And I don't know what I'm doing with my life.'

Roshan blinks. I'm not quite sure why I'm telling him all of this.

'None of you know us at all.' I trace the lines of sand and salt on my legs. 'None of you have a clue.'

He doesn't answer at first. We gaze at this glistening beach, the shoreline of Colombo city a faint curve in the distance. The fronds of the palm trees sway gently. There is beauty all around us.

His voice, when it comes, is quiet. 'Then I would like to get to know you.' He turns, the orange glints in his eyes catching the light of the falling sun, no squint there now, meeting me without flinching.

The fire in my chest is fading. This guy isn't responsible for me or my family. It's not his fault that I've been pushing away the worries about my sister, like I've always done, trying to keep them contained. I'm not going to find the answers in men. Not even Ernie. I knew that when I met the WBM; I knew that when I met the Architect. I lean my head against Roshan's shoulder, easier now that we are sitting down, and he puts his arm around my back. It feels pretty comfortable. Maybe Mum was right about our horoscopes. Maybe for the first time in this country, I have a genuine connection with somebody, even if it isn't a matrimonial one. We sit like this on the cooling sand for a while, letting our bodies dry.

'Shall I get you home?' Roshan asks gently. 'Your mother will be worried.'

He pulls on his crumpled clothes and I adjust my damp dress and the two of us, looking exactly like we have recently plunged into the sea, start walking home, heads bowed against any locals who would be shocked by our antics. It takes little in this community to raise gossip. Fortunately, our section of beach has stayed fairly deserted.

From time to time, I glance at this Eastern Brown Man. It's funny to think that in another time, we could have had a chaste conversation around a table with a pot of sweet Sri Lankan tea, and then some time later, unclothed ourselves for our wedding night. It's funny to think that in another time, I could have spent the rest of my life with him.

*

202

It is starting to get dark when we arrive back at Aunty Mala's place. The frangipani and palm trees twist in the shadows, the crickets beat out their steady rhythm.

'Shall I go?' Roshan asks.

I shake my head. I need to face the music. But if Mum sees me with Roshan, her anger might be softened a little.

The veranda is deserted, the doors closed. No voices can be heard within. Bracing myself, I open the door and step inside. I'm expecting to see them all, Aunty Mala, Uncle Garmony, Aunty Kalani, Aunty Lakmani and Mum, lined up on the wicker chairs, arms folded, frowning, waiting to ask me what I'm playing at. Jet lag, I'll confirm. I'm too weary to argue; I'll just tell them I'm sorry and that I'm not myself. Then I'll ask Uncle Garmony to put on his Kenny Rogers CD and we'll all sing 'The Gambler', in harmony. That'll be bound to help.

But the room is empty. The day is slowly fading away, long shadows crossing the furniture. The lacy curtains flutter against the iron rails at the windows. A mosquito flits through the air and lands on a corner of a seat cushion.

'Anjali?' I turn to see Mum sitting alone at the dining table at the far end of the room. She is all but lost in darkness.

'Mum?' I go over to her, Roshan hanging back. 'Why are you just sitting here? Is everything all right?'

The mirth and anger of the afternoon has left her face. She looks drained, lines around her mouth where her smile should have been. She presses the edge of her index finger to the tip of her forehead.

'What's the matter, Mum?' My heart is thudding.

'Shanthi's gone,' she says.

Eight

The family appear from quiet corners, congregating at the dining table. Mum is in the middle, her head in her hands. My aunties' words are whispered, mumbled. My sister missing. Her things gone. There's a numb feeling in my chest, a distant ringing in my ears.

'Where have you been, *duwa*?' Uncle Garmony suddenly booms, as if he has only just seen me. He's halfway through putting on another XXL shirt and has changed out of his sarong into trousers.

'The beach,' I say.

'The beach,' he repeats, then turns to Mum. 'The beach. I will fetch the car.'

He finishes buttoning up his shirt, slips his pudgy feet into flip-flops and grabs his keys. 'You will come and help me look for her, Anjali?'

He can't quite meet my eyes. I know that he doesn't want to discover Shanthi by himself. I gather my thoughts. 'No, we have to split up, Uncle. You go to the beach. Try the hotels and ask if anyone's seen her. I'll get a three-wheeler and go into town.'

Roshan is still at the front door. I don't look at him. I don't want to see the embarrassment in his eyes.

'Mum, you come with me.'

Mum lifts her head. Her eyes are red and swollen. Beside her, Aunty Mala is twisting the brown prayer beads at her wrist with jittery fingers. Kalani and Lakmini are studying the wooden grains of the table. If Shanthi does return, she can't be greeted by these terrified relatives.

'Second thoughts, Mum, you stay here in case she comes back.'

'Where will you look?' Mum asks.

'I don't know,' I say. 'Have you searched her room? Is there any clue in there?'

Mum hesitates.

'Keep your phone on, *duwa*,' Uncle Garmony calls as he pushes past Roshan, out of the door.

I touch the damp pockets of my green dress, panicked, then remember dropping my phone earlier on my bed. Retrieving it, I head towards Shanthi's room.

'Anjali . . .' Mum is saying.

Opening the door, I stop.

When we arrived, Aunty Mala led us around the bungalow: *Here, Anjali, you have your* amma's *old room; here, Shanthi, you will be comfortable in Deepthi's old bed*. Deepthi's room was as bare as Mum's, just a cold tiled floor, sparse sturdy furniture, plain walls with one picture of the Buddha.

The Buddha has been taken down now. The walls are half covered with scraps of old paper. The twisting bodies of tiny crawling serpents fill the white space, taped up at different angles so that I am surrounded by snakes, creeping towards me.

It feels as if someone is running their fingernail down my spine. I think of the paper I found in Shanthi's bedroom a few days ago, of the notebook filled with similar drawings. For a moment, it's difficult to breathe. Why did I let it go? Why didn't I tell Mum? Why didn't I try to talk to my sister and find out what was going on in her mind?

Mum comes to the door, face stained with tears, but I hold up my hand and shake my head and she backs away. If she comes closer, I will cry too.

I'm still holding my phone and realise it was only a couple of hours ago that I was staring at the message from Jack, wrapped up in my own world. I think of the past few months and how I've barely thought about anyone but myself.

Before I can change my mind, I scroll down to Jack's number and press *call*.

I remember me and Shanthi lying on her bed once, one Saturday afternoon when Mum was working. I'm maybe six years old, Shanthi eight. *My Fair Lady* is over and Shanthi is sketching as usual. I'm fascinated by the scratching noise her HB pencil makes as it shades in the creamy white paper. Miss Harrison gives Shanthi all her supplies, even though she's probably not supposed to.

Who's that you're drawing, Shanthi?

Dad.

What was his name?

Sarath.

What's he doing?

That's you in the bath. You're really small. He's washing you.

Are you helping him?

Yes.

And is that Mum?

Yes.

206

What's happened to our faces?

We're laughing, Anjie.

There's a funny feeling in my tummy, like the kind I get on sports day when we're lined up behind the little track, waiting. Except when the race is done, the feeling goes away and everyone laughs. Laughing. It's something you do – with your friends.

Did we used to laugh a lot?

All the time.

Mum too?

Mum the most.

Shanthi puts her pencil away. *Come on.*

Where are we going?

Maybe this isn't how it happens. Memories can fall into one another, until you're left with a beautiful lie that you treasure always. The moment I treasure is pulling on my plimsolls and running after Shanthi, and it's exciting, because we're never supposed to go out if Mum's not home; the white people might be lined up outside to take us away. But the corridor's empty, just the dying spider plant beneath the barred window. We're running out of the building and rushing past the people walking along the road, and nobody notices us. We're invisible.

Shanthi takes me along the railway path, up to a gate. She's unlocking it with a rusty-looking key that she's taken from her pocket.

How come you've got that key?

I don't know where we are. There are plots of overgrown grass on a sloping bank, and grey corrugated sheds and small greenhouses. Shelves of soil are boxed in by wooden boards, and the place is deserted apart from an old woman sitting on a wooden chair. She's wearing a wide-brimmed straw hat; it must be summer.

I pull on Shanthi's shoulder, because we should get out of here now that she's seen us. But the old woman says, *Back again?*

And then she disappears inside the corrugated shed behind her.

What's this place, Shanthi?

It's Dad's garden.

The old woman comes back with Ritz crackers and paper cups of lemonade. She goes back to her chair and Shanthi and I sit cross-legged on the ground, drinking fizz and eating biscuits. The old woman hasn't really stayed with me. All I remember now is the straw hat and the varicose veins on the backs of her calves, like purple worms. I don't know if she was the one who gave Shanthi the key or if Shanthi had kept Dad's key or how often my sister visited her; I don't know if we ever went back.

I just remember sitting on the ground and gazing at the sea of flowers in front of me. Just a pool of colour then, pale pink, bright orange, purple, deep blue. Now I think maybe hollyhocks, Cape daisies, corn marigolds, wild marjoram, lavender. These were probably flowers that the old woman had planted. But sitting on the grass eating salty crackers and watching the bees drink their nectar, I pictured Dad, many years before, digging up the soil, sowing these plants and tending to them with gentle, patient fingers.

'Anj?'

A bit of me was hoping that Jack wouldn't answer. A bit of me didn't want to hear his voice coming back at the end of the line, deep and clear. His voice is the same, but it's different too. Or maybe the memory of it has slipped too far away.

'I can't believe it. I thought I'd never hear from you again.'

His words are light and hopeful, a little breathless. In my mind, he's pacing up and down a room, pushing back his auburn hair. I wonder where he is, whether he's still in Bristol, or somewhere else, writing up an assignment or visiting friends or maybe just moved away altogether. Ten years of being so close, and now I don't even know where he's living.

'Are you still there?'

'Shanthi's missing.'

'What? Where are you? The connection's weird.'

'Sri Lanka.'

There's a delay on the line, and I hear my voice a second after I speak, quiet and flat.

'What d'you mean, she's missing?'

'She's not been right. And now she's gone.'

There's quiet. Ten years of being so close, of not needing to finish our sentences. He'll have stopped pacing, be standing completely still, scratching his right eyebrow, the way he does when he's thinking, except he doesn't know he does it.

'Where have you looked? Could she have gone to one of the guest houses?' He pauses, and in those seconds I feel each pulsation of my heart. 'What about ... Have you tried your dad's place?'

As soon as he speaks, I realise I didn't have to call him. I didn't need him to say what I already knew.

I just needed him.

'See you.'

Roshan comes with me. We hail a three-wheeler at the end of the road and get in. The guy takes off, the pink and white garland hanging from the rear-view mirror flying up in the sudden breeze. We rush past the stores packed with lurid orange bottles of Fanta, past the roadside caravan selling egg hoppers and onion sambal, past the men carrying bundles of fish. The buildings along the main street are crammed together, shops and homes and offices in tower blocks reaching high into the sky. Mum remembers a time when none of this was here, when once she could stand on Aunty Mala's veranda and gaze at the sea.

Roshan is quiet. His white shirt is creased. Streaks of sand run down his jeans. At the calf I see a spot where the seam has come away; someone has stitched it carefully back together.

'You know about my sister, don't you?' I say.

He nods. He isn't looking at me. There's a tiny birthmark in the shape of a curling leaf just beneath his right ear.

'I know there's gossip.' I flinch as the three-wheeler squeezes itself between two fast-driving cars, horns blazing. 'My family are scared. That's why they never speak to her.'

There'll never be a horoscope for Shanthi, a Roshan placed beside the bougainvillea for her.

Still Roshan doesn't say anything. He's buttoning and unbuttoning the cuff of his shirt-sleeve, and I want to take hold of his hands and make him stop. I feel the anger building up inside me at how nervous everybody is at the mention of my sister.

'Are you scared too?' I blurt out. 'And if you are, why are you here with me now?'

His hands stop moving. Was it really only earlier this evening that we were standing side by side in the ocean? The cuff of his sleeve falls open and he turns to me. His nose is long and fine, his cheekbones chiselled. His brow is furrowed.

'Why would I be scared?' he asks. Then he says something that surprises me. 'We all love Shanthi.'

We don't say anything else then, and I'm staring at the stretch of grey road ahead, dotted with cars, but not seeing it. I'm seeing the hospital ten years ago, the mental health ward; seeing myself waiting outside the nurses' office, staring at my sandals, the chipped pink nail polish on my toenails, not able to look up at the other patients walking by, the ones in jeans and T-shirts who chattered and joked and seemed no different to the nurses; the ones who were quiet, or who sometimes burst into unnatural laughter; the one who talked non-stop to another person who wasn't listening; the one who touched the wall, leaving an arc of fingerprints. The ringing in my ears shuts off the sound of Sri Lankan traffic, and instead I'm hearing the television in the ward lounge, the low murmuring, the tap-tapping of the ping-pong ball in the games room, the regular tread of footsteps coming in and out of the smoking garden.

I'm seeing myself following the nurse, head down, counting the steps, fifteen, sixteen, seventeen, till we got to Shanthi's room. Peering through the door window at the thin figure cross-legged on the bed, hunched over a sheet of paper, drawing furiously, the blanket on the floor, covered in other papers, the serpents still crawling their way towards me, their mouths open wide. My sister sometimes looking up, eyes terrified, darting around the room, listening to a voice that didn't reach my ears, her hissed words as she held onto the sleeves of my dress: *It was me, I did it.*

Did what?

Killed Dad.

What do you mean? He was sick, Shanthi, he had cancer.

The snake-covered paper pushed towards me.

I gave it to him. With my mind. Stay away, I don't want to give it to you.

Shanthi . . .

Stay away, I said. Go home.

211

'What is the road you are wanting?' I jerk to attention as the driver barks from the front of the three-wheeler.

'Adamaly Place,' I tell him.

'We are almost there.'

I try to focus again on the road, aware of Roshan by my side, glancing at me. But there's a film covering my eyes, the tarmac dissolving. I'm seeing Mum trooping out of our flat each morning, her back stooped with the weight of her carrier bags. I'm seeing myself the day I walked away from home, packing up my stuff when she was at the hospital. Standing in the middle of the flat, holding only a small case of clothes; all the rest of my things dumped at the charity shop, even my books, because I didn't want to keep any of it. I'm looking at the chipped porcelain and the second-hand Buddhas, the cheap brass trinkets in the glass cabinet, carefully polished every week. I'm walking away, my throat clogged, shooting pains stabbing at my eyes, knowing I'm a coward for not saying goodbye to my mum, knowing the telephone call tonight will never make up for it, no matter how much time passes. I'm seeing myself as I'm about to close the door, putting my case down and running back to the living room to take the two photographs from the mantelpiece.

That very first time, Shanthi was in hospital for three months. By the time she got out, the leaves on the trees were turning rusty and golden. Sometimes I picture the day she arrived home with Mum. Walking into the flat with its echoes of curry and sandalwood; maybe Ordie coming over and rubbing her soft body along the back of my sister's calves. The tiny, tidy kitchen, the dusted and hoovered lounge. None of my clutter there, no CDs beside the cheap Tesco player, no book open on the sofa.

Walking into our room and discovering my bed stripped and the cupboard empty, the rest of my things gone.

'Are you all right, Anjali?' Roshan has turned to face me, his voice just a whisper. I can't look at him; can only stare beyond him at the cars and buildings whipping past the open sides of the three-wheeler, wondering what he might see when he looks at my face.

Here in Sri Lanka, I hated that I was the focus of my family's attention. Feeling that they'd forgotten about my sister, or worse, had given up on her, too discomforted by the waves of her condition. But looking at Roshan's slim hands on the passenger bar, his body edging forward, I know it isn't the family who is fearful of Shanthi's mental illness.

Because while Mum visited the psychiatric ward every day, her bags stuffed with curry and home-made samosas, not just for my sister but for all of the patients on the ward, because that was the only way she knew to show how much she cared, I stayed away. The years passed, I moved into the house share with Jack, then our private flat, and whenever Shanthi was sick, I was never there.

Because I'm the one who's always been scared. Who's still scared.

'We are here,' the driver says.

This place was grand once. At some point every holiday, Mum brought us here, and we would stand at the iron gates and peer in at the bungalow within the grounds, whitewashed and sprawling. Sometimes there would be people standing against the white pillars of the veranda: a mother, her three little children, another older woman – a grandmother, perhaps. We never saw the father, and I didn't want to see him, because I had a strange feeling, watching from the road, that maybe my dad wasn't dead, he was just here, with another family.

The gate is unlocked. The last time I visited was with Jack. It was the only time I let any family stuff intrude on our holiday. We'd expected to do just as Mum, Shanthi and I always had: hang around outside for a few minutes and then go down the road to drink some faluda in a café. Except the gate was unlocked then too. I lifted the latch and we crept inside. The place was deserted, boarded up, no sign of the family who had once lived here. Jack and I wandered around the yard, expecting someone to shout at us any minute for trespassing, but nobody came. Not even my father, who I'd unreasonably hoped might have been sitting beneath the mango tree, waiting for me.

The yard has become overgrown in the three years that have passed. In the darkness, Roshan and I step on thick weeds that have sprouted amongst the gravel, Roshan holding onto my arm to steady me. Bushes have turned wild, mountains of leaves blocking the path and scratching our arms, scattered with flowers whose magenta colour I pick out in the torchlight of my phone. Hibiscus.

Cracked steps lead up to a rotting veranda. The doors and windows are still boarded up. The old brilliant white walls of the bungalow have slowly greyed, streaked now with lines of dirt.

'I think it's empty.' Roshan peers through one window that has lost its board, into the darkness beyond.

I shine my phone on the space inside. An abandoned room; a few discarded pieces of furniture – a chair, a table, an overturned chest. I wonder what happened to the people who once lived here, and why their home has been left like this with nobody to care for it.

Roshan goes around the building, looking for a way in. One of the larger windows at the back is also unboarded and open; we are able to climb through into the house.

'Shanthi!' I shout, but my voice only echoes around the empty space. The bungalow smells of damp and the salty scent of a wild fern growing in a crack beside the door. We find more scattered pieces of furniture; old pans and crockery still stacked in a kitchen, now home to cockroaches and spiders. Roshan tells me to be careful of scorpions. The bedrooms are completely empty, except for the small one with an iron bedstead and a cupboard. In the cupboard I find a stiff, yellowing exercise book, a couple of notes in Sinhala scribbled inside that I do not understand. I go to the window and rest my hands for a moment on the ledge. Perhaps this was once my father's room; perhaps he once stood where I am standing, gazing out into the blackness. When I remove my hands, they are covered in dust, the outline of my fingers left against the sill.

'She is not here.' Roshan comes to stand beside me. 'I do not think she came here, Anjali.'

But if my sister is not here, then I do not know where she is. We start to leave and I am checking behind the chair and the table and going back into the kitchen as if maybe she has been following behind us the whole time, stepping out of our way. Roshan gently guides me back to the open window.

'What shall we do now?' he asks when we are outside again. He takes my hand. 'Shall we go back to Aunty Mala's?'

I shake my head. I cannot return without Shanthi. My phone has stayed silent; Uncle Garmony has not found her either. We are walking back to the gate, and I'm holding Roshan's hand and remembering three years ago when Jack and I were also walking away, hand in hand, and there was an urge inside me to break free and run back to the mango tree, to check one more time beneath the fronds of its leaves.

I break free from Roshan and run.

I push past the hibiscus bushes, past the broken pots near the veranda, almost tripping on the weeds. I run around the side of the bungalow, past the cashew nut trees that I cannot see clearly now but I know are there, past a huge rhododendron, its slippery leaves brushing the side of my face.

The mango tree is around the back. Its shape stands out in the darkness, the outline of its hanging fronds like splayed, drooping fingers. I crouch down and crawl beneath the branches.

In the darkness that smells of soil and leaves, I find my sister.

The old memory is clearer now. I am three, my sister five. She's inside our bedroom and I'm standing outside, watching through the door crack. She's sitting cross-legged on the floor in a huge jumper, and for a moment I'm confused, because I've seen that jumper before and I don't know where.

I'm on my tiptoes, reaching up to the gold handle of the door. It's too high up to grip properly, but that doesn't matter, because in the end all I need to do is push. The crack of the door widens, the chink of light expanding. At first I think my sister is drawing, but she's only staring at the red swirly pattern of the carpet, tracing it with her fingers. She's been in here for a long time. What's Mum doing? Normally she would have called us by now; we would be eating poppadoms or samosas or having a drink; she would have set out a jigsaw or be reading us a story. But her bedroom door is shut, and my little hands can't open it.

'Shanthi?' I say.

My sister doesn't look up, just keeps rubbing the carpet round and round, round and round.

The jumper comes down over her knees to her ankles; it's made of royal blue wool, it's soft and bobbly. There's a hole underneath one of the sleeves; I can't see it but I know it's there. Because it's Dad's jumper.

'Shanthi?' I whisper.

I don't know why I'm whispering when it's just us. Roshan must still be at the gate. My sister is sitting cross-legged, crouched to avoid the branches above her, drawing a circle in the ground with a stick. Inside the circle is a pile of cigarette butts. Beside her an empty plastic bag, her few belongings scattered. She isn't looking at me, but I know that her lowered eyes will be wild and bright.

'Shanthi, it's me, Anjie.'

That old memory, my first memory, is so vivid now, burning a hole in my mind. I don't remember any times with my dad. Just the day of his funeral, the unnatural quietness in our flat, my absent mother and the sister I could not rouse no matter how many times I whispered her name. Mum must have come out; I cannot believe that she would have left us for long, even in her grief. But in that memory, I am alone.

'Stop talking, Anjali.'

Shanthi's voice is the one I expect, the low, hissing tone that I once tried to run away from. It's quiet and careful and vigilant. She points at the circle she's tracing in the ground.

'Can you see?' she whispers.

'See what?'

'Don't you see?'

'See what, Shanthi?'

She pauses.

'Shh, they're listening.'

'Nobody's here, Shanthi.'

'They're here, here, here.'

The leaves of the mango tree pitter-patter in the breeze.

The sky's gone ... they wake up ... this will break ... don't stop going round ... don't let them ... they took him ... go round ...

Shanthi's voice is even quieter now, muttering odd words that I can't piece together and that do not make any sense to me, but I know that the people are tormenting her again. The ones who put her down. Who tell her she killed Dad.

'Shanthi, can you hear them now? Are they talking to you?'

She raises her head and her bloodshot eyes peer into mine. In the glow of my phone on the ground, her hair looks lank, greasy curls falling down her back. There's a bruise on her forehead and grazes on her cheek, and I wonder when she came here and what she has been crawling through. Her lips are dry and bleeding; she must have walked all the way from Aunty Mala's; she won't have had anything to drink.

'Shanthi, are you thirsty?'

'Thirsty, thirsty.' She is smiling like it's a joke, but then her face falls. 'Shh,' she says. 'Don't speak.'

I swallow. I take away the stick and hold her nicotine-stained fingers, her nails chewed down, a weeping gash across the back of her left hand, mosquito bites on her forearms. My head hurts and I'm wondering how many nights of sleep she has missed, and how I could have turned my back on her.

Because you were thinking about yourself, the voice in my own head is telling me. *Because you've always been scared.*

'Shanthi, I don't think you're very well,' I say quietly. 'I think you've got sick again.'

'Sick ... sick ... sick ...'

'Can you listen to me, Shanthi?'

'They're listening.'

I stop talking but I don't let go of her hands. I watch her pupils

218

flickering and listen to the dribble of words coming out of her mouth, and I nod and close my eyes because I don't know how I'm going to get my sister home, and what we're going to do even if we get there.

Then I hear the scuff of footsteps. Shanthi's eyes dart to the noise; she pulls her hands away from me and starts to push herself further back into the undergrowth.

'Shanthi?'

I'd almost forgotten Roshan was here. He's kneeling down now in front of the tree and is looking in at us. Shanthi's eyes are crossed in fear.

'Roshan, I don't think . . .'

'Aunty Mala called me.' His voice is slow and gentle and he is talking to Shanthi. 'She said it is time for you to come back.'

For a moment, none of us say anything. There are expressions on my sister's face that I do not understand, that indicate that she is listening to someone or something. I hear the skittering of an animal, maybe a rat or a mouse, making its way through the bushes to its home.

'We must be careful,' Shanthi says.

Roshan nods. His diamond-shaped face is steady and kind. I wonder what it is about him that makes Shanthi scramble out and crawl into his arms. That allows her to let him support her as she walks, resting her head on his shoulder. There is another three-wheeler at the gate; Roshan must have summoned it.

Gathering up Shanthi's spare clothes and stuffing them back in the plastic bag, I walk behind the two of them. There's an odd sensation in my chest and my tummy, like I'm three years old again and following my sister and father, putting my feet into the shadow of their footsteps.

*

When Shanthi is sleeping in her room, I creep out and close the door. Aunty Mala is sitting in the chair beside my sister's bed; the family will take it in turns to watch over her. Shanthi refused food but accepted some coconut water and took Aunty's sleeping tablets. In the morning, we will call a doctor. Shanthi's own prescription tablets weren't in her toiletry bag or her suitcase. I guess she's not been taking those for a while.

As I left the room, Aunty Mala was still twisting those prayer beads. But it wasn't for nerves. She was saying a blessing. She leaned over and kissed Shanthi's grazed forehead, and when she turned to me, there was no fear in her eyes. Only worry and kindness.

I say goodbye to Roshan on the veranda. Light filters out from the front room, but everywhere else is lost in darkness. In the distance I can hear the flitting wings of a bat. Roshan is rubbing his eyes. He can't have expected this exhausting day when he met me by the bougainvillea.

'I can't ever thank you enough,' I tell him.

He stops rubbing his eyes.

'I can come and see you all tomorrow?' he asks.

I hesitate. I feel so comfortable with this man with whom my horoscope matches, so grateful for everything he has done for us. In another life, our marriage would be a steady and peaceful one, quiet evenings on a small veranda, gazing up at a distant moon, at moths darting about a candle. But I guess some marriages are only ever built on friendship. And trust.

He's watching me carefully. 'It's all right, Anjali,' he says. 'I am not asking for anything. I would just like to get to know you. And your family.'

And friendships? Well, they're built on friendship, too. The distance between me and the people in this country doesn't feel quite so huge after all.

I watch him walk away, up the red path.

Mum and I sit together in the early hours of the morning, watching over my sister. Shanthi opens her eyes after a while. They look vacant now, still influenced by the sleeping pills. She says very little, turning to the corners of the room. I take her hand and stroke it. 'Anjie,' she whispers. 'My gift.'

A gift or offering. It's what my name means.

Shanthi means peace of mind.

Holding my hand in both of hers, her eyes slowly close again and she drifts back off.

Mum hasn't said much since we got back. I can see the pain in her eyes as they go over Shanthi's cuts and grazes, the gash at the back of her hand. She will bathe the wounds tomorrow and dress them with gauze. She will offer Shanthi food and pour her more coconut water. She will listen to the stream of her thoughts and will not interrupt her.

'It was like this for your father,' she says suddenly.

'What?' I've slipped my hands out of Shanthi's and turn to face her, confused.

'He came to see me one day,' Mum says. 'Before we were married.'

I hold my breath as I always do whenever Mum talks about Dad.

'It was unusual,' she says. 'In those days, when the marriage was arranged, you did not always spend much time together until after the ceremony.'

She pauses.

'He told me that sometimes he was hearing people talk to him, when there was nobody else there.'

221

I stare at her.

'He said that his family did not want him to tell my family, because they would call off the wedding. But he said to me that I did not have to marry him.'

'He had the same illness as Shanthi?' I ask.

'It was similar.' With trembling fingers Mum tucks a lock of hair behind her ear. Her hair has grown out a little now and she seems to have stopped dying it, almost all of it grey. 'I do not know if it was the same.'

'And you married him anyway?' A lump is building in my throat, a pressure behind my eyes.

'I did not see why it mattered. I did not see why I should change my mind.' In the dim light coming from the lantern, the fire in Mum's eyes is back. But it's different. She doesn't look like the woman I see most Sundays. She doesn't look like the person whose only concern is finding me a good, brown-tinged man. I gaze at the lines of her tough, weathered face. It feels like I'm meeting her for the first time.

She takes my hand and inspects the palm. Ernie's words come back to me. Strong lines, he said. Like Mum's.

'I used to worry for him,' Mum continues, her jaw tight, the tiniest crack in her voice. 'When I would wake in the night and he was gone and I would find him on the beach, watching the fishermen. But he was not there because of a sickness. He was there because he loved to watch the boats. He said they made him feel happy. He loved Sri Lanka, Anjali.'

'Why do you stay in England?' I squeeze her dry hands, seeing tiny shadows of myself in the shining gold of her rings. 'You seem unhappy there sometimes, Mum. Is it because of looking after me and Shanthi? If it wasn't for us, would you come back here?'

Mum kisses my forehead, the softest brush of her lips against my skin.

'Shanthi is getting stronger,' she says. 'You are both strong girls. You do not need me.' She smiles. 'It is me who needs both of you.'

She settles back in her chair and closes her eyes, hands folded in her lap. Hands that have held Shanthi, held me. Hands that once held my father, that lowered his head to rest on a final pillow. Hands that touched, two years later, the still bodies of her own parents. 'You two are in England. And your father is there. When I go to his stone, I feel him. I am not always happy in England, *duwa*. No place can make you always happy. But it is where my family are, and it is my home.'

Later, Mum sends me off to rest while she waits out the last hours with my sister. She won't be able to sleep now, she tells me. I'm not sure that I will either.

In Mum's old room, someone has put a bowl of jasmine on the side table, the sweet, fruity fragrance drifting from the sprays of yellow anthers inside the white petals. I lean over to breathe in the scent. These delicate flowers are a symbol of hope and love. Curling up on the bed, I think of the life that Mum and Dad once shared together, that I once had a little part of. I think about the gap that has been left in all of our lives, and the different ways we have tried to fill it.

Picking up my phone, I start a message to Jack. Across the other side of so many seas, I know he'll be wondering if Shanthi is OK and if I'm OK. I stare at the picture I have of him in my contacts, the deep blue pools of his eyes, his wide smile. I don't remember taking this photograph. So many memories are starting to slip away, and maybe soon we will be strangers.

I don't know how to put into words everything that I'm thinking and feeling.

In the end, I just write: **We found her. Thank you.**

Before trying to settle to sleep, I find myself scrolling down to Ernie's number. There's no photo there; I have no pictures of him or the two of us. I count nine and a half hours back to Canada. I hesitate, then put my phone away.

Nine

Most of the time I forget to count my blessings. It's so easy to get caught up in your bills, your insomnia, your waistline, your mother, the little army of neuroses that march along with your days. Or mine, at any rate. But in the days after finding my sister, I just feel grateful to get her home safely.

Aunty Mala's doctor prescribed some medication to cover her. Uncle Garmony had contacts at the airport who helped sort out new flights and get us boarded on the overnight plane. We realised my sister hadn't slept properly for days, maybe longer, the doctor's medication allowing her to drift in and out of sleep for the twelve hours of the journey. Mum and I drink coffee and play round after round of rummy, neither of us taking the other's offer of rest.

At Gatwick, the three of us stumble through Arrivals into a world that is only just waking up. And into a tall woman in dreadlocks standing there in the sparse crowd.

Clara.

I'm too touched to speak. I phoned her before we left, explained a little bit of the situation. She's always known

225

something of Shanthi's illness, although not the full extent of it. How much she seems to understand, though, without being told. How much you can hear in the gaps between words, if you listen hard enough.

She squeezes my shoulder.

We're all still in flip-flops; outside, the February chill bites at our toes. Clara helps Mum and Shanthi into the van, and I get into the back after them. Clara passes us blankets and a thermos of sweet tea. 'You got everything you need? Let's see if we can beat rush hour.'

Before she slides the doors shut to get into the front, Mum leans forward and kisses her pierced cheek.

We drive without stopping. Shanthi is in between Mum and me, groggy with the drugs. She stares out of the window, down at the footwell, upwards at the ceiling, her gaze fixed so long that I gently put my hand on her wrist. 'OK?' I whisper. She doesn't hear; she's listening to something else, someone else, someone who isn't there, whose voice isn't drowned out by the passing cars. Her eyelids are drooping again, her head beginning to nod forward. I roll up a blanket and make a pillow on my shoulder, and eventually my sister rests her head there and drifts off into sleep once more. Even in sleep, though, the lines don't slacken on her face, as if she needs to stay vigilant in her dreams.

I glance at Mum watching my sister, the worry and fierce sense of protection embedded there in the deep cleft of her forehead. I think of how long she has quietly endured this pain. First for Dad, then for Shanthi.

'Why did you never tell me?' I ask.

Mum hesitates. I see a young woman in a sari arriving in this country, pregnant, her husband and two-year-old daughter by her side. Then three years later, alone with two small girls. I see her as an older woman, walking home with her Tesco shopping bags, opening the door to a silent, empty flat.

'You were young. You had your life to lead,' she says eventually.

I think of the things I have never told my mother. I know there are some things she can never tell me either.

Once home, Shanthi is visited at first by a crisis team. They get her going on her proper prescription, they keep her out of hospital. A good thing, we're told, as there aren't any beds anyway, and we'd be looking at an out-of-area placement forty miles down the road in Swindon. Mum has a panic attack over the commute that never was. Then the team transfer Shanthi over to her new care coordinator, Lucy, a young nurse with a partially shaved head and the fullest heart.

Lucy visits Shanthi at home in her room, sitting cross-legged on my old bed with Ordie on her lap. She chats with Mum in the kitchen, never complaining that her tea always comes with three sugars. Mum for her part never comments on Lucy's visible scalp. Not once.

'I have made this drink.' Lucy comes into the kitchen late one Friday to say goodbye to Mum and is greeted by a glass of green liquid. I'm out in the hallway, about to pull the old camp bed out of the cupboard. Glancing through the kitchen doorway, I see Lucy taking in the herbs and spices and green leafy vegetables cluttering up the work surface. The blender is whirring, mulching more green liquid. Mum pushes the glass further beneath Lucy's nose, the smell possibly making the nurse gag, because she backs off, hitting the counter top behind her. 'It is a remedy from my childhood days,' Mum is saying. 'My own mother made this for us when we were not well. I do not know why I have not given it to Shanthi before. Look, I have the recipe here.' She shows Lucy the pages scattered beside the sink, Sinhala scrawled across them: Mum's notes from the late-night phone calls to Sri Lanka.

'Mrs Chandana . . .' Lucy begins gently.

'Oh, I know Shanthi must take her medication too. But this drink, it is very good, it is calming, Aunty Mala says.'

'Aunty Mala?'

'Do you think it will help?' Mum carries straight on. 'It is worth a try, no?'

'Mrs Chandana.' Lucy puts her hand on Mum's arm.

'You do not think it will help?' Mum asks. She eyes the glass suspiciously. 'Will it make her worse?' She whirls around and sloshes the green liquid down the sink and heads towards the blender.

'Mrs Chandana, I think you just need to slow down a little.'

'Slow down? Why?' Mum looks around the kitchen, panicked. 'Am I making Shanthi worse?' She starts packing away the bottles and herbs in a frenzy.

'No,' Lucy says, a little more forcefully, making Mum pause in her tracks. 'I'm not thinking about Shanthi right now. I'm thinking of you. You're doing enough. You really are.'

Mum comes to stand beside Lucy. She stops the blender, pours another glass of green mulch and downs it in one. 'I do not know what else to do. She is a bit better than in Sri Lanka, but she is still not right. And she does not eat enough. And this drink does not taste good.'

'Shanthi will be OK.' Lucy takes Mum's glass and puts it on the counter. 'You know she will be. She made a good recovery before. She'll do it again.'

'I keep thinking about all of the things she was saying in Sri Lanka. Sometimes she is saying them now. Maybe the medication is not strong enough.'

'The doctor will keep it under review.'

'She does not have an appointment for some time.'

Lucy sighs. 'I know. We're under-resourced. But we keep the doctor aware. And it's early days.'

'I just . . . It is hard. Seeing her this way again.'

'Of course it is.' Lucy picks up a stray green leaf and toys with it. 'But you know. These symptoms. They can tell us something too.'

'Tell us?'

'I've worked with a lot of people. What we call symptoms are their experiences. And there's meaning behind them.'

Mum is quiet, watching Lucy carefully.

'I'm trying to listen harder,' Lucy says. 'To try and understand.'

I turn back to the cupboard. Hauling out the camp bed, I drag it through to the living room, pondering Lucy's words.

Over time, I see my sister become slowly less distracted and more able to focus in conversation. Her voice stays quiet, but the whispering gradually stops. It's the only time I've known her to be without her art; sometimes she sits in her room with her sketchpad on her lap, but her hands are still and the paper is blank.

'Do you think you might want to visit the studio?' I ask her one morning as I'm about to leave for the shop. She is over by the window, looking down onto the front yard. 'I could go with you if you liked.' Once the words are out, I wonder how she would feel about me being there, whether Donna told her about my trespassing there once before. I wonder if the people at the studio, the person who might be her boyfriend, know anything of what she's been going through.

My sister doesn't answer for a while. Her stereo is already on, volume turned up, Bob Marley strangely agitated.

'Shanthi?'

She's starting to put weight on again, but her frame is so tiny; she's stopped putting her hair up, and from a distance she might be mistaken for a child. As is so often happening these days, I am remembering both of us as children, the times when she might often be at the window, not always hearing me. I've been thinking a lot about what Lucy said. I imagine my sister as a five-year-old, at six, seven, struggling at school. We both lost Dad, but I was so little. He slipped quietly away from me like a dream. I wonder how it was for my sister, how her mind might have tried to make sense of why he wasn't there any more.

'Sorry.' Shanthi turns around. She's still in the big blue T-shirt she wears to bed, the one she's been wearing for a few days and Mum is tiptoeing around asking to wash. 'What did you say?'

'Do you want me to go with you to the studio? We could go one day after I've finished work.'

It seems to take a while for my words to register. Then she shakes her head. Picking up a pack of cigarettes from the windowsill, she lights one. 'Not today. I can't just now, Anjie. Maybe later.' After two or three drags on the cigarette, she stabs it out into the clay ashtray. 'I *said* I'd cut it out,' she mutters. I'm not sure who she's talking to.

I hesitate at the door. The wounds on her body are healing and the red lines are fading from her eyes. I want to ask if the voices are still talking to her, but I don't. I don't have Lucy's way, I don't know how to do it.

Bob Marley's 'Sun is Shining' has come on. It's a song that has followed us from our small days, one that Mum said Dad used to play. A soundtrack to breakfasts, to lounge picnics, to the afternoons when it was just me and Shanthi, to the night-times when Mum would eventually come in and turn off the stereo, tut-tutting. It's a song I remember too after Shanthi's first episode of illness, when for months after leaving hospital she was holed up in her room, barely talking to me on my rare visits. But one afternoon this song was playing as I walked through the door. Shanthi was in the lounge, bent over one of the intricate jigsaw puzzles Mum had bought. My chest swelled with hope. I sat beside her, and although we didn't say much, we didn't move for hours. The CD was on repeat and we steadily fitted our pieces, tapping our fingers to the beat of the music.

I want that hope to be there today. But the melody is that bit too loud, the singing voices a little too insistent. My sister is facing the window once more, following an unseen line down the pane with her finger. Lost again, wherever she goes in her mind.

'I'll see you later,' I say.

I want to tell her that I love her, but I don't. As I leave for work, closing the door quietly behind me, I wonder if I ever have.

It's the end of March. In front gardens, along the grass verges, daffodils are starting to poke out their heads. They've been late to arrive this year. I've always loved these flowers, standing on the doorstep of spring. Yet I'm still in my duffel coat and can barely feel the tips of my fingers. Winter is holding on tight.

While walking, I take out my phone from time to time.

There's one message from Jack there, the only one he has sent since our last communication in Sri Lanka. *Hope you're OK*. My fingers hover over the message, never sure how to reply, how to sum up both the gladness and the sadness that is pooling in the pit of my stomach.

I wish I could tell Ernie.

'She's getting there, though, right?' Clara calls to me from out the back. It's the end of the day. I'm standing in the middle of the shop, gazing at the daffodils in their buckets, their yellow colour a little dazzling.

'Slowly, I guess.'

'Is this how it normally is?'

I sigh. 'I don't know. I wasn't there for her before.'

Clara comes out, a small glass of whisky in her hand.

'You know I hate this stuff, right?'

She passes it to me anyway. 'It's good for you.' She touches me on the shoulder as I take a tiny sip. 'Don't be too hard on yourself, Anj.'

I pass the glass back to her with a grimace. 'It's true though, Clar. Watching her come through this makes me realise how much I've let her down.'

'But you're here now.' Clara pulls me to sit on a stool behind the counter. 'That's what you need to focus on.'

My mouth is open to reply, but she puts her hand over it. I smile. I take my phone out again. It'll be lunchtime in Vancouver. Maybe Ernie is eating lunch with colleagues, or at his desk; maybe he's sitting outside somewhere in the Canadian sun.

'What?' Clara turns to me.

'What?' I blink.

'What are you thinking about right now?'

I shake Ernie away, urgently. He needs to stop coming to me like this. 'Nothing.'

Clara's observing me suspiciously. 'It's him, isn't it?'

I screw up my eyes in apology. 'Kind of.'

'Stop it.' She takes a big gulp of my whisky.

'Sorry.' Clara's right: this mooning isn't going to get me anywhere.

'Remember what he did to you.'

'What? He didn't do anything. You mean, him going away?'

'No, I'm talking about *her*, you idiot.'

'Who?'

'The burlesque dancer!'

'Oh.' I grin, taking back the whisky and wincing over another sip. 'Jack.'

'Well, who were you . . . ' She stops. 'Ah. The Ernster.'

'Is that better than thinking about Jack?' I allow Ernie, sitting under blue skies, to drift back into my mind.

'Isn't it about time you called him?'

'What?' I see Ernie looking up at me, surprised, putting down his sandwich.

'Come on, Anj,' Clara grabs the whisky and downs it in one. 'Remember what Robin Williams said, in that film?'

'Good morning, Vietnam?' I hazard.

'Seize the bloody day, you dimwit.'

He's working. When he answers my call after two rings, I can no longer feel my heartbeat. I touch my pulse, wondering if I'm still alive.

'Anjali?'

'Um,' I falter, not being clear for a moment exactly who I am. 'Yes.'

'Are you all right?'

I falter once more. Clara's out the back again, tidying up. She's going to kill me if I don't actually say anything.

'I think so.'

'Hold on a minute, I'll go outside.' His voice is the same as the one that sneaks into my dreams, deep and warm. There's the sound of a chair being pushed back, footsteps, a door opening. 'I'm here. Are you sure you're all right?'

It's started to rain, a steady pitter-patter against the window. There's so much I want to tell him. About the flowers. About my sister. But now that he's there, on the other end of the line, the words that I've practised won't come. So much must have happened to him too these past few months. It's arrogant to expect that he would have been thinking about me. I wonder if he might even have met someone else.

'I just felt like talking to you,' I say.

The line is clear for a moment.

'Ernie?'

'It's good to hear from you,' he says, quietly.

'Where are you? Exactly?'

'A place called Victoria, it's in—'

'Vancouver Island.' I wonder if I've spoken too quickly, if he'll guess just how much Wikipedia I check while lying in bed at night.

'That's right. I'm not normally based here.'

'What's it like?'

'I'm near the parliament buildings. There's a harbour. It's beautiful at night.'

'Is it sunny?'

'Yes. And getting a little warmer. Not like Bristol, I'll bet.'

'Did you have a sandwich for your lunch?'

I can feel him grinning. 'I haven't had lunch. Now you mention it, I'm starving. Are you calling from home?'

'The shop. We'll be closing up soon. Clara probably needs my help.'

'Don't go yet.'

We both pause. For a moment, I hear him breathing, remembering that time in the meditation hall, before everything got complicated. I wonder how things might have been in another world, a world where perhaps I hadn't met Jack, where I'd looked after my sister.

'I think about you a lot,' he says, finally.

I hesitate, my heart lifting.

'It's good here. My colleagues are relaxed. I'm getting to know my niece and nephew.'

'That's great,' I say, meaning it.

'But there's a lot I miss.'

Clara's come up beside me. She waves her hand to indicate that everything's done, and drops the keys on the counter. 'Call me,' she whispers, before she leaves, pulling up her hood.

'What do you miss?' I ask him.

'Big things. Little things. My mates. The guys at work. The Rising Sun on Gloucester Road. Can't find any Liverpool supporters here.' He laughs, and I close my eyes, trying to make a memory of the sound. 'My old neighbour Billy. You never met him. He was always on the front doorstep when I left for work, smoking his pipe and playing his harmonica. Feels like I wasn't back long before saying goodbye again.'

I listen to him breathe once more.

'Sometimes I go out walking by myself. There are daffodils here,' he says.

'Here too.'

'Tell me a story, Anjali.'

There's a lump building in my throat. 'Narcissus,' I say.

'Ah.'

'The self-absorbed guy. He was cursed with unrequited love. In one tale he mistakes his reflection in a pool.'

'And falls in love with it?'

'Yep.' I swallow, trying to clear my throat. 'In the end, he lies down beside the pool and dies. Those who looked for him found only a daffodil where his body had been.'

'So I'm walking past unrequited love?'

My head throbbing. 'Something like that.'

Another pause on the line.

'There's cherry blossom here too.' He waits for me to say something, but my voice is lost now, listening to his. 'I keep thinking of that morning at the flower market. I miss you, Anjali.'

Tiny streams trickle down the window, blocking the view. It feels like too much to bear.

'I've got to go,' I whisper.

I walk. The rain seeps into my uncovered hair, slipping down my neck, beneath my duffel coat. I walk past the Rising Sun, catching Ernie in another life, with a pint of cider and a small group of friends. Past some of the shops I recognise from my childhood, wandering in and out with Shanthi when Mum was at work and we should have been at home, some of our favourites now closed down in austerity. I keep going, into Stokes Croft, past the Tesco Express that caused riots when it first opened, the community trying to fight back. But the people lost in the end. Past the cafés, the vintage clothes and furniture shops, the graffiti, bold and brave and questioning.

When I turn up outside Shanthi's studio, maybe I'm not surprised. Maybe this was always where I was headed.

The lights are on; gazing up, I see movement at the window. The blurred image of Donna coming to look out, a flash of brilliant red hair.

I wait for a while, for what reason I'm not sure, before turning around to go back to Mum's. I walk a few paces, then stop, turning back on my heel and pressing the buzzer.

Donna leads me up to the studio. This time we're not alone. There's a man, older, late forties, maybe early fifties, skinny, in corduroy trousers and a thin cotton shirt, bent over by the desk where the giant-mouthed sculpture used to be. He's sketching on a piece of card, stopping and jumping up when he sees me.

'Anjali? Shanthi's sister? It's so good to meet you. I'm Ben.'

I wipe my feet on the mat and shake his hand, rough and marked with pen, taken off guard by his warmth.

'It's good to meet you too.'

There are deep laughter lines around his mouth, creases around his eyes, a darker blue than I've seen before, the kind I imagine my dad had, if you were able to get up close.

'Drink? Orange juice? Hot chocolate?' Donna says.

'Coffee?' I ask.

She smiles. I see her reminding herself I'm not my sister. 'Coming right up. Get that coat off. You're soaking.'

She takes it from me and hangs it over the radiator. Ben opens a cupboard in the corner and finds me a thin towel; I wring out my dripping hair. Donna brings me my coffee and sits me down on a chair. Their care and attention is touching. The studio seems less intimidating than it did last time, warmed now by the glow of two electric fires.

When Donna is over by the percolator again, fetching their drinks, Ben looks across at her. 'How's Shanthi?'

They know.

'The café.' Ben senses my unasked question. 'Your mum went in. And she left us a note here.' It surprises me that Mum knew where the studio was. I wonder if Shanthi asked her to do it.

Donna brings over their espressos and they pull up their chairs. They ask me everything. I don't want to say too much, not knowing how much my sister, usually so guarded, would share with others. But there's a sense that she is more open with these guys than she has been with anyone before.

'Why wasn't she admitted to hospital?' Donna asks.

'It's different now,' I say. 'There aren't enough beds. But the crisis team was good. And I think she's better off at home.'

'Is there any reason it happened?' Donna's speaking quietly. 'I mean, now?'

I pause, again not sure how much to say. 'I don't think she was taking her meds.'

'Why not?'

I shake my head.

'She never follows the rules,' Ben says, after a while, almost to himself.

Maybe I knew this. I remember my sister at school, eating lunch by herself, or in our bedroom when we were growing up, when everyone else was outside, playing. A loner, that was how we put it. It's odd, seeing her from someone else's perspective.

'Can we do anything?' Donna asks. Her face is smaller than I remember, her eyes large and clear and amber, brown specks spreading out into an orange glow. I've never seen eyes like hers before. How much they intimidated me that first time in the studio; how full of concern they are now. 'Can we come over?'

I hesitate. 'I don't know. It might be better to wait until she comes here.'

'Does she ask about . . . the studio?' Donna glances at Ben.

I hesitate again, looking away from both of them. 'She's not talking about anything much at the moment.' We fall into silence, our conversation replaced by the ticking of the heaters. Footsteps sound overhead; outside we hear people calling to one another. Ben is looking down, studying something imperceptible on the floor. 'Is the exhibition going ahead?' I ask. It was scheduled for next month.

Donna shakes her head. 'We postponed it.'

'I was wondering,' I begin, not sure what I'm going to say until the words are actually out of my mouth, 'if I could maybe take back something of Shanthi's. A painting. Something she could work on.' When I've spoken, I wonder how I'll be able to confess to Shanthi that I've visited her space and met her friends. It feels like going behind her back.

But Ben is getting to his feet. I put down my coffee cup and he takes me over to Shanthi's desk. I realise my error as soon as I see the size of her pictures, larger than any of the other canvases she's used before. I stop in front of one that is almost the height of the wall.

I stare.

Snakes. Everywhere. Giant and small. Some on their sides, some with mouths open at me. But not the silvery ones on the screen in Shanthi's bedroom, not the snakes of her illness. These creatures are magnificent, unreal, the canvas covered in so many vivid and shining colours. The serpents' bodies are made up of stars, of moons, of suns, of teardrops, of blood, of leaves, of irises, of tiny, tiny hands.

'We couldn't do the exhibition without her,' Ben says softly. 'We need her.'

My throat is choked. I'm prying by being here, I'm invading Shanthi's space. But I'm greedy to know her after all my years of absence. To see not just my sister unwell, but my sister in all her glory, not dependent on us, on the mental health system, on the small tablets she swallows down every day; not solely made up of the sum of her symptoms and medication, but a whole person, sparkling, vibrant, alive. Where her madness is a part of her but not all of who she is.

Donna comes to stand beside us. Turning, I glimpse again the peacock feather tattoo that troubled me so much the last time I saw it. But I know now that in some cultures, the feather symbolises compassion, kindness and patience. Donna lays her head against Ben's narrow shoulder, and for a moment I can see Shanthi doing the same. I wonder how it would feel to rest my own there, beneath the dark blue gaze that might be just like our father's.

April days pass, brisk and cloudy. I while away lunch breaks alone on the grassy bank of St Andrew's Park, a little bit down the road from the shop, not minding the cold. I haven't called Ernie again; he hasn't contacted me. I watch other couples as they stop briefly at the small kiosk to buy coffees, their heads bent in chatter. It's not clear to me why I couldn't talk to Ernie properly, why I couldn't even tell him that I think of him, that I miss him too. Why I couldn't confide in him about my sister so that his voice could come back to me as clear and warm as it always is. So he could tell me, *Shanthi will be all right*.

I see him in that hi-vis jacket, gazing at a thousand flowers bright beneath the strip lights. I see us in the van, stopped before the burning eyes of a fox.

'Ring him again?' Clara touches my arm one day, finding me paused once more in front of the daffodils. 'You need to talk.'

But when I pick up the phone, I lose my nerve.

Shanthi draws a picture of Ernie.

I find myself telling her about him on my visits after work. Tentatively at first, not knowing exactly what to say. Then, seeing her interest, a little more each day. It's kind of nice not to be continually interrogating her about how she is and what she's been doing with herself. Instead, I sit on my bed in her room, answering her questions. She's cut right down on the cigarettes, and her fingers are restless for something to hold. One day I pass her a pencil and her sketchbook, and the man she has never seen before starts to come to life on the page.

'What do you think?' she asks me.

I'm stunned. I watch her fingers shade and enhance Ernie's features, the tiny hook of his nose, the crooked lower tooth; there are differences, but the resemblance is clear. I turn to my sister, thinking how incredible she is, thinking how much I've missed her, not just in these past few weeks, but in all of the years that have drifted by.

'Could I have it?' I ask. She nods and passes the picture to me.

Every day that follows, there's a new drawing in Shanthi's room. The old frown of concentration is back between her eyes as her pencil moves. Music still plays constantly, but the volume is a little lower and there is space to hear. Some evenings when I come over, she isn't home, and Mum tells me she's gone for a walk, no look of worry in Mum's eyes about whether she will return safely. I sit alone in Shanthi's bedroom, noticing that her easel is out, breathing in the smell of drying oil on canvas rather than Benson & Hedges. The pictures are smaller, simpler, easier than the ones in the studio, but I feel the heart of my sister in them, pushing through.

I see the small gifts to Shanthi that have been sent from Sri Lanka, the cassette of Buddhist prayers (we don't have the heart to tell them we haven't had a tape player since 2000), Aunty Mala's cards crowding the surface of my sister's dresser. In the middle of them, one from Roshan. *Be safe and happy, my dear Shanthi.*

I eat dinner with Mum when Shanthi gets back, her cheeks bright from the wind, perhaps from a visit to the studio. I sleep over again in her room, the two of us tapping the serpent screen and chatting until Mum comes in, tutting. 'Anjali, remember you are working tomorrow!' She turns out the light, the room flooded with darkness, and for the first time in so many years, Shanthi and I giggle.

I feel like a child again.

It's the anniversary of Dad's death in the middle of May. His headstone is at Arnos Vale Cemetery, south of the river. It's a beautiful place, forty-five acres of green land, where we used to walk as a family. In other years we've visited him separately; on this day Mum goes by herself in the morning, but Shanthi and I make the trip together.

Spring is still being undecided. The daffodils are all but gone, just a couple on the outskirts of the cemetery.

We are settled on the grass beside Dad's stone. Mum's left a little pot of tulips there, bright yellow against the grey concrete. It reminds me of the story she once told me about the day she and Dad and Shanthi first arrived in Bristol. It was spring then too, bitterly cold, their suitcases containing no coats or jumpers. Shanthi was two years old, terrified of this freezing and unknown place where the people looked at her strangely. Mum said she felt equally nervous, not sure whether they could make it here. Only Dad was calm. Getting off the bus, he gazed at a crop of yellow tulips on the edge of the verge and told them that if the country could care for flowers as beautiful as these, it would care for them too.

My sister pulls paper bags of Mum's short eats from her satchel. Vegetable cutlets, rolls and patties, the best of deep-fried Sri Lankan fare. I notice the faint tremor in her fingers as she passes me the food. Lucy suspects it is due to the tablets, but Shanthi has refused to make an appointment to discuss this.

I force my question out. 'Why did you stop taking your medication, Shanthi? Was it because of the shaking?'

Shanthi folds and unfolds a corner of one of the paper bags. Her hair is coiled up on her head once more, little hairs visible on the back of her neck like baby down.

'I wanted to feel something again,' she says.

'Do the tablets stop that?'

'Sometimes.'

I think of the paintings I saw in the studio, the places her mind can reach when free of the drugs.

'We could go back to the doctor's. I could come with you.'

She shakes her head. 'It's OK for the moment. I don't want any more doctors, not just yet.'

I look at the tiny indented mark beneath her left eyebrow. It was from the time as a little girl she tripped down the bottom of the stairs, her face meeting the corner of the radiator. Mum said she was running to the door to see Dad getting in from work. I glance at the heavy scar on the back of Shanthi's hand and think of her body, bruised and battered, when we found her in Dad's old home. I wonder if I'll ever know how things are for my sister, deep in her mind. I heard her tell Lucy that she'd never been aware of when the voices had started; it seemed as if there had always been someone there, someone she couldn't see, talking to her. At first maybe just a murmur in the curl of steam from the spout of the kettle. Sometimes a low voice in her ear; sometimes a whisper creeping beneath the door like sandalwood fumes. Gentle, like a friend. Then the other, stronger voices had joined. The ones who say she is to blame for Dad's death.

What else they say, she has never told us.

'I'm sorry, Shanthi,' I say.

'What for?'

'For moving out.'

'What do you mean?'

'When you were in hospital. The first time.'

My sister reaches for her pocket, then stops. There are no cigarettes in there; she's trying to quit altogether. She goes back to the paper bag, folding the corner over and over again.

'I get it, you know,' she says. 'I saw Dad once when he wasn't well. I know what it's like.'

'Why did nobody tell me about that?'

'You were so small.'

'So were you.'

I think again about my sister losing Dad at five years old. The fears that might have settled deep inside her while Mum was busy attending to me, the louder, more demanding one.

We fall into silence. I study the weathered inscription on my father's stone, the letters of his name fading away. *Sarath Eshan Chandana.* I wonder if any of us can ever be free of the voices inside our heads.

'I've missed you, these last few years,' I say.

Shanthi lays her hand on mine. There's a thick fading line now to mark the place where the gash was. Her nails have grown again, shaped now into small ovals. She's washed her hands, but there are still some spots of paint. There always are. 'I've missed you too, little sis.'

'I know there are things you keep from me,' I say. 'Do you think you'll ever be able to tell me about them?'

She pauses, and I see her fingers twitching, desperate now for a cigarette. 'There's something I will tell you, Anjie. In time. I promise.'

Ten

Maybe that was my sister's way of letting me know she was in a relationship. Even after meeting Ben at the studio, I still couldn't be sure. Maybe he was just a good friend; it's not like she explicitly said she was seeing anyone. But the more I talk to her, the more certain I become.

I start to notice real differences in my sister and feel convinced the two of them are meeting up again. It isn't just her growing well-being – I know better than to attribute contentment to a member of the opposite sex. It isn't just that one day she trims her hair and puts on a dress – she did this once before, when she stopped smoking.

Maybe it's the way I'm woken early one Monday morning, after sleeping over at Mum's, to the sound of singing out in the hallway. It's my day off and I'm frustrated that my lie-in is being interrupted. When I call out, 'Mum! Can you please shut up!', I realise that my mother left ages ago for her shift at Tesco, and that the unusual, pretty sound is actually coming from my sister.

Getting out of bed and pulling on my clothes, I dash out to the hallway – but there's only a shining Buddha and a mewing

Ordie to greet me. Footsteps echo from the outside landing. Crossing to the window, I see Shanthi go through the gate and cross the road. Her footsteps seem light, like there's a song in her head. It reminds me of how I walked, when I first met Ernie.

The official confirmation comes on leaving the building myself. The postman has just delivered the mail. My discovery is a postcard to Shanthi, of a painting from an exhibition at the Arnolfini. There is a heavy mass of bold colour covering the card, and on the back all that is written is Mum's address and the words: *To Shanthi, my love.*

Ping.

Leaving the mail on the shelf beside the door, I make my way back home. It feels kind of nice to think of my sister in a relationship, and to know that she is happy. It fills me with enough energy to tackle the washing-up and to clean out the fridge. However, it isn't long before Mum has interrupted my spurt.

'What is my love?'

'I'm sorry?' Slightly disorientated on picking up the phone, I'm not sure if Mum is asking a deeply philosophical question. 'I don't know, what is your love?'

'I am talking about your sister. Who is this calling her "my love"?'

Ah.

'Oh, the postcard.'

'You know about the postcard?' I can hear the accusation in my mother's voice that she is being kept in the dark about the first bit of romantic love we've ever known to happen to my sister.

'I saw it this morning,' I say. 'I don't know who sent it, Mum. But it's good news, isn't it? If Shanthi's got a boyfriend, then doesn't that show how much things have changed? She's never had a relationship before.'

'It is not good news!' I'm having flashbacks to when I first told Mum about Jack, when she placed the long edge of her index finger against the tip of her forehead and wailed, *Oh, my Anjali is with a suthu!* (*Suthu* means white person in Sinhala.) 'Is this why Shanthi became sick again?'

'It might be one reason why she's getting better,' I point out.

'Who is this man?' Mum's voice still sounds loud but at the same time quite distant, as if she is whirling around the living room. 'Who is this man who is destroying my little girl?'

'Mum, he's probably not destroying her,' I say, as reasonably as I can. 'And for God's sake, Shanthi is thirty-one. She's old enough to have a boyfriend if she wants one.'

'There you both go, ganging up on me!'

Over the past few months, it's felt as if my relationship with Mum is changing; growing. But sometimes I'm right back to where we always have been, in a confusing pit of persecutory beliefs.

'Mum, calm down. Nobody's ganging up on you. It's just that Shanthi has a boyfriend' – and this, I note, has somewhere along the line of our conversation become an actual fact – 'and I think we should be happy for her.'

'I will never be happy,' my mum declares, 'when both of my girls are running wild with *suthus*.'

'Mum, first of all, *I* am not running wild with *suthus*,' I inform her, realising at the same time that a few months ago this wasn't exactly true. 'And secondly, can you stop being so melodramatic? This is no big deal, but if you keep going on about it like this, it will become one.'

For once, reason appears to have an impact on my mother.

'I am just so worried about her, Anjali.'

'I know you are, Mum.'

'She may be thirty-one, but she has already been through so much.'

'I know, Mum.'

'I don't want her to be hurt.'

'Of course you don't.'

'It is enough that one of my daughters has already been hurt.'

'I'm OK, Mum.'

'But that boy hurt you, Anjali.' At first I wonder if she is talking about Ernie, although I haven't ever spoken to her about him. But of course she means Jack.

'I'm OK, Mum,' I tell her again. Not that I've ever confessed to her about Jack being unfaithful, for fear of having to use a second plot at the Arnos Vale Cemetery.

'But you have been sad.'

'I guess. But I'm fine now.' I think about Ernie's voice on the phone, the silence left behind after we hung up, and I'm not entirely sure if that's true.

'I do not want Shanthi to be sad.'

'Being in a relationship doesn't automatically mean she'll end up sad,' I say, not sure if I really believe in that, either. I sit down on my sofa. Glimpses of the men I have met over the past few months come into my mind. The encounters didn't always make me feel good about myself. Yet I guess each one meant something, however good or bad that was. Sometimes I picture the Architect turning up with his umbrella on that Gothic walk around Bristol, and seeing his future wife standing there with a guidebook on top of her head. Or the Saxophonist's true love flying out to surprise him, her rucksack on her back; or the Western Brown Man making his mother a chapatti. 'But maybe being sad is OK.' I wonder if I can put what I'm feeling into words. 'We miss Dad. But we're happy for the time we had with him. We would rather that than never having known him at all.'

I see Mum coming to sit at the table, gazing at the bright streaks of colour covering the postcard. 'I hope you are right, Anjali. I hope you are right.' She pauses. 'And are you really all right now, my *duwa*?'

'I'm fine,' I stress. 'I have you and Shanthi and my friends. And I have my flowers.'

'I'm giving up the shop,' Clara blurts out as soon as I get into work the following morning.

I stand in front of the sweet peas, stunned.

'You know I've been thinking about what I'm going to do for a while.' She comes over and takes my arm, as if afraid I will fall. She leads me to the counter, sits me down on the stool and pushes a vase of sweet peas beneath my nose like smelling salts. 'The truth is, I did this for my aunt Sammy. I didn't want to sell the shop, I wanted to keep it alive for her, and I did it for far longer than I planned. But I can't stay here any more, Anj. Sometimes my feet only ever get as far as the traders' market. I need them to go further.'

'But I love the traders' market,' I whisper. A woman has come into the shop and is perusing the peas. Normally I would go over, relishing the chance to revel in their beauty with strangers. 'Where are you going to go?'

'Back to Bali.'

'Bali?' I turn to her. Clara's face is flushed; she looks more excited than I've seen her for a long time.

'I woke up at three a.m. and knew that's where I have to be.'

'For a holiday? For a year? For how long?'

'For as long as possible.' Clara's green eyes are glistening with life. 'I'm going back to him.'

And *him*, I know, is the one-handed percussionist. The one she almost made a commitment to before her aunt died and she took over the shop instead. The one she hardly ever speaks of and who, I now realise, has never left her heart.

'But it's been what – almost eleven years?'

'I know.'

'He might not be there.'

'He is, he emails me.'

'He might have met someone else.'

'He hasn't emailed me that.'

'He might have lost the other hand.'

'Then there'd probably have been no emails.'

'He doesn't know how much I'll miss you.'

'Oh, Anj.' Clara moves the flowers away to put her arms around me. I'm entangled in her heavy dreadlocks, and the thought of no longer feeling their coarse frizz against my upper arms fills my eyes with tears. 'I'm going to miss you too. But you'll email me, won't you? And we can Skype. And you'll come to visit me. And I'll come back sometimes. My mum would kill me if I didn't.'

The woman comes up to the counter and has to wait while I extricate myself from Clara's hair.

'Sorry,' the woman says. 'I don't want to interrupt your moment.' She puts her bunch of sweet peas on the counter, and my eyes swim for a second in powder blue and pink and violet.

I hunt out the most delicate paper we have to wrap the bunch for her. 'These flowers are so beautiful. I almost don't want to sell them to you.'

'They're my favourite,' the woman says.

'Mine too.'

'I'm just sad they don't last for ever.'

'Me too.' I nod, vigorously.

Clara cashes up the order. 'But they come back next year,' she tells us both. 'And all the ones after that.'

In between customers, we talk through Clara's plans. She's agonised for hours, but the most practical option is to sell the business and rent out the flat above. Then she'll live off the income for a while. 'I feel bad for Aunt Sammy, but I know this is the best decision,' she says.

We gaze around the shop we love. It's like I'm catching glimpses of our previous selves in the shadows: my nineteen-year-old self, on my first day at work, bending down to smell the giant daisies, to run my hands over the ferns. Realising I didn't know the proper names of any of these plants, but feeling the excitement grow inside me that one day I would. The end of that first day, sweeping up the fallen petals and knowing that I was never going back to university. 'Say that when you've worked a sixteen-hour day, your hands are numb and I'm making you get up at four a.m.,' came Clara's wry reply. I'm seeing her making two cups of cocoa in the kitchenette and hesitating over the hip flask of whisky. Then the two of us sitting on stools on either side of the counter, slurping the hot, sweet liquid and exchanging the stories of our lives so far. I'm seeing us in the same position the next year, and the year after that, hearing the door open and seeing another shadow, Jack, coming to pick me up. 'Do you two ever stop laughing?'

I look away from the shadows; if I picture anything else, I'll just start crying again.

And this guy, the one-handed percussionist. The man she once met sitting alone beside a stretch of Bali sea, tapping an astonishing, intricate beat on his drum. Despite everything Clara has ever said, all the rants I've heard over the years about the futility of relationships, turns out she's never stopped loving him. 'I couldn't admit it,' she says. 'I couldn't see how we had a future, with him so far away and all, so it was easier to try and believe that I didn't care about him.'

She hasn't emailed to tell him her plans; she doesn't want to put any pressure on him. She'll just turn up, see what's what. Maybe it will work out, maybe it won't. They'll both have changed over the years; they might want different things now. She doesn't want children or a traditional life. She wants music, adventure, someone to share these things with. If none of it's possible, she'll move on. There are other places in the world to see. 'I'll be like Uncle Bulgaria,' she tells me. It takes me a moment to work out she's referring to the Wombles, not a member of my extended family.

I think about Clara sending a series of postcards about her lone travels. I can't see it somehow. Instead, I see her lying on a beach next to her man, sand drying between their bare toes, talking to the fading sunset. As I tell her this, her green eyes start to glisten again.

And as for me ... We talk about this too, and throw ideas past each other, wacky and serious. I'm not sure. It's time to move out of my flat. I've finally started opening some bills. I'll be going back to Mum's, tail between my legs, stuffing aubergines down my throat while listening to a summary of my failings. Or maybe not. There is something different about Mum these days – or maybe something different about me. We both seem to be changing.

But as to what I'm going to do next, I don't have a clue.

'So it's sweet pea season, hey?' a deep voice calls as the door opens. The sun is shining into the shop, bright light around the person who has just walked in. 'Man, I love those.'

Ernie.

*

'Hey, you!' Clara runs out from behind the counter and lets him catch her in a bear hug. A wistful feeling passes through me for their long, uncomplicated friendship, and I find myself wishing it was my mother who had cooked his weekly roasts, vegetarianism aside.

I hang back at the cash till. I'm tracing the stickers that have landed there over the years, and I cannot lift my head because then Ernie will know that it's my heart he can hear, thumping inside its walls.

'So what's new?' He puts Clara down. If I look up, I'll see the strong line of his jaw, his dark skin maybe a little darker now with the Vancouver sunshine. Maybe there will be more flecks of grey in his fuzzy hair. He's right there, on the other side of the counter. Close enough to touch his stubble, to hunt for the cleft in his chin. Close enough to search in those eyes, those warm and tender eyes; to find out why he's here.

'Everything, actually.' Clara begins to give him the lowdown.

When she's finished, there's a pause, and I know that they are both probably looking at me now. There's no way I can continue to make out that the cash till is so interesting. Plus my neck is starting to hurt.

I raise my head, slowly.

There are his warm and tender eyes.

'What about you, Anjali?' His voice still carries the deep echo that leaves an ache in my throat. 'What are you going to do?'

Not cry again, not cry again.

I glance at the clock and try to gather myself. 'I was going to head home, I guess. We're about to close.' On the counter is another little bunch of sweet peas. They were going to be a gift to my mother. But she hardly ever notices my flowers anyway, so she can wait a while. I hold them out to him. 'It's good to see you again.'

He takes the flowers and breathes them in, and I notice the deep contours of his face, the grey creeping into his stubble, the thick veins in the hands holding the fragile stems. He looks a little thinner, his head shaved now, his arms even more taut in a festival T-shirt.

'Can I walk with you?' he asks me.

I'd kind of like another montage. Although I'm not sure if you can have them twice in your life. I'm pretty certain I've never seen more than one in a film. But walking down the road with Ernie, our hands swinging side by side, getting closer and closer, I've got all kinds of ideas; like Clara maybe lending us the van so we can take off on the valley walk in north Bristol. We can kick off our shoes and wade through a brook lined with stones as soft as cotton wool buds. Or maybe out to the Cotswolds to breathe in the wild garlic and sausage-roll down a sloping field of buttercups before feasting at the bottom on an avocado and goat's cheese granary bap. Although that might not really be for the montage and more because I'm hungry. Or maybe we could head down to the harbour to pop into that Arnolfini exhibition and bump into Shanthi and Ben, their faces when they see us lighting up with montage surprise. Though again that's possibly taking advantage of the medley for my own selfish purposes.

And I guess, if I can slow down the racing of my mind, let it take in the reality of being so close to this man again, of our hands almost touching, maybe a montage isn't needed this time. Maybe this time around, I don't need to embellish anything. A lot has happened since the two of us were together. Maybe this time it can just be me and Ernie, and the truth. Or my version of it, anyway.

*

He tells me he's back for only two weeks, staying with his aunt in Bath because he's renting out his flat for these few months.

'Why didn't you let me know you were coming?' I ask him.

'I wanted to. But you sounded different on the phone; I wasn't sure what you'd say.' He's looking at me, but I've gone for neck strain again, studying a tiny breadcrumb on the corner of the table.

We're in Shanthi's café. Around the corner from the studio, on the edge of Stokes Croft, it's a crowded, jostling kind of place, with vats of bean soup and plenty of goat's cheese granary baps, and all manner of vegetarians engaged in meaningful chat. It's a place I haven't visited for two years, not since Shanthi started working here. At the time I told myself that it was important she establish her own life without us encroaching on her privacy. Now I guess this was just another way to keep my distance.

'Is your sister working today?' I sense him looking around at the waiting staff in their jeans and aprons as they chat away to the customers.

I shake my head, still concentrating on the breadcrumb. Shanthi's only doing a couple of shifts a week at the moment; they're letting her build up again gradually. Mum said that her manager, who had known about Shanthi's illness, showed only kindness when Mum first came to tell them that Shanthi wasn't well. I feel touched that my sister has been able to find these places that have become so supportive of her.

'So I'm a bit worried,' Ernie says, 'that I'll go back to Canada and I'll have only seen the top of your head.'

I look up slowly. I'm expecting to see Ernie's smile, but there's an anxiety in his expression that hasn't been there before.

'Sorry,' I say.

He's observing me closely, as if trying to work me out.

'I've been concerned ever since you called. I've got to ask, and you've got to answer me properly. Are you all right? What's been going on?'

Something's loosening in my chest.

'Is it your mum? Your sister?'

I nod.

'Did something bad happen?'

I think of everything that has happened these past three months. I think of my sister's torn body, the hissed words, the whispering. I think of the panic building up in my chest on the plane, that she would never fully recover.

Then I'm looking around this café, at the friendly faces of the staff, the noticeboard crammed with adverts for yoga and Pilates and meditation and also for mental health groups. I'm thinking of the warmth of the studio, my sister's amazing paintings. I think of all that I've started to share with Shanthi, and she with me, however much she's holding back too. Of how I'm coming to understand something of her illness, and with this knowledge, allowing the fear to drip away. I think of my mother, her hair cut and dyed black again, the swelling going down on her fingers, the way she's started to bounce to Tesco, even though to some it's an alarming sight.

'It's not really bad,' I tell Ernie. 'It's not bad at all.'

I flick the breadcrumb off the table. The sweet peas are between us, giving off their gentle fragrance. Our hands rest on the surface, fingers so close, but not quite touching.

'You are cleaning?'

Mum sounds surprised, but then I don't think she knew I owned a feather duster.

She piles her ample body into my flat, then stops short. The vacuum cleaner's in the lounge and there's a tin of Pledge on top of the coffee table.

'Are you moving?' she asks.

'Not yet.'

She follows me into the kitchen, where a large saucepan is bubbling on the gas ring.

'Chicken?' Her nose is almost in the pan; she turns around and regards me like a sniffer dog.

'Quorn.' I hold up the empty packet. She views it with suspicion.

'It's a vegetable casserole, Mum. I'll come over to yours and cook it for a Sunday dinner. That would make a nice change, wouldn't it?'

Mum looks aghast. She's had curry every single day for over fifty years, starting off in the amniotic sac.

'Tea?' I ask, while her mouth's still open. Mum gets to the kettle first and peers inside.

'Limescale,' she says, and closes her mouth, like the world is finally making sense.

It's Saturday, I've got the weekend off and Ernie's coming over for dinner. His flight back to Vancouver is tomorrow. We've seen each other four more times over these past two weeks, meeting in cafés and restaurants and talking until all the other customers have gone and the staff are waiting by the door. But this is the first time he'll have come here. I glance at the clock: it's three, five hours before he is due. Surely Mum will have left by then.

'You should pull out this furniture.' The limescale has given her the confidence to go back out into the lounge and struggle with the sofa. 'And get the vacuum cleaner behind it.'

'I've finished vacuuming.'

'And where is your stepladder? There is a cobweb on the ceiling.'

'I don't have a stepladder, Mum.'

'No stepladder?' She looks at me in astonishment.

'Use the chair. Actually, don't use anything at all. It's just a cobweb.'

'Anjali, if you don't take care of your home, you will never find a man.'

I was wondering how long it would take her to fit that one in. I'm kind of tempted to tell her about Ernie. An engineer is definitely in her top ten career choices; after the failure of the WBM and Roshan, she might be willing to accept his Nigerian-Irish origins – and one mention of Buddhism and she'll be anybody's.

But I'm not clear where things are going with Ernie right now. We've talked a lot, but nothing else. His lips have only brushed my cheek at the end of the night, even though I've been aching for so much more. I'm not sure if it's him who's holding back, or me, or maybe both of us, not knowing where we stand.

'Shanthi OK?' I go for the safer option.

Mum looks down from where she's wobbling on my chair. 'She is not home very much.'

'Better than how it used to be, when all she did was stay in.'

'I think she is with this man a lot.'

I glance up at her furrowed brow, and realise why she's turned up at my flat. 'You're worried.'

'We do not know a thing about him, Anjali.'

Guilt edges my spine. If I explained a bit about Ben, she might relax. But then a sculptor isn't anywhere near her top career choices; she's probably never even said the word out loud. And if I mention his age she'll topple from the chair to her death and

I'll have to explain to Aunty Mala that I have cobwebs on my ceiling.

'Mum, you've just got to trust her.'

Mum sighs. She steps down from the chair, the unused feather duster cradled in her arms. 'You are right, Anjali. I know you are right. But she is my first baby.'

'We need to let her live her own life.'

'Yes, yes, Lucy told me.' Mum sinks into the pulled-out sofa. She runs her hand through her short hair, a tiny tuft sticking up on the crown. 'My girls must be independent. It is time to stop interfering.'

I blink.

'Let me just stir the casserole.' I go back into the kitchen, not quite sure how to handle a rational mother.

'And what are you going to do now?' Mum calls to me. 'Now that Clara is going?'

'I'm not sure. Find a job somewhere.'

'You must go back to university.'

I pause, wooden spoon in hand. 'Mum, what did you just say about interfering?'

'This is not interfering, Anjali. This is making a suggestion. Can a mother not make a suggestion to her second-born?'

'I don't think I want to go back to uni.'

'You can get your degree. And then your master's. And then a PhC.'

'PhD.'

'And then you will be a DOCTOR.' She shrieks the last word.

I go back to stirring the casserole. It would be weird if Mum changed too much. But her words are nudging the little ball of anxiety in the pit of my stomach. The shop will be sold soon,

Clara gone. I cannot imagine my life without them. And Ernie? What if things really could work out between us, as I lie awake in the early hours of the morning hoping that they might? Would I just go back to the way I was before, with Jack? Working long hours somewhere, no time to think, always feeling like I didn't know what I was doing with my life?

My phone beeps.

It's funny the way people contact you just when you're thinking about them. I pull out my mobile to reply to Ernie. But the message isn't from him.

It's been so long, Anj. But if you ever want to talk, I'm still here.

Jack.

'You don't know how close you came to meeting my mother.'

Ernie's arrived. He's sitting on the sofa with the peppermint tea I only just remembered to rush out and buy, minutes before he was due. He's been here for almost half an hour, and I haven't been able to slow down yet, checking on the casserole, the rice, pulling down the hem of my green linen skirt (the final choice out of eight hundred items of clothing), showing him things: my dog-eared florists' manual, my fresh sweet peas, just how squeaky shiny I get those rubber plant leaves. I'm not clear if he's interested in rubber plants; I only know that for some reason I can't stop talking about them.

'We'll eat outside, right?' I say. 'It's lovely. The weather, I mean, not the food. I've got no idea about the food.'

When it's all laid out on my tiny table, and I've finally got him out there, next to my roses and the lavender that soon will be in bloom, the fresh May breeze mixing with the aroma of the casserole, I still can't sit down.

He takes my hands. I've been wanting to feel his hands on mine for so long, to remember their warmth, the feel of his knuckles under the pads of my fingers. Everything is thudding – my chest, my head, every tiny pulse in my body.

'This is great. It's all great,' he says. 'And I would have loved to meet your mother.'

'No you wouldn't.' I'm aware he's still holding my hands. 'It would have been an inquisition. You would have missed your flight.'

'My mum was the same,' he says. 'You wouldn't have escaped either.'

'Maybe it's an immigrant thing. You move for your safety and security, then you can't stop manifesting it over your kids for the rest of your life.'

'Will we be the same?' he muses.

I get an odd sensation then, thinking of the kind of parents we could be. I shake it off, because children are so far away from the plans I don't have, and I haven't given this man his dinner yet. I let go of his hands, and we sit.

'Did your mum make Nigerian food every day? And tell you about Abuja while you were eating it?' I ask him.

He laughs, the sound I have bottled up and played back in my head every night. 'Not every day. Dad needed his potatoes. But a lot.'

'What did you have?'

'Man, I miss her jollof rice. And pepper stew. It makes me rethink vegetarianism.'

'Are there Nigerian restaurants in Vancouver?'

'There's everything. It's a good place, Anjali. Trudeau might get in; it feels hopeful out there.'

I want to say: *But you'll come back, won't you?*

We eat. I pour wine, trying to keep mine to just a glass. I don't want to get drunk and blot out our last evening. Ernie eats steadily, praises the food, but there's something quieter about him tonight, something he seems to be holding back, waiting there in the cleft between his eyebrows, the pauses between his words. The light is fading, the breeze picking up, the hair I tried to pat down as much as possible now threatening to unleash itself, to take flight. I clear our plates away and we go back to the lounge.

Ernie looks at the photographs on the mantelpiece of my mother and sister. Taken so many years ago now, but their essence still captured there in the pictures: my mum's fiery eyes, my sister's always searching.

'I'd have liked to meet your sister too,' he says. 'I'm so glad the two of you are getting closer again.'

Glancing down at the coffee table, I see my phone, with Jack's message inside. It feels odd, like he's somehow there between me and Ernie, telling me that I'm not quite being truthful.

'Anjali, who did this?'

'What?'

Looking up, I see Ernie holding a piece of paper that was tucked behind the photographs. He's staring at an image of himself sketched out in pencil.

'Shanthi.'

'From a photo?' I can see him thinking that we haven't taken pictures, that he doesn't have a Facebook profile.

'I told her about you.'

He's turning it this way and that, touching the ridge of his cheekbones, the base of his jaw. He hands the picture back to me, astonishment etched into the lines around his eyes.

I look down at the paper. I see the pencil in Shanthi's hand, her frown as she sharpened some lines, loosened others. Working away until it was done, hot chocolate growing cold beside her. Her own face lighting up as she passed the drawing back to me.

'It's funny,' I say, softly. 'How I didn't realise. That I was the one who was scared of mental illness.' He's looking at me, but I'm not sure now whether I'm talking to him or to myself. 'I didn't realise I was just as responsible for the stigma. For the stuff that made my dad's life harder. My sister's life harder.'

I listen to the sound of Ernie's breath.

'It stopped me,' I say. 'From seeing who she was all this time.'

He touches my shoulder, a wave of warmth travelling down my spine. 'But you see her now.'

We both look at the picture in my hands, the clear lines of his features, the shadows of his skin. I rest the drawing back behind my sister's photograph. Looking up at the image of her, taken before she went to Goldsmith's, before any of us knew what lay ahead.

Ernie turns me around and cups my face in his palms, more warmth coursing through my body from the press of his fingers. I see myself in his pupils, wild-haired, waiting.

I kiss him.

It's funny how things change. I remember how his lips once made me want to be consumed, and excreted with a left-wing national newspaper. But it's different now. When our mouths touch, I feel like I'm dissolving. But not fading away or disappearing into him. More like becoming part of something else. I reach up into his warm body, his arms tightening around me.

After a while, we break apart from each other. I take his hand.

I haven't brought a man to my bed since the Architect. The

sheets and pillows are free of Jack's dents. Ernie takes the place where Jack used to be, and for a moment I'm expecting the old ache to come back, the one that has been lodged for so long in my chest. But I'm only aware now of its absence, of how much easier it feels to breathe.

I slip off the linen skirt, unbutton my grey top. Ernie has taken off his T-shirt and I rest against him, touching the outline of his ribs, kissing the spaces where his own aches may have lain; might still lie.

We're fully unclothed. Once, I would have tried to cover myself up, to shield myself from being seen. It was always too much to look down on the soft, movable flesh of my body. To compare myself to the thin women in magazines, to the women who came into Jack's life. But it occurs to me that I haven't thought about the burlesque dancer's beautiful physique for a long time now.

Ernie lays me back on the mattress. I feel the warm press of his lips and the tender touch of his fingers as they travel down my body. When I come, there are tears in my eyes, but it isn't like last time. I'm not crying because of fear, or distress. The tears touch my skin now for this intimacy, for finding myself in a place I could not have imagined almost a year ago.

He pulls himself up. Stroking my cheek, smoothing away a tear. When we go on to have sex, I think about how things were when I first met him. How desperate I was to be saved, to be carried away on a life of meditation. To be connected to the Buddhism that had always been part of my family. Falling in love with the idea of who I could be.

Opening my eyes for a moment, I study his closed ones: his long, curly eyelashes, the little crinkle of his lids. I gaze at the deep cleft in his brow and listen to his steady breath go in and out, in and out. I wonder if he might be the person I could share my bed with for always. The person who might talk to me into the early hours, telling me about the love he once knew with his own family, the love he lost. The person who might never hurt me. Who might hold me tight and never let me go.

But my phone's still out there, in the other room. Those few words on its screen, telling me the past isn't quite ready to let me go either.

'There's something on your mind,' Ernie says, when we are lying back on my pillows, side by side. I look down at our bodies, our arms and legs touching, remembering the channel of loneliness I once felt between me and the Architect.

'I think there's something on yours too,' I say.

'You first. Is it Jack?'

I wonder how he knows. Maybe I've always been too easy to read.

'I got a message from him today.'

'You've still not spoken to him?'

I shake my head. 'Not properly. A phone call in Sri Lanka, when I was looking for Shanthi. But nothing else.'

He is quiet for a while. 'Maybe you should see him.'

My eyes follow the faded scar over the back of his upper arm. I'm not sure that I want to see Jack, not sure what I would say to him now. But that message is there in my mobile, and with it the thought that somehow I'm not being honest with myself. 'Maybe.'

Ernie's quiet again. The clock is ticking out in the hallway, counting down the hours until he has to catch his flight.

'I've thought about you a lot since Christmas,' he says, eventually. 'There were so many times I wanted to call you.'

'Why didn't you?'

266

'I was never sure. There seemed to be so much you needed to sort out here. I didn't know if I would just complicate it all.' He looks upwards at the ceiling. 'They offered me a full-time position out there. In Vancouver.'

I close my eyes. I knew, deep down, that these words were coming.

'I could apply for a permanent resident card if I want to,' he says.

'Do you want to?'

He turns to me. 'I came back here to find out.'

My head is throbbing.

'I thought I'd sorted myself out, Anjali. All that time away in India. Meditation, herbal teas, that was all I needed, right? Then I met you. And I saw all the stuff that was missing in my life. It's been so good hanging out with my bro. Spending time with his kids. Seeing my sister. All that time, being alone. I had no idea I was drifting. I forgot I was lost.'

I stare at his wrist, making out the faint beat of his pulse.

The clock is still ticking. Tomorrow, he'll be boarding a plane. Maybe his brother will be there to meet him at the airport, to drive him back to his place for a meal. His nephew, six years old, his niece, a little older, waiting on the doorstep for the uncle they love. Scouting him out for presents, their father telling them to give Ernie a chance, he's only just got back.

He sits up, turns to face me.

'If you ask me to stay, I'll stay.'

When I was a child, I always wanted blue eyes, like my dad's. I've never realised how many shades of brown there are. Ernie's eyes are sometimes chestnut, sometimes caramel, sometimes just as they are now, shining with deep flecks of gold.

I know what I want to say. To tell him, without a doubt, that

I'm over Jack, that the message on my phone means nothing to me. To tell him that he isn't lost. That I've been waiting for him all these months to come home.

But there are other pictures in my mind. Of a man broken after burying his parents. Of a man waking up in a hospital bed, listening to the sound of monitors, unfamiliar footsteps tapping the hospital floors, feeling totally and utterly alone. Of a man now, years later, meeting his family again. Who might, a little while down the line, have a chance to meet someone special. Someone who lives over there, who won't separate him from all that he's found, who isn't lugging around baggage of their own.

There's a pricking behind my eyelids. I can't stand in the way of Ernie's happiness. Not when it's been so important to me to sort things out with my own family. Not when I don't know what I can offer him, when I don't know what I'm doing with my life. I can't make him give up his.

'I think your life is there,' I whisper.

I find his hand. He clasps mine back tightly. For a while we lie together, our fingers cradled, not moving. Then he starts to pull on his clothes and gather up his things. I think of sitting on the floor of this room, my knees bunched up to my chest, when Jack was packing his small bag. I think of sitting in this bed, watching the Architect pulling on his jacket. But back then there was something hard and painful in my heart; now it's soft and won't stay contained.

Ernie looks back at me from the door. The stubble bristles the smooth curve of his scalp and I want to feel it once more, running beneath my fingers.

He frowns, like he's going to speak, like he might tell me this is all bullshit and we should be together. And despite everything

I want for him, there's a big part of me hanging out to hear these words.

His face softens.

'You should stay true to your experience,' he says, gently.

Seconds later, I hear the door close.

I sit on the bed for a long time, listening to voices coming and going on the street and the sound of the cars outside. Couples and families tucked up inside their houses, doing the washing-up, sitting around the television, maybe already asleep.

Eventually I pull on my dressing gown and go out into the lounge. Ernie's mug on the side, the remnants of our dinner in the kitchen. My phone still sitting there on the coffee table. The sweet peas there too, resting in a little glass of water.

Soon I will be leaving this flat; soon I will be leaving the shop. With each day that passes, the feeling of disorientation is starting to increase. And soon Clara won't be here to help me make sense of things.

I crouch down in front of the sweet peas and take in their honeyed scent. I can't imagine my life without the flowers. No matter what happens to me, they always seem to stay steady.

My thirtieth birthday falls in the middle of June. Once, I would have hired out a bar, invited school friends and friends from that first year at uni, caught up with people I hadn't seen for months and drunk so much wine that all conversations would be blotted out the next day. Back then it wouldn't have occurred to me to invite Mum and Shanthi along. It's strange now to imagine cele-brating without them.

So when the day comes, I put on a black dress and Clara prepares a feast. Her flat above the shop doesn't have a dining room. She clears a space and sets up a fold-out table on the shop floor, decorating it with fat white candles and the last of our sweet peas.

It's funny seeing Mum in the shop, looking out of place in the red and gold sari that's been at the back of her wardrobe for years. She wanders past our pots and buckets, bending low every now and again to sniff the flowers. Maybe she's hunting for cannabis.

Shanthi looks out of place, too. I realise she's never once been to the shop, despite my almost eleven years of working here. She gazes at the displays, the indigo freesias, the plump peonies, the peppery scented stocks. She's quiet like she usually is, and a little awkward in the cornflower-blue shift dress Mum bought her for the occasion. But there's something in her eyes that I can't quite put my finger on, a new kind of brightness maybe. When the four of us are crammed around the table, Mum eyeing with suspicion the Quorn Thai dish Clara's brought down from upstairs (I stipulated that for my mother's sake it had to be some form of curry), I notice Shanthi take a breath and wonder if she's going to tell us what might be on her mind. Then the moment passes and she's back to studying us all, taking in the conversation.

Which is mainly Mum quizzing Clara.

'So you are not knowing what you are going to do next?' she's asking.

'Not a bit,' Clara says happily.

'You are giving up this business ... and your home ... and going away ... and you do not have a plan?' Mum's getting a little high-pitched.

'That's right.' Clara's voice is gleeful.

'Not even a small plan?'

'Not even a tiny one.'

270

'What about your security?'

'I hate security.'

Mum turns to the front door, panicked.

'There's an alarm,' Clara reassures her. 'I didn't mean that kind of security.'

Mum turns back, a little relieved. 'But what if you are making a mistake?' She glances around the shop that she's been begging me to leave for over a decade. 'What if you change your mind?'

Clara chews another mouthful of Thai curry. 'I've thought about this for a while, Mrs C. I've realised I'm happiest in transition.'

'In trans . . . ?'

'When I'm between places.'

Mum's looking at her in disbelief.

'I think I might be like that too,' Shanthi ventures shyly.

We all turn to my sister. She looks discomforted, like she didn't realise she'd spoken out loud.

'What d'you mean?' I ask her.

'When I'm not too sure what the future's going to bring.' She nods, avoiding our gaze.

Mum seems now in danger of a heart attack.

I study my sister keenly, noting again that brightness in her lowered eyes.

At the end of the meal, Clara brings out a coffee and brazil nut cake, crammed with candles, and the presents I specifically didn't ask for, including a framed photo of the two of us from years ago, in dungarees, holding buckets and brushes, laughing as we painted the shop walls pale blue. I stare down at our happy faces, a lump in my throat, and wonder if Jack took the picture. Mum hands me an envelope of money that I desperately need despite my protestations.

Shanthi doesn't give me her present until later, when Clara and Mum have taken the dishes upstairs to wash up. She passes me a canvas wrapped in brown paper. Pulling it out, I see a painting of a fox at the end of a road, its eyes burning orange in the glow of oncoming headlights. She looks at me apologetically.

'I've been working on this for a while. Then I wasn't sure whether to give it to you.' She knows what happened with Ernie. 'But I thought you might want it anyway.'

The fox gazes back at me, the streaks of its red coat shimmering in the candlelight. I wonder, as I so often do, where Ernie might be now.

'Is it OK?' Shanthi asks. 'Do you mind . . . being reminded?'

I shake my head. I think about what Ernie said all that time ago, that keeping out the pain only keeps out the good as well. No matter what, I'll always be grateful for the brief time the two of us spent together, even if there'll always be a sadness that comes with it.

I squeeze Shanthi's shoulder. 'I love it. Thank you.'

Later, when Mum and Shanthi have gone and Clara is cleaning up the last bits ready to open again tomorrow, I wander around the shop. I feel grateful for everything it has given me: a space to shelter in all these years, a space tonight to hold my family. Clara's still waiting for a buyer, and more than once I've hoped that things could just stay as they are. Unlike my best friend and my sister, I guess I'm always searching to be settled. It's funny, to think this might be something Mum and I have in common, neither of us really taking to transition. I wonder if Shanthi takes after Dad. I wonder again about the sparkle in her eyes and what it might mean.

*

At the end of the week, I find out. When I arrive at Mum's on Sunday, I find her sweet peas wilting. That's what happens when you leave them in the dark with no water, I think a little irritably, picking the vase up from the dining table and examining them. I take the flowers through to the kitchen and stop short. The counters are overflowing with dirty pans, chopping boards and open spice bottles.

My mother must be dead. It's the only possible explanation for the mess. She didn't even come waddling when I opened the front door. The flat is silent; there is no sign of Ordie. Putting the vase down on a turmeric stain, I rush back into the hallway.

'Mum? You home? Where are you?'

It's Sunday – she has to be dead because there is nowhere else she can be. She would never work Sundays; family time is far too sacred to her.

As I stand in the hallway pondering the possible demise of my mother, I realise that I don't want to lose these Sundays either. I look into Shanthi's room. Empty. There is a fear gripping my chest that I am losing them both.

'Mum?' I call again, pausing outside the closed door of her bedroom. From the cracks in the frame comes the scent of sandalwood, but nothing new is burning. I can't hear any movement.

'You in there?'

I turn the handle of the door and walk in. The curtains are drawn and it's gloomy, but there she is, lying in bed, the duvet pulled up to her chin. She's definitely alive: the covers are moving up and down – she's always been a bit of a heavy breather, my mum, owing to all the weight her lungs have to support – and her eyes are open.

'Mum? What's the matter? Are you OK? Are you sick?' I pull

open the curtains and flood Mum's body with evening sunshine, making her wince. 'Have you got a temperature?' I lay the back of my hand against her forehead, panicked that I've never seen her like this before. What if she really is sick? I berate myself for my selfish lack of a medical degree and never becoming a doctor to help her on her deathbed. Then I remember the National Health Service. 'Shall I call the out-of-hours GP?'

'There is no need,' Mum says, drawing out each word like an invalid. 'It is too late.'

'What d'you mean? What's happened? What's wrong with you?'

'It is too late for help.' Mum reveals some final strength and shifts herself up the bed. I see she is fully clothed, in her favourite Persian-rug dress, and she smells of newly toasted spices as if she's not long come in from the kitchen. Her hair is shining and her skin is a normal kind of warm. This woman is not sick. Relieved, I sit down on the bed beside her.

'Stop talking in riddles, Mum,' I say, 'and tell me what's happened to make you get into bed on a Sunday when you've just finished cooking and are going to make the sheets stink?'

That works. She almost leaps off the mattress. '*Anay*,' she says, bending down to smell the covers. 'You are right, Anjali. I am going to have to wash these.'

'So tell me more,' I say.

'I'll have to take the sheets—'

'No, not about the washing, Mum. About what's happened. Why are you behaving so weirdly?'

She pauses, then sinks back onto the bed, obviously deciding it doesn't matter now, the sheets are done for anyway.

A thought occurs to me. 'Is it Shanthi? Is she OK? Has something happened to her?'

Mum nods, in slow motion. 'Yes, Anjali, something has happened to your sister.'

Panic is starting to rise again. 'What's happened? For God's sake, just tell me what's going on!'

I'm sure that if this was someone else's mum, this would be the point where they would divulge everything. But my mum is my mum and it takes a good half-hour more to get the full story. Even then it comes out in slightly puzzling words that require a bit of time to put together.

I think I've got this straight.

Shanthi is moving in with her boyfriend. Except it turns out Shanthi's boyfriend isn't a boy.

Eleven

When was I first told about The One? Was it the magazines (*How to know if he is Mr Right: ten helpful signs!*) or books I read, the films I watched, the stories people passed on to me? Was it a combination of all of those things? Probably. I guess it's not just about The One; I guess you assimilate a lot of ideas and opinions over the years and find yourself, a way down the line, mulling it over, wondering why you took it all to be fact when the truth is ... life is much more complicated than that. Nothing is ever so clear-cut. Girls don't always fancy boys, neurotic mums can (sometimes) be reasonable, sworn players of the field can fall in love with percussionists, one-night stands can provide a useful workout, and people who cheat on you with burlesque dancers are not always bad people. Although it might be helpful to think so for a time, if only to have some of those one-night stands and raise your heart rate a little.

Eleven years ago, I thought I'd met my One. It was July. I'd just turned nineteen and was standing outside a flower shop. It was the university holidays and I'd scraped together enough money for a couple of months' rent in a shared flat. But I was sick of the bar work and smelling like a chippy. I wondered if this was how it would be if I moved out of Mum's.

I was contemplating the future when I saw the sunflower. Sunflowers have always seemed a bit magical to me. The Incas used to worship them as a symbol of the sun god. Way back in the 1500s, they discovered gold figures of sunflowers in temples in the Andes. I like to think about the people of this Peruvian empire gazing at these plants in awe, watching the faces of the flowers turn east at sunrise and wondering if they followed the earth's star westwards. A lot of flowers do this; they call it heliotropism. But in the sunflower it's only the immature buds that show this motion; by the time they're mature, they're fixed. Usually eastwards.

That day, the particular flower that had caught my attention was standing in a pot outside the shopfront. It was wearing a sign. ASSISTANT NEEDED. ENQUIRE WITHIN.

I walked into the shop and was surrounded by the tall plants, dazzled by bright yellow heads. The room was filled with the scent of summer fields. At the counter was another sunflower. And a dreadlocked woman, having some kind of fight with it.

'This bugger won't stand straight.' The woman turned to me, dreadlocks bouncing around her shoulders.

'You're looking for some help?'

'Nothing doing. Nothing's going to get this fella to stand up for itself.'

'No, I mean, you need an assistant in the shop?'

'Oh.' The woman took me in for the first time. I wondered what I was wearing and looked down at my jeans and flip-flops. 'What do you know about these guys?' She held out her invalid sunflower and a pack of seeds.

'I know the Incas used to worship them,' I told her.

'And?'

'I know that a sunflower head is actually made up of lots of little florets. It's a head of flowers.'

'And?'

'I know that Vogel proposed an equation for the pattern of the florets in 1979.'

'What?'

No, no, I'm kidding, I didn't actually say that, although I did find it on Wikipedia years later.

'But what about their growth season and when to plant them and what soils they thrive in and how much sunlight they need?'

'Oh,' I said. 'I didn't realise you meant useful stuff.' I looked down at my feet. 'I don't know any of that.'

'You can't wear those if you work here.'

'What?' I looked up again.

'Flip-flops.'

'Oh. Why?'

'Because it's freezing in a florist's. You'll get frostbite. My name's Clara. What's yours?'

'Anjali.'

'Can you start Tuesday?'

'You're giving me the job?'

'Yes.'

'Why?'

'Because I like your flip-flops. Havaianas, aren't they?'

I left the shop on a high and stumbled into Jack.

I've made it sound like a particularly fortuitous day, meeting both Jack and Clara in one morning. Truth is, of course, I'd actually met Jack for the first time a few days previously, when he opened the door of his flat to me. He showed me a living room crammed with guitars and surfboards, a cluttered kitchen, and the tiny room that would one day be mine. We sat on his sofa and started chatting, and afterwards I couldn't remember what we'd talked about, only the heady sensation that had come with the words. And a realisation that for the first time in a long time, I hadn't thought about my sister and the situation at home.

'Do you want the flat?' he asked, at the end.

A yearning filled my chest. The same feeling I was experiencing a couple of days later, when we bumped into each other outside the shop.

It's funny how you can't know how significant a person will become when you first meet them. At that point, Jack was just a man who gave me goose pimples during a July heatwave. A future flatmate I might have always had a crush on, who might never have felt the same way about me.

'You're actually wearing a genuine Cheshire cat grin,' he informed me.

'I've just got a job.'

'Where?'

I jerked my thumb to indicate the shop.

'For the summer?'

'Maybe.' I still wasn't sure about university.

'Nice one. So are you all set to move in with us?'

The room wasn't going to be available for another month, when the current flatmate left for his travels. Nothing was signed. I hadn't mentioned it to Mum. I could pull out later, if I needed to.

I nodded. 'Definitely.'

He was looking at me curiously. 'This is your first time away from home, right?'

'Right.'

'You saw our place. It's messy.'

I thought of Mum's shabby but pristine flat. Her daily rounds picking up my sister's cigarette butts, spraying our bedroom with air freshener, the nausea of tobacco and sandalwood and vanilla. 'It's perfect.'

'It's hard to get Andy to do the washing-up.'

Mum's whirlwind cleaning sprees were growing in frequency, the Marigolds discarded, her hands cracking and bleeding. 'That's fine.'

'And one of us is usually playing music till late.'

'Are you trying to get me to change my mind?'

He smiled, a dimple in the centre of each cheek. His face was scattered with freckles as fine as gold dust, his auburn hair tinged with summer sun.

'I'm just worried we'll disappoint you.'

An image of my mum, sitting alone at the dining table, came into my mind. Of my sister, lying awake in bed, unreachable, the pale sheets stained with grey ash. I didn't know that by the time the house share was available, she would have already been in hospital for a couple of weeks. I didn't want to think about what was going to happen. If I could push those images away, they didn't exist.

'You won't disappoint me.'

We stood there for a while, the sunflower like a gooseberry between us, and I couldn't think of an excuse to keep him talking. In a moment we'd have to walk away.

'So if we're going to be flatmates,' he broke the silence, 'd'you fancy a drink?'

When he smiled again, his blue eyes were lost in crinkle. When he smiled, I thought he was The One.

*

So one year has passed since Jack and I broke up, and the shop is bursting once more with sunflowers. These seem more beautiful than any I have ever seen, because each time I look at them, I remember how I met Clara, and I remember too that I am saying goodbye to her.

'I'm not gone yet,' she keeps telling me. 'We've got a lot of shit to sort out first. You can't get depressed till I'm actually on the plane, and even then, you don't have time to mope. You've got to be in possession of all your faculties.'

I really do need to be in possession of all my faculties.

I'm buying the business, you see.

It started after Ernie left my flat. An idea that I didn't pay attention to at first because all I could see was the way his hands had held the sweet peas. But it returned on the evening of my birthday, then again when I was crouched beside my mother's false deathbed, staring at her panicked, but very much alive, face. She was consumed with worry about Shanthi, and all I could think was: Shanthi's got courage. She's being true to her experience.

You can do this, Anjali.

That's what my dad would have said, I'm sure of it. I'm so grateful that my imagined conversations with him are always so supportive.

I love the flowers. I always have. I never wanted to leave them.
I can do this.

Maybe I can't. I'll be broke. I couldn't do it without Mum, who lent me the deposit. I found a cheap suit in a charity shop, and begged the bank for the rest. I still can't believe the loan went through. I'd love to rent Clara's flat above the shop as well, but that's no way affordable right now. I've got to move back into my mother's for a while. It's not only my deceased parent who is being supportive. I can't believe how much Mum is backing me.

'I am proud of you, Anjali,' she said to me sometime last week when my back was turned.

Although I'm not completely sure whether she did say it, or whether I am now making up conversations with both of my parents, dead and alive. I swung back round to her asking, 'What was that?'

But she didn't say it again.

Turns out she's been putting away for a wedding fund all these years for me and Shanthi. Now, deciding I'm too much of a geriatric and Shanthi's too much of a lesbian (she hasn't caught up about gay marriage), she thinks the money needs to be otherwise spent. Shanthi said she'd help me in the shop too.

Maybe we'll never be able to pull this off, and eventually I'll just pack up my belongings on the end of an old stick and go off in search of Clara and the percussionist.

It's kind of exciting, not knowing. Maybe I'm OK in transition after all.

You can do this, Anjali, you can do this.

I'm not sure if that's me, my live parent or my dead one.

So this is it, this is me. The 4 a.m. rises, the trips to the traders' market, the deliveries, the conditioning, the watering, the arranging, the internet orders, the demands, the stock takes, and all of my plans for the future. Greeting cards that Shanthi will design. Weddings: there are going to be a lot more; it's going to mean even longer hours for free consultations and a hell of a lot more scissor-induced blisters. The last wedding we did, we had to snap the ends off over a thousand carnations.

All of this without any of Clara's laughter, just our ghosts hanging out there in the shadows with the scent of old roses. But

I'll be spending more time with my sister. And Anna, our student assistant, makes me laugh. She's hardly been around, what with her dissertation and all, but after graduation she'll be helping out until she decides what to do next. I'll be her manager. All of this responsibility is getting a bit daunting.

'Breathe, breathe.' Clara hits me on the back when she catches me about to hyperventilate one afternoon.

'What if I mess this up?' I'm mindful of not putting the fear of God into her before she hands me the keys.

Fortunately, as a mild Buddhist, I can't put the fear of God into anyone.

'Then you'll be fucked,' she says, cheerfully. 'But you'll sort it out.'

My laptop's open, the screen full of figures, and I'm wondering how proud Ernie might also be, if he knew. But I'm doing my best to put him out of my mind. Even though there's a growing emptiness in my stomach when I think of never seeing him again, I'm glad that he might be happy. I look back at the screen, and try to concentrate on the accounts.

'Whisky?' Clara catches my frown.

'Clara, I have to make this official. I detest whisky. Dad's favourite drink or not.'

'Not even in preparation for tonight?'

I gaze up into the ocean green of her eyes.

'OK, just one,' I concede.

Mum's reading up about art. The library books are spread open on her kitchen counter, dangerously close to the turmeric.

'This man, Hockey. He is painting for children, yes?'

'Hockney. And no.'

'Then what does it mean, Anjali? All of this colour?'

'I think it's about sexual freedom, Mum.'

'What?'

No, no, I don't say that, although it's kind of on the tip of my tongue.

Mum puts the lid on the rice cooker and turns the book upside down. 'And what about this, Anjali? All of these circles?'

I squint at Kandinsky, then close the book. 'Mum, maybe you don't need to try so hard.'

'But she will be here any minute.'

'And you can't learn all of this in a minute. Besides, she's a sculptor.'

'Those books were heavy.'

We hear voices outside; going to the window, we see the backs of two people coming in the front door.

Mum can't go pale, but she sort of does.

'Don't panic, Mum.'

'I must spray the house.' She gets out the can.

'No, you mustn't.'

'What should I say about Hockey?'

'Hockney. And nothing, Mum. Don't say anything. Just listen instead.'

'Listen?' Mum looks startled.

The door opens. They're here.

The four of us are squashed into the kitchen, the library books stuffed hurriedly in a cupboard. Donna kisses me on the cheek. I catch the coconut scent of her cropped, shimmering hair, reminding me of gorse flowers in spring.

'I wanted to tell you,' she murmurs in my ear.

I think of the assumption I made about Shanthi and Ben, the assumptions I've generally made for all these years about everybody:

my mother, my father, Clara, Ernie. About mental illness; about my place in the world.

'I'm really happy for you guys.' I squeeze her hand and hope she'll believe me. Her fingers are long, the skin rough. I imagine the hours she worked away on the sculpture of the giant woman, who Shanthi says I'll see again at the exhibition.

I see Mum taking Donna in: her sandalled feet and the gold ring on her toe, the tattooed bracelet of thorns around her ankle. Her shorn-off trousers, her velvet shirt. Upwards to her neck, to the peacock feather gleaming in its iridescent colours. There is alarm in Mum's stretched temples. 'Food is ready.' She bustles us out to the dining room.

Her table maybe reflects her state of mind, covered in so many dishes of food there isn't room for our plates. She's never one to sit much during big occasions, but now she won't stop hovering, filling up plates the minute a mouthful is taken, the rest of us trying to make conversation in the brief intervals between servings. I glance at Shanthi. In her usual baggy jeans and T-shirt, scruffy hair scooped into its bun, there's a different sort of calmness about her. About twenty-five minutes in, when our bellies have been tested beyond breaking point, she catches my eye and says, 'Mum. It's your turn to sit.'

Then she gets up, small hands on Mum's shoulders, and deposits her into the spare place at the table. I serve the lentils up onto her plate, Shanthi adds the rice. Donna rises, goes over to Mum's side and starts spooning on the aubergines. Mum looks bemused by all the attention.

'I must just . . .' She attempts to get up.

'No you don't,' says Shanthi.

Mum looks from me to my sister, then she starts eating. Our natter has now dried up, and I'm becoming all too aware of the silence, broken by clinking cutlery. Mum's still eyeing Donna up warily, every so often pausing. Then she opens her mouth, about to say something. I brace myself. It's going to have the word Hockey in it.

'This is just fantastic food, Manisha.' Donna gets in first.

Mum blinks. I don't think Jack ever called her by her first name.

'These aubergines – they're something else,' Donna goes on, undisturbed. 'Have you got a recipe, or is it just in your head?'

Mum hesitates, as if not sure whether to curb her evident pleasure in the question. 'You must salt them thoroughly,' she says finally. 'And slice them very, very thinly. Anjali does not do that.'

'It's true,' I concede.

'Do you have a good knife?' Mum asks Donna.

'Not for cooking. That's the secret, is it?'

Then they're off. Donna takes her through every dish on the table, her quiet, interested voice moving Mum on to talk about her childhood meals, her early life in Sri Lanka, the change in her cooking when she moved to this country and couldn't locate the tamarind.

'There are more things now,' Mum says. 'The other day I saw a coconut. A *king* coconut.'

Donna's eyebrows rise.

'But you will taste all of these things for yourself. When you come to Sri Lanka.'

Donna's eyes light up.

We leave them to it, Shanthi and I going out to the kitchen to wash up while Donna and Mum sit side by side now, heads bent together. Shanthi washes, I dry. For a while we don't speak, following the same rhythm we have for years, the only sounds the slosh of the sink water, the occasional squeak of the tea towel against glass. Then I find the courage.

'I already knew Donna,' I tell my sister. 'I went to your studio.'

Shanthi turns off the tap. 'She told me.'

'I'm sorry. I shouldn't have gone behind your back.'

Shanthi rinses off another plate and passes it to me. 'It helped, you know. I'd told Donna to leave me alone. After seeing you, she came and found me again.'

I hold the wet plate, water dripping onto the scratched lino. 'I'm glad for you, Shanthi. For how happy you are. You are happy, aren't you?'

Shanthi doesn't answer. I notice how her hand still shakes as it grips a bowl. I think of the reasons she came off her drugs, wondering how hard it might be to maintain a relationship when the bits that make you up have been dulled.

'I think so,' she says, after a while. 'But what is happiness anyway, Anjie? I only know that this feels right.'

I think about this. 'I envy you. I'm never sure what's right.' I see Ernie beside me in bed, his shining brown eyes saying that he would stay if I asked. The shadows in his face as he stood at the door. I'm hearing the quiet after he left, the finality of it.

I take the final bowl, wiping it clean and setting it back in its place in the cupboard.

'You know, maybe you're not supposed to have the answers.' Shanthi leans over and kisses my cheek. 'Not just yet.' Without the cigarettes, I breathe in her old scent, rose-water soap, paint, and something else, unfamiliar, like blossom; maybe something from Donna.

Shanthi goes back out. I fetch a cloth and start to wipe down the surfaces. Listening to the sounds of the chatter in the dining room, I remember the first time Jack met my mother. She hadn't wanted to like him, but despite everything she would go on to say to the contrary, she couldn't help herself. I'd known she wouldn't be able to.

Finishing up the cleaning, I lean against the sink, phone in hand.

I'm still here.

Here's what I remember: the good things and the bad. The nights when we were out and I'd catch Jack looking at other women. The conversations he had with them, their smiles lodging like a stone in my throat. The way he made me feel afterwards that it was all in my head, all just my jealousy. That stuff was true. But when I met the Saxophonist, I told him about the other things too. The times Jack made me feel beautiful. The times we would be in my favourite position, slightly turned in towards one another, my head on his chest, listening to his laughter coming through his bones. Or the other position, wrapped around like spoons, my finger measuring the little mole beneath his shoulder blade. How hard he tried with Mum during those Sunday dinners, the number of times he invited her to our flat; the number of times he rehearsed Lionel Richie songs for a woman who never showed. The times that he was there for me. That was true too.

I remember that holiday to Sri Lanka. The way we packed up our rucksacks and sleeping bags and left the UK full of a glee that sort of discharged itself along with the diarrhoea that overtook us right at the very beginning of the trip, in the first guest house we stayed in. There's nothing like your bowels for ruining your glee. We were grumpy and tired and useless, unable to find a kind word for one another. But eventually our guts cleared and we managed to hitch a lift on the back of a man's jeep to cover some lost ground.

There is one memory that has stayed with me from that time: a headache, a leftover pain in my tummy, and nausea from the jeep wheels going over potholes. The sun was hurting my eyes and it was too much to gaze out on the dusty broken road, at the reddish-brown earth, the spiky fronds of the palms. We pulled over for a break, and there was a local man, sitting cross-legged on the ground, shaded by the outstretched branches of a fig tree. A little herd of ebony elephants was spread out on a colourful patchwork cloth in front of him.

'No, thanks,' I told him when he approached us, too queasy for a sales pitch. The man didn't say a word and returned to his spot beneath the tree. He had beautiful hands, long, sculpted fingers, holding each elephant with tenderness as he tap-tapped out their strong legs. He frowned in concentration, looking back only once at our dirty faces.

We returned to the jeep, and as it started to pull away, I glanced again at the man, working in peace. I thought about how many interactions we have, how our lives can cross with others in so many different places, leaving a story at the intersection, if only you notice it.

'Those were cool elephants,' Jack said to me. He was scratching his right eyebrow. I often had the feeling, when we were together, that we were thinking the same thing.

'They were.' I nodded. And then I smiled.

'Hey, mate,' Jack leant forward to tap on the rear window separating us from the driver. 'Can you stop again for a minute?'

He took my hand as we swung ourselves off the jeep and ran back to the man underneath the tree. A Tamil guy, called Eeshan. He'd been making those statues right in that spot for years, calluses embedded into his elegant fingers. He had a wife and a baby boy, a mother who had taught him how to carve the

289

splintery wood. He had a dreamy look on his face, his mind shaping stories while tourists in all their shapes and sizes came and went. He carved these elephants for peace in his country, which had too long been scarred by war. For love and for safety, he told us.

Jack paid for the elephants. 'To keep you safe too,' he said to me.

We got back on the jeep and waved at Eeshan as it drove away. But he was already lost in his work, waiting for the next story.

Jack and I meet at St Andrew's Park, just down from the shop. We have maybe sat like this a hundred times before, him cross-legged, me with knees bunched up to my chest, watching the students and the kids, and the squirrels scuttling in the trees. I stare at the scuff of his green canvas shoes, shoes I've never seen before; catch a glimpse of dark auburn from the corner of my eye. But I haven't been able to look at him properly.

'You took the elephants away,' I say, after a while.

'I paid for them.'

'To guard over me.'

'I was hoping it would make you return my calls.'

'Sorry.'

'Or my texts.'

'Sorry.'

'Or my emails.'

'Sorry.'

'Why didn't you?'

'I just couldn't.'

'It's me who's sorry, anyway.' I can feel him closing his eyes, can picture the ray of lines stretching out each side towards his temples. 'I can't believe what I did to you. I'm so sorry, Anj.'

I look down at the daisies poking out among the grass. Eleven years ago he carefully looped these flowers into a chain and tied it around my ankle, a shiver rushing upwards in my body with each press of his fingers. It wasn't long after I'd moved into the shared flat. We were quieter that evening, making pasta, tiptoeing around each other in the kitchen, watching the television instead of chatting over it. I was aware of the rustling of his clothes, the movement of his shadow, more shivers crossing my skin every time our bodies brushed past each other, which seemed to be happening more often. '*The Great Chelsea Garden Challenge?*' I smiled at one point, gesturing for the remote, knowing he would protest. Looking up when he didn't; finding his kiss instead.

I lie back against the bank of grass, listening to the calls of the children in the play park. I never expected that kiss to lead to the years we went on to spend together. Although as the days drifted by, there was something about our time that seemed hard to believe in. 'You really hurt me, Jack. But it's OK now.'

It feels so strange to say those words. I never thought it would be OK. But in the year that has passed, somewhere in the space where dahlias turned into sunflowers, it became that way.

'What changed? What made you text?' He's turned to me.

I make myself face him. To look once more into the well of his pupils, to see again the fine gold dust of his freckles.

'I'm not sure,' I say. Ernie's face still there, hovering in my mind.

'I've missed you.' There's a sadness about Jack, and yet he is smiling as well. There are his two dimples again, tucked into his cheeks, both of them asking me if he could still be The One.

'I've missed you too,' I tell him.

*

When Jack was a little boy, his mum was only a visitor. His parents had divorced when he was two years old, and the way things worked out, he lived with his dad. Sometimes weeks passed without a visit from his mother. Then she would show up with a new bike, a radio, one time a sledge for the freak fall of snow he'd woken up to one morning. 'Christ's sake,' his dad said once, only once, when shoving the radio or whatever to one side. Jack didn't understand the venom in his voice and why his father seemed to hate those visits, and those gifts, so much.

Over the years, he got to understand. He got to see how a person could work hard every day, paying for the unseen things like the gas and electricity, buying the boring things like his gloves and his school blazer. He got how a person could strive to do those things and how they might feel if their endeavours were dismissed with one bike, one radio, one sledge.

He remembered how his dad stared at the best present, the silver Rotary watch, his face as sour as lemons, while Jack felt the joy pass out of him, through the hole in his blazer pocket.

Later, Jack stamped on that watch, crushing every last piece of glass, until it was completely destroyed.

Are relationships gifts? he wonders. We have come back to my flat now – our old flat. It's only early in the afternoon, but we've opened a bottle of red wine. For both of our nerves. He pours out a glass and stares at it for a while. 'Remember how much you liked the word meniscus?' he says, and I frown. It's something I've forgotten. 'You said we should drink more wine, just so we could say meniscus more often.'

He remembers how I loved things like that; certain words, smells, little details in stories like holes in blazer pockets. 'You'd go quiet and I'd know you were lost for a minute in something so small and simple. I could watch you all day, watching the flowers.'

He winces and puts his hand to his temple like he's been struck with something sharp. 'I fuck up everything I care about, Anj.'

He tells me, like he did on that first day, that Julia didn't mean anything to him. He didn't care what she did, he wasn't interested in the burlesque thing. He doesn't know how it started; he liked her tattoos, he'd been thinking about getting one, then suddenly one drunken night became more, and he doesn't know why he didn't stop it.

I put down my glass and let the meniscus settle. I lay my hand over his. 'We don't need to talk about this,' I tell him.

Over the past year, I've played out what would actually happen if we saw each other again. I imagined all kinds of outcomes. Tears and anger, dignity and sorrow. Maybe I would pass him in the street with one of my men; perhaps I would glimpse him in the distance with Julia, or another woman I didn't know (but who might be equally good at dancing). Or maybe we would find each other and make the decision to try again. Maybe.

I look around the flat. It's tidy for once, the furniture empty, most of my things boxed up. I have more than a suitcase now – I have books again, some trinkets, the baggage of a life. Jack picks my florists' manual out of one of the boxes, battered and dog-eared, held together with tape. He's looking around too, like he's watching the ghosts of our old selves hanging out in the shadows.

Putting down his glass, he walks to the kitchen window. I'm going to miss the garden. I wonder if Jack's mind is running through its collection of memories: the tiny mess of weeds and concrete we discovered when we first arrived, the hours I spent out there with a fork and a trowel and a pair of oversized gloves. He marvelled because I was kind to spiders, laughed because I

293

am terrified of ladybirds (I always have been; it kind of unsettles me when they break in half to fly away).

He looks older than just the year that has passed, a little thinner. His shoulders are slouched; it feels like a long time ago that I would bring him coffee while he sat at his desk and nag at him to buy a better chair. Where does he do his work now?

'Where do you live?' I ask.

He doesn't answer me. He turns around, and I look into a face that seems at once both familiar and completely unknown.

Then he crosses the room and kisses me.

At first it's like kissing a stranger, but after a while, it's as if my body knows him better than I do. My head knows when to tilt to one side, my lips know when to part. My tongue knows his, even though I am surprised by the texture of it, and the way it tastes, of spearmint chewing gum.

'You've stopped smoking?' I ask, when we break apart.

He holds up his hands. 'It's bad for you, someone said.'

Taking my hand, he leads me into my/our old bedroom. Except it doesn't feel like his or mine. There's only the made-up bed, a couple of my toiletries on the chest, everything else dusted and empty. I've taken down my curtains and put back the ones that came with the flat. They're red and gold and make the room seem as if it's trapped somewhere in time, in a place that no longer exists.

We take off our jeans and he lies back against the sheets, Jack-shaped dents in the pillow and the mattress. I wonder for a moment what Clara would say, what my mother would say, what Shanthi would say, and then I stop, figuring they might say a lot of things, and I'll have to listen to them all later. Jack starts to lift off my T-shirt, but I put my hand against his, and he leaves it on. We lie there half dressed, and I am remembering the worry I had about my body in all of our time together. Then I'm thinking about Ernie again. I think about how it felt to lie right here beside him, to feel his warm hands running over my skin. The way I could expose all of myself to him, the good and the bad.

Jack gathers me towards him. I can feel his ribs, the extra hardness of his thighs (he's started basketball, he told me), and see the shiny bruises on the pale skin of his arms (he's not very good at it, he admitted). He starts kissing me again.

We stopped using a condom during our relationship, so it feels odd to ask for one now. He leans over to find his jeans and his wallet, and as he does so, I see the burlesque dancer again. Her long, slim legs wrapped around his, the tattoo of an uncoiled snake slithering along her calf. She startles me; it's been so long since she took up a space in my mind, but now she won't go away completely, her dark, glossy locks falling onto my pillow.

When I close my eyes, Ernie is there. The way he looked at me with all of the passion and love and kindness that fills up his soul. He travelled the world looking for a place where he belonged. He came back to find me. And I told him to go.

Jack takes the condom out of his wallet.

There's a lot of advice on what to do about infidelity. In the early days I googled it constantly. The answers varied depending on my search questions. Should I take him back? *A guy that's perfect for you can still cheat on you!* Cosmopolitan UK assured me. Should I leave him? *Ten signs you should run for your life!* shrieked Oprah. I haven't got a fucking clue; what should I do? *You're a fucking coke-head slut, I hope you fucking die!* suggested Eminem.

I clicked on website after website, and in the end I had to stop looking because they were full of people in the worst kinds of misery, going over and over their decisions, wondering if they'd made a mistake.

When I open my eyes, Jack is looking at me.

'Are you OK?' he asks.

I can't torture myself with my mistakes. I guess I'm a fairly lightweight Buddhist, but I've gleaned enough to understand that the Buddha was a decent kind of person, who would have told all of those people in all of their miseries to think about how they could accept their choices and learn from them. To carry on with their journeys. To find a way to live with it all, the bliss and the suffering, the joy and the pain, success and failure. Treat those two imposters just the same. Although it's possible I've just slipped into Rudyard Kipling.

'What are you thinking about?' Jack asks.

He has moved onto his side and is looking back at me, lines running across his forehead.

'I'm sorry. I can't do this, Jack.'

For a moment, he is still. Then he turns onto his back and gazes at the yellowed swirls on the ceiling.

We don't say anything for a while. I put my head on his chest and we turn slightly in towards one another, my old favourite position. I listen to his voice coming through his bones.

'Is it that guy?' he asks me.

'Which guy?' Although I know who he means.

'The one I saw you with . . . in the shop.'

I think back to Christmas Eve, caught in Ernie's arms, my mouth lifted up to his. I think of all the chances I had to be with him.

'He moved away.'

We fall silent again. I find myself counting five hours back to Vancouver once more. I wonder where Ernie is now; picture him behind a desk in an air-conditioned office, or maybe walking with a colleague, deep in conversation, heat beating down on their backs, irises blooming on the roadside. Maybe in his brother's home, playing a board game with the kids.

'I don't want to lose you,' Jack says. 'I never wanted to lose you.'

I put my arms tighter around him. I think about the day we first came to this flat, lying on the bed like this, waiting for Mum. I remember wondering how it might feel for Mum, not having someone to hold. I think of my dad, with his blue eyes and his long sideburns. I don't remember him, no matter how hard I try. I don't remember the day he died. I just remember the day Mum shut herself in her room and my sister could not move from her position crouched on the floor. We lived every day of our lives after that with something missing.

I watch the rise and fall of Jack's chest as he breathes, my head moving with the gentle rhythm. The two of us spent ten years together. I wonder how it will feel to spend the years to come without him.

'I don't want to lose you either,' I say.

'Then don't.'

But I guess the truth is, people don't leave you. No matter how long you are without them, no matter how briefly you knew them. You will always carry something of them inside you.

We turn around, wrapped together like spoons, and I put my finger over the mole beneath his shoulder blade and am glad to find it unchanged. There is a bit of me that wants to ignore the voice in my head, to wonder if there is any way we could make this work. But right now a dragon has opened its mouth across a beautiful woman's shoulder, and it is telling me – just me, not any of the other people in their own separate circumstances – that I'm on a different path now, and I might want to let that carry me for a while.

I used to think Jack was my One. I'm not sure if I believe in The One any more. I think life is a lot more complicated than that. It's difficult; my mind changes a lot and I never know if what I think is the truth. But for now, this is my experience.

Mum's making patties. She's whirling around with the pastry and the fork and the vegetable filling. She's making a mess. The flat stinks of spices and urine. Ordie's become incontinent.

'You poor thing.' I pick up our little cat and press my nose into her soft face. She mews quietly, asking to be put down. She doesn't like to be picked up so much any more. I lay her on the sofa and stay there for a while, stroking her bony back.

Shanthi's moving out today. Mum's trying to blame her damp cheeks on the onions. The hallway is blocked with boxes; a few of Shanthi's, a few of mine. We keep knocking over Buddhas, which is causing my mother increased agony.

'Can you girls pull yourselves together?'

'Do you mind if I take the screen?' Shanthi asks when I come to the door of our bedroom. The windows are wide open and the smell of Benson & Hedges has all but gone. The beds are stripped, the furniture empty, the pictures taken down, two darker squares on the pale green walls. It was Mum who painted the walls while Shanthi was in hospital that first time. There isn't much evidence of my sister left in this room. She's lived here for so long, but now the little that she has is packed neatly in the hall. I think about how long she's been tucked away in here, on the sidelines.

'Maybe it's time to get rid of it.' I touch the screen, gazing at the snakes and wondering how my sister can move on, with their glittering bodies around her.

Shanthi turns to me, her eyes bright. 'I couldn't get rid of it. It reminds me too much of you and me, growing up together.'

Her exhibition painting comes back to me, the huge, vivid canvas covered in serpents, their bodies made up of so much life. Pinpricks start up again behind my eyelids, images of so many years flashing by, of being children in matching gingham pyjamas, teenagers in deeply unfashionable Sri Lankan nightdresses, adults in oversize T-shirts; each night waiting for my sister to tap her side of the screen just so I could tap right back.

I gaze down at the red circles on the carpet. 'You know I love you, right?'

For a moment, I think she won't say anything, then there is the gentle touch of her palm on my shoulder. Her words so quiet I almost miss them. 'You too, little sis.'

Picking up the screen, she puts it out in the hallway. The last thing to pack is the old gilt-framed mirror in the corner of the room. She lifts it up and I see the two of us. Her small face, the darkness beneath her eyes, but her eyes as clear now as they have ever been, as if she is finding it easier to see. The tiny holes in her ear lobes. Mum got our ears pierced when we were very small; we spent our youth with matching gold stars, long since lost. The little scar above her left eyebrow, from the time she was running to the door to see Dad.

The mirror is trembling as she holds it. She still refuses to see the doctor. They'll only say it's risks versus benefits, she tells me.

I turn to my own reflection. For a long time I haven't been able to look at myself directly. Now I witness my cloud of hair, long overdue a cut. There are my almond-shaped eyes, like my sister's, like Mum's, mapped by the fragile red lines of broken sleep. The curve of my mouth that I've always hoped is Dad's. I've got my own tiny scar, at my right temple, but Mum doesn't remember how I got that. *You were always running around, I could not keep up with your falls. The doctors must have thought I was beating you, it is a wonder I did not end up in prison.*

'Hello, hello?' comes Donna's voice at the open front door.

She comes in wearing shorts, a magnificent eagle in black and green covering almost all of the back of her right calf. I think she's revealing her tattoos slowly, one by one, to minimise the impact on Mum's blood pressure. Shanthi said Donna had been at the studio a few months before my sister started to rent a space there. Their relationship started with conversations about art, sitting on cushions on the studio floor, talking as the light faded from the sky, still deep in discussion as it began to filter into the room again.

'You all ready?' Donna asks Shanthi now. She kisses that scar above Shanthi's eyebrow. It seems like a touching, intimate thing to do, and there's a lump in my throat.

'All ready.' Shanthi nods.

Mum comes out of the kitchen, wiping her hands on a tea towel. There's no hiding her tears. It's impossible to blame the onions.

'You've got to stop worrying, Mum,' Shanthi says. 'I'm only round the corner, remember.'

'We're just swapping places,' I remind her. 'You're going to be stuck with me now instead.'

'My baby girls.' Mum shakes her head, unable to say more.

'I'll take some things down to the car.' Donna kisses Mum's cheek. 'I'll give you all a few minutes.'

We're not good at these soppy moments, Mum and Shanthi and I. We're much better when there's curry on the table and we can pass each other the aubergines. When Donna leaves, my mother wipes her eyes and tries to pretend that she is no longer crying. 'Just a minute,' she says, and goes off into the lounge. I rest the mirror against one of Shanthi's boxes and she folds up the serpent screen.

Mum comes back with a photo. It's the one we found in the closet all those years ago. Me and Shanthi and Dad, down by the harbour. Mum's put it in a frame. 'I thought you would like this,' she says to Shanthi.

My sister takes the picture.

We're not good at these soppy moments, our family. So I'll leave us here: me, Mum, Shanthi and Dad, just like this in the hallway.

Epilogue

It's in the early hours that I feel the changes most. Unloading the flowers from the van I bought off Clara (for a pittance, really), and bringing them into the shop, I stop a few times to stand on a grey street that hasn't fully woken up. I listen to the blackbirds singing in the gutter and wave at the man putting up the board outside the organic grocer's. I smile at the still-drunk students finding their confused way back home.

I think about how many thousands of times I've walked along this road, from my early childhood with my mother and my sister, to now.

Instead of attending to the flowers, I find myself wandering around the shop floor, adjusting the pots and setting the signs straight. I'm still expecting Clara to come through from the kitchenette with a tea or a hot chocolate, asking me if it's too early for whisky.

We're halfway through September. Sunlight is beginning to find its way into the day, the steady thrum of cars starting rush hour, people appearing from their flats, or stepping down from buses.

Pausing for a moment at the window, I wonder where Clara is. She left a couple of weeks ago, to spend some time first with a cousin in Australia. Her flight to Bali should have landed not all that long ago. She might be getting a bus, or a taxi, straight out to the beach and the hostel she has booked. She might be changing into loose beach trousers, an oversize blouse; Clara clothes. Maybe she will head straight for the percussionist's place, or maybe she will turn cartwheels in the sand and gaze at the horizon for a bit. I know she won't be sure, but her palms will be tingling with hope.

It's colder today. The mornings start off a little darker, the days are a little quicker to end. Time is passing by so fast, and maybe one day I will wake up and realise I haven't thought about him.

I need to get on with some work.

Something is sparkling on the floor. Bending down, I pick up one of Mum's gold rings. She always takes off her rings before helping out. She's helping out a lot. At some point I might have to tell her that I have worked in the shop for over eleven years and know what I'm doing, but to be honest, I don't mind her being here all that much. Anyway, Shanthi's exhibition is next month, and her attention will soon be focused on helping them getting the space ready for that. The ring goes inside the drawer of the cash till with a Post-it on the top to remind me that it's there. Next to the note is the flyer on the evening course. I pick it up. I was thinking of giving it a go. Not to feel closer to him.

Maybe to feel closer to him.

Get on with it, Anjali.

There are always voices in our heads, aren't there? Mine has turned stern and critical, forcing me out of the daydream that comes so often into my mind these days. *Do some work, what's got into you?*

Maybe somewhere inside me, I knew it was going to happen today.

'So what's it like, being in charge?'

There's someone at the door. I am still looking down at the flyer in my hands. I don't want to lift my head, in case it's not true, and it isn't really him. His voice as deep as always, echoing to the same place in my throat.

'Can I come in?'

There's no Clara to help me out this time. I have to look up now, otherwise it'll just seem weird.

Ernie is in jeans and a short-sleeved shirt, a brown satchel slung over his back. I'm gazing at the curly fringes of his eyelashes, the grey dusting of his stubble, the firm swell of his arms. He's wearing a black beanie, and I can't help seeing him as he might have looked as a child.

'Anjie, are you going to say anything?'

Anjie. My heart is too loose, too soft.

'I thought you were in Vancouver.' I force the words out.

'I was.' He is standing by the counter now, right in front of me, and I am gripping the cash till.

'You're back for a break?'

'Maybe.'

I press my tingling palms flat against the cool metal. 'How did you know I'm in charge here?'

He smiles. I love that smile. I love how I can't help but smile back. It's a useful skill, I always forget to tell him. He could use it more, set up a business.

'Clara phoned.'

'When?'

305

'Last week.'

'How was she?'

'Anjie.' If he says my name like that again, I might start running around the shop. It might freak him out and send him back to Canada. 'I didn't come here to talk about Clara. Well, not yet, anyway.'

'Do you want something to drink?' I'm dashing out to the kitchenette, not sure how to control the pitter-patter of my stomach. 'I haven't got peppermint; did you bring some peppermint?'

'Coffee will be fine.'

'Coffee?' I swing around. 'Decaff?'

'Caff.'

'White?'

'Black.'

'Black, fully caffeinated?' My eyes are wide.

'Black, fully caffeinated.'

'When did you start drinking coffee?'

'Around the time I stopped meditating.'

I look down at the flyer I'm still holding, the six-week course in meditation and mindfulness. I throw it over my shoulder.

'When did you stop meditating?'

'When I started waiting.'

My heart is beating hard. But maybe there are engineering exams in Canada; maybe he's waiting for a house to come through.

'Anjie,' he begins.

'Stop calling me that.'

'Sorry.' His face falls.

'No.' I recover. 'I didn't mean to say that out loud. Did I say that out loud? I don't mind you calling me that; I love you calling me that.'

He's starting to laugh, and I am gazing into his eyes, now a deep golden brown in the morning light. I am thinking it's Mum's day off from work and there's a chance that she might pop in. I'm thinking I wouldn't mind introducing them.

One of these days, I'm going to have to stop thinking about my mother.

He is standing so close to me now. His skin is much darker after months of Vancouver sun. I can smell the freshness of his shirt, the lemon scent of his aftershave. And something else, something that reminds me of long summer days, many, many years ago, of a childhood that existed before my memories began; running into the warmth of outstretched arms.

'What were you waiting for?' I whisper.

Just behind Ernie, on a shelf, is a poinsettia from last Christmas. It was the only one I kept back from last year. It lost all its leaves; I pruned it down until it was only four or five inches above the soil. In the spring, I started to water it more. The leaves began to grow back in the sunlight, staying a deep green throughout the summer.

We are heading towards October. As the days shorten, the plant will need twelve hours of sunlight per day. Then twelve hours of darkness.

Soon I'll be hoping for red bracts, velvety beneath my fingers. Perhaps tiny yellow flowers.

I look at Ernie's black beanie, and for a moment, I feel like a child too, breaking into a smile, fingers crossed behind my back.

So long

307

Acknowledgements

It has been a long journey. I couldn't have made it on my own; I have a lot of people to thank.

To my wonderful agent, Diana Beaumont, for believing in me and to her then assistant, Aneesa Mirza, for picking my manuscript out of the slush pile.

To my writing family without whom I would have long ago fallen by the wayside. Thank you Victoria Finlay, Emma Geen, Susan Jordan, Sophie McGovern, Peter Reason, Jane Shemilt and Mimi Thebo for seven years of stories, laughter and mountain tree analogies. Also to Hadiza El-Rufai and Vanessa Vaughan for early readings.

My gratitude to Maddie West, Thalia Proctor and everyone at Sphere for making this dream possible. Thanks especially to Manpreet Grewal. It was a privilege to work on the manuscript with you those first few months, I learned so much under your guidance.

To the friends who have encouraged me. Thank you to Stephen Middleton, my dearest buddy, for a lifetime of support. To Natalie Davies for reading/watching everything I have ever done, sometimes against your will. To Toni Wood for endless advice and Lydia Berry for endless positivity. To Nathan Filer, for always believing in me.

Thank you to Sophie Lambert for invaluable advice and to Tessa Hadley, my creative writing MA tutor, for telling me not to give up.

Thank you to my parents for your practical support. To the Mattingleys; Kate, Jonny and Lucy, for always being interested. To Ray . . . you are missed always. I wish you could have been here to see me published. To Penny King for your encouragement and to Bud Atapattu, for following your own dreams, my inspiring older bro.

To my amazing daughters, Eliza and Bibiana, for supplying happiness whenever it is needed.

And finally to Daniel Mattingley. I don't know what I would do without your endless support, understanding, reassurance and cooking. Thank you for coming with me on this journey, and for the detours we took along the way.

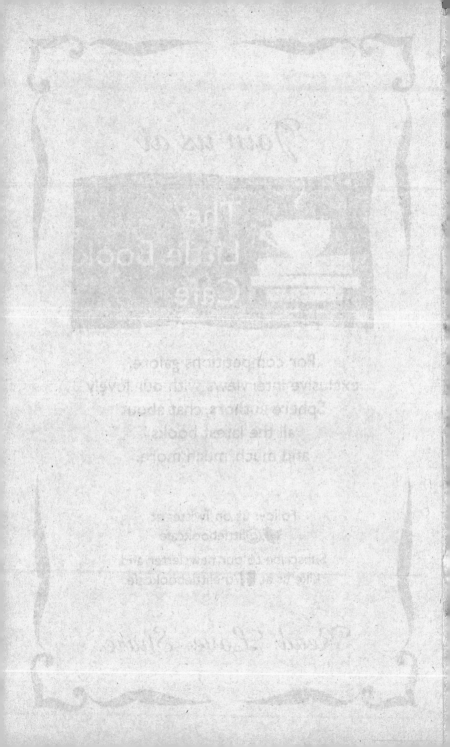